The Homestead

BlackPit Publishing

Group

For Carl,
I appreciate the
support, man! I hope this
knife serves you well!

Published by
BlackPit Publishing Group
P.O. Box 179
Centerville, Massachusetts 02632
BlackPitPublishing.com

ISBN 978-0999407479

Printed in the USA

For Post, Kopps, Schranz, Doc, and all the other brothers we've lost to the war back home.

Acknowledgments

I owe a debt of gratitude to all those good friends who took the time to test read and provide feedback on the manuscript. I need to thank my incredible family who instilled in me the love of reading at a young age and have supported me in all my endeavors since. I also need to thank my brothers from the Marine Corps. Those filthy, alcohol-fueled bastards of Charlie Company, 1st Battalion 9th Marines helped shape me into the man I am today (for better or worse). Special thanks is due to Professor Cornelius Sebacher for his eye-opening seminars and pushing me to pursue a career in writing. Lastly, and most importantly, I need to thank my beautiful, brilliant, loving girlfriend and editor, Patience. Her countless hours of hard work and dedication have helped transform this story from a nonsensical jumble of words into the novel you're reading today.

The Valley

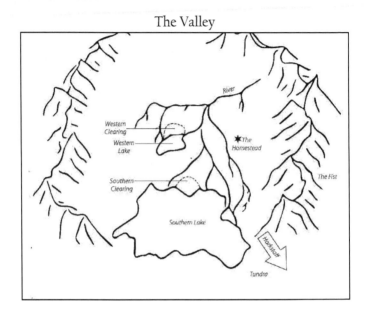

The Homestead

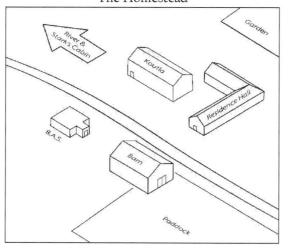

Harkstaff

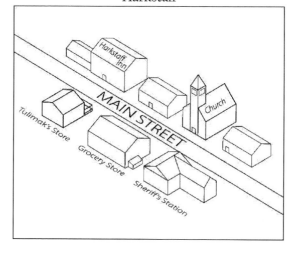

Prologue

Agent Donson knocked again. For the third time. And for the third time there was no answer.

Stepping back from the quaint, suburban ranch house, he called out to his partner, "how's that side door?"

"Locked." The younger agent's voice carried over the hum of the nearby highway. "I think I can jimmy it, though."

"Sure you can..." Donson muttered. There was something so insufferable about agents fresh out of the academy. Their constant need to prove themselves to the more seasoned vets made for a younger sibling dynamic. Only Donson hated his younger brother.

"Excuse me!"

An elderly man in comically high neon blue shorts waddled across the street brandishing an archaic Nokia cellphone. He cast a horrified glance to where the younger agent crouched fiddling with the side door's lock.

"You can't just break into that house, you know! Who do you think you are?" the geriatric neighbor called out, pointing the phone like a weapon.

"Calm down, sir," Donson responded with the same lack of enthusiasm as every other time he was forced to deal with some obnoxious neighborhood watch or passing do-gooder. "We work for the Federal Bureau of Investigation. We have a warrant to search this house."

The old man gave Donson a cockeyed look as he pulled his badge from his jacket pocket and flipped it open.

"Got it!" Fender yelled from around the corner. Donson pocketed the badge and made his way along the overgrown cobblestone path that led around the side of the house.

"Now, wait a minute!" the old timer protested. "I'm going to need to see that warrant…"

"Fuck off," Donson muttered, ignoring the old man and pushing past Fender, who stood beaming with pride in the doorway.

The house was humble enough. Though it hadn't been lived in in years, it showed little sign of neglect. A hardwood and marble kitchen gave way to a comfy den littered with all the amenities of modern suburban life. Donson let his eyes wash over the nuances of the room. A handful of photos hung in perfectly measured intervals, revealing a young couple: the man was bulky and dark skinned, with a thick mane of black hair, while the woman was slight and surprisingly attractive despite her apparent inability to smile in photographs.

"Start in the living room. I'll take the office," Donson ordered.

"What exactly are we looking for?" Fender was too eager. *Fucking rookie.*

"I'll know it when I see it," Donson grumbled and made his way down the hall.

The office was barely an office at all. The couple had thrown a writing desk and an ugly, 70's era filing cabinet against the wall opposite a paint-stained futon. Donson started with the desk, milling through the folders and loose papers that littered its surface, searching for the distinct yellowy parchment that was his target.

Nothing.

He turned his attention to the filing cabinet. As he fingered through the contents he felt a twinge of annoyance.

Where did these fuckers hide it?

Just as he was about to move on to the second drawer, it caught his eye. Its dull, bone yellow hue gave it away against the stark white sheaf of printer paper it was stashed between. He pulled the letter out and glanced over it. It read almost the same as the other half dozen he'd recovered across the country over the past week:

Dear Mr. and Mrs. Durrs,

My name is Augustin Stark. As you read this letter, I have no doubt that you are still a bit shocked at the bizarre proposition our mutual friend, Frank Erikson, has just presented to you. I asked him to deliver this note as a personal invitation to join us in our fledgling community. I hope whatever Frank has told you hasn't scared you off yet.

Now, before I begin, I know what you're thinking: that this is a cult; that Frank drank the Kool-Aid and got himself tied up with some weirdo fanatics. I can assure you this is not the case. Our community, which I and the others refer to as the "Homestead," is just about the furthest thing from an overbearing religious organization as there is.

Frank came to me months ago in the hopes that we could open up our home to you. As the summer months begin to wane and we look back at our progress over the past year, I believe we now have the capacity to house both of you quite comfortably.

The Homestead is small, but our numbers are rapidly growing due to current members insisting on inviting those whom they think this place can help. By next summer we expect our numbers to reach north of thirty. We have a handful of buildings already constructed and more are popping up with each passing month. Most of our members live in a residence hall where they each enjoy their own quarters, including our newly set up indoor plumbing (we tried the outhouse thing at first – that won't happen again). World-renowned neurosurgeon and close personal friend of mine, Dr. Alwan Freeman is among our ranks, accompanied by two highly trained nurses who always stand ready to care for any injuries or illnesses in our fully stocked, state-of-the-art clinic.

I must warn you that while the community itself is quite safe, it lies deep in a nearly uninhabitable parcel of land that is entirely cut off from modern society. Coming here will be wrought with sacrifices. There is no internet, no phones, and the only contact you will have will be the very occasional opportunity to travel by horseback or ATV through rough terrain to Harkstaff, the nearest town. A large number of predators and wildlife that do not fear us roam the valley and surrounding mountains. Please do not let this intimidate you. Despite the foreboding nature of such isolation, our community members are safe so long as they are responsible.

I will assume that, since you are still reading, at least some part of you is interested in what I have to offer:

Freedom.

Not the hillbilly, flag-waving, whiskey-drinking nonsensical battle cry of overly patriotic Americans. No, I am offering something far more genuine.

I am offering real, chaotic, primal freedom. A tribal society where the overbearing powers that be cannot restrict your free will; where your nine-to-five captivity in indentured servitude is a nightmare of the past. While you will be expected to pull your weight, we operate as a true democratic republic and you will find yourself entirely in control of your own life. Even more importantly, your voice will carry legitimate weight when it comes to deciding the future of our community.

The Homestead is many things. To most people it is a personal experiment — a means to immerse yourself in a more visceral and natural life. It is my hope in founding this community that we can, together, create a new home void of the misgivings of the modern era. What I am offering you is a unique opportunity: a break from the daily monotony of cubicles and sedans. An opportunity to invest yourself in the primitive art of survivalism. An opportunity to discover for yourself whether the issues in your life really are the fruits of your own decisions, or rather a product of existing in a toxic environment.

If you choose to accept this invitation, I can promise you two things: financial security and an eye-opening experience. While you are with us, your home and belongings will be expertly cared for, and when you choose to return, you will be heartily compensated to make up for any lost time in your career field. I say "when" because this experiment is not an attempt at creating a utopic prison, only a sustainable, remote, and free community where people may come and go as they please. You may try it for a month and decide to leave. You may decide to spend only summers with us. Or you may, as most of our current members have, decide to make the Homestead your permanent home.

If your answer is yes, and you are ready to undertake something outside of the numb repetitiveness of modern life, please let Frank know. Any and all logistical arrangements will be made by—

"Donson, I really gotta know what I'm looking for here, man," Fender interrupted, leaning on the office door.

Donson hoped he was subtle enough in slipping the letter into his jacket. He turned to face his younger partner. "Uh, fuckin'…" The little bastard caught him off guard. "Explosive residue, fertilizer, shit like that."

"Oh shit." Fenders eyes lit up, then he paused and seemed to debate his next words in his head. "I know I'm not supposed to ask, but, uh… weren't you up there when it happened?"

"No," Donson stated flatly. He noticed Fender's eyes drifting toward where the parchment was concealed in his jacket. "I got called in right after, though," he added quickly.

Fender's eyes snapped back up to meet his.

"Yeah, it was a fucking bloodbath," Donson continued. "Go grab the bomb kit from the truck and start swabbing the kitchen utensils. You'd be surprised how many of these freaks eat with the same shit they use to mix HME."

Fender nodded and disappeared down the hallway. Donson waited until he heard the side door shut then grabbed an ashtray from atop the filing cabinet. He pulled out a pack of cigarettes, lit one, and drew in hard, letting the acrid smoke fill his lungs. Then he pulled out the parchment letter, folded it twice, placed it in the ashtray and lit it too.

Part 1

1

Jackson Durrs gently finagled the bait branch into a chest-high wooden deadfall trap then stepped back, eyeing the contraption with pride. If someone had approached him three years earlier while confined to his dreary cubicle at an accounting firm and told him he would be spending his days chopping down saplings in the depths of the Alaskan wilderness to fashion frontier-esque small game traps, he would have scoffed. Yet here he was, completing his eighth of the day.

He pondered the surrounding snow-spackled wilderness. Spring thaw was in full effect: brown mud and mottled leaves shone through the remaining carpet of quickly melting snow like giant, earthy freckles on the forest's floor. Around him, the magnificent pines of the taiga stood in staunch resistance to the elements. Thick and ancient, their bristling peaks swayed gently with the breeze coming off the nearby mountain. Closing his eyes, Jackson savored their cool, sweet scent.

This was his happy place — his not-so-metaphorical escape from reality. Out here in the arboraceous valley he now called home, he couldn't help but wonder if everything in his life before had been a fever dream.

He had grown up in a small town, raised by a distant mother and an abusive, white-collar father. Jackson left his home as soon as he graduated high school. It was in college where he met his wife — a beautiful, brilliant, young woman named Amy. Not long after they married, they bought a house and stockpiled the humble earnings of his accounting job in the hopes of one day starting a family.

It was five years after graduation that his college roommate Frank Erikson showed up at their door with a very strange proposition and a letter from a mysterious millionaire. Things in the Durrs household were not going well; Amy had just been let go from her job managing a local bar, while Jackson had found himself suffering from an ever-expanding hatred of his career. His misery at work had begun bleeding heavily into their marriage. With their savings account still nowhere near what they had planned and their mortgage and taxes eating most of their paychecks, they listened eagerly as Frank laid out his pitch.

Frank had sounded more like a Jehovah's Witness than the loveable nerd who had taught Jackson how to shotgun Budweiser. "What if I told you that there was a place out there where you could get away from *all of this*?"

A sharp series of cracks drew Jackson from his deliberations. The trap's trigger bowed heavily under the weight of the eight-inch-wide log it held up. Glaring at the thin stick, he willed it not to break. Replacing the trigger and resetting the trap would be an easy task, but he dreaded the prospect of doing so; the waxy numbness of his fingertips had just begun to dissipate within the warmth of his pockets.

After a moment, he decided that the trap was sturdy. He pulled on his pack and began the short trek to his ATV parked a hundred yards away on the well-worn game trail that led back to the Homestead. Though his boots were already soaked from the slush of the melting snow, he made the conscious effort to hop between the raised islands of dry earth, making it a game to see how far he could go without having to sink his feet into the soggy forest floor. After a few minutes of entertaining himself this way he caught sight of the ATV through the dense foliage.

Something's wrong.

A primal feeling overtook him, causing his neck to tingle as the hairs stood up straight. Crouching, he cast a wary glance around the surrounding forest. Absolute silence had replaced the cacophony of birdcalls and squirrel chirps that usually littered the spring air. He inched forward, cringing as dry leaves crunched beneath his feet.

Seconds dragged by. The silence was abruptly shattered by a high, warbling moan. Jackson felt his heart skip against his ribs as a dark brown ball of fur shuffled into sight. The bear cub meandered along aimlessly, rooting at the earth and occasionally calling out to…

"Fuck…" he whispered under his breath, drawing the word out as he scanned between the budding trees for the cub's mother.

A rumbling growl emanated from directly behind him. Jackson froze. Every muscle in his body tensed as the grizzly's heavy footsteps thudded through the forest at his back. The Colt 1911 at his side offered only the slightest bit of comfort as he slowly closed his hand around its stippled wooden grips. Ahead the bear cub halted its plodding stride and looked directly at him.

Time stood still as Jackson gazed into the furry animal's big eyes. If it weren't for the menacing growl behind him, he might have marveled at the heartwarming beauty of the young creature. He sucked in a shallow breath, mentally begging it to move on as the tingle of adrenaline flowed through his body.

The cub moaned again, and the growl stopped.

Like an Olympian at the pop of the starting pistol Jackson launched himself toward his ATV. He sprinted through the trees, his eyes darting from root to root to avoid tripping, refusing to look behind him; he didn't need to. He could hear the crashing foliage and panting grunts as the mother bear catapulted through the forest in pursuit.

He burst through the tree wall and onto the game trail. The crashing behind him morphed into heavy thuds as the bear reached the open trail as well and gained momentum.

The ATV was positioned facing him on the trail ahead. Without slowing he yanked the pistol from its holster and fired repeatedly over his shoulder, knowing the .45 caliber rounds would do little to stop the massive predator. The bear roared. Her guttural howl echoed through the trees and surrounded him, but her heavy footfalls did not so much as pause.

Jackson reached the vehicle and spun in a half circle to leap aboard, gripping the clutch with white knuckles and slamming his thumb into the starter. The engine roared to life as he looked up to see the beast closing in, his eyes immediately snapping to its snarling, fang-filled maw whipping long strings of spittle.

It was too close.

Without hesitation, he slammed the accelerator and the ATV lurched forward toward the oncoming bear. At the last second, he threw himself off the seat, splashing into a puddle of slush as the machine smashed into the massive beast, sending her sprawling.

Run!

Something deep inside screamed the word through the fog of panic that hung in his brain. He complied, scrambling to his feet and sprinting into the forest. He couldn't hear if the beast was still behind him — his own heavy footfalls sounded too loudly in his ears along with his pummeling heart. The trees passed in a blur as he crashed through their low hanging branches. Twigs clawed at his face; he swatted desperately to keep them out of his eyes as he stumbled over the uneven earth. The pack on his back seemed to catch on every passing object, but he dared not slow his stride to wrestle it off.

Jackson had no idea how far or how long he had run by the time he broke through the foliage and stumbled into the shallows of the wide river where he finally stopped. Grasping his knees and trying to catch his breath, he scanned the tree line from which he had just emerged, but aside from the trickling water that ran over his shins, the forest was silent. There was no sign of the grizzly.

His legs burned and his throat ached as he sucked in deep breaths. He bent and scooped the ice-cold river into his hands and gulped it down. He reached to his hip to check his pistol, pulling it out of its holster and ejecting the magazine.

Four rounds left.

The freezing water left his hands numb and shaking, and as he replaced the magazine the pistol slipped from his quaking grasp and splashed beneath the surface.

"Goddamn it!" his voice echoed across the open water as he scrambled to recover the gun from the riverbed. He felt a wave of relief as his hand closed around the smooth metal, but it was immediately cut short by a terrifyingly familiar grunt. He spun to see the monstrous grizzly trot out from the tree line. She stopped, panting at the edge of the water and reared up on her hind legs. Her sheer size wrenched Jackson's stomach into a knot and his whole body shook. He raised the pistol level with the bear's chest and yanked the trigger. *Click.*

The 1911's hammer fell dead against the back of the pistol.

Jackson stared at the gun in horror then yanked the slide back. A waterlogged round flipped out of the chamber amidst a spray of water. The bear dropped to all fours and barreled toward him. He yanked the trigger again.

Click.

Jackson froze. He didn't think to reach for the Bowie knife at his side, or to scramble for the razor-sharp wood axe strapped to his pack. Only one image filled his mind: the face of his wife Amy.

Her luminescent green eyes glinting over soft pink cheeks as she smiled.

Her curly amber hair bouncing over her delicate neck.

Her perfect, pillowy lips forming the words *I love you.*

The grizzly smashed into him with the force of a dump truck, sending him hurtling backwards into the shallows. The icy water enveloped his face and forced its way up his nose and down his throat as his lungs fought to regain the air that had been knocked out of him. The image of his wife disappeared as the distorted blue sky above his submerged eyes turned dark and a massive, leathery paw slammed down on his shoulder. He gagged against the water as his collar bone snapped under the immense weight. He couldn't even scream. Desperately, he flailed his free arm above him, smacking at the hard, shadowy mass with the useless handgun. There was a crushing pain as the bear bit down on his wrist.

Just as quickly as it came on, the pain was growing distant; everything was beginning to feel surreal aside from the burning water that filled his lungs. He kicked his legs against the beast's underside and for a second the bear released its toothy grip. Wrenching himself out from under the meaty paw, he scrambled to get to the air above.

As his head breached the surface and he felt the blast of

hot, rancid breath roll over his face, he knew he'd made a mistake. In that split second, he wished that he had sucked in the freezing mountain water and let it gently pull the life out of him. The enraged grizzly glared down with furious eyes, then opened her mouth wide and latched her vice-like jaws over his face. The last thing Jackson Durrs felt was a two-inch long fang erupting through his temple with a sickening crunch.

2

Augustin Stark lay alone at the base of an ancient alder tree that skirted one of the valley's few clearings. The mess of intertwined roots ran underneath his prone form like hardened veins, digging painfully into his hips. The sun rose slowly in the eastern sky before him, the fields and forests of snow gradually dissolving into mud and emitting clouds of eerie, drifting fog. Tiny streams of water burrowed under the melting snow, pooling in the mud impressions of his elbows and soaking through his worn, canvas jacket.

Before him stretched a vast tundra of glistening snow, mottled only by sparse winter shrubbery and occasional patches of half-frozen earth. The field marked a rare gap in the heavily forested area; the eight-hundred-meter semicircle bordered the northernmost edge of a small lake, which was otherwise entirely encompassed by the dense foliage of the taiga.

Stark had arrived at the clearing hours before dawn, dragging the upper half of a partially rotted elk carcass to its center. The rancid stench of its torn, decaying flesh had caused him to gag more than a few times as he staked it into the frozen predawn earth. From there, he meticulously executed a pace count directly back to the tree he now lay beneath, measuring the distance at just under four hundred meters. It wasn't a particularly easy shot, even for an experienced marksman as he, yet the extra distance between him and the bait served as a comforting cushion should he not be able to immediately kill his prey.

Beside him, propped across two exposed roots to protect it from the melting snow, lay a worn Lee Enfield rifle. The wooden stock was weathered and scarred by countless nicks and gouges while its metal barrel and action shined bright from lack of bluing. A modern scope was fixed to its top, an anachronism atop the century-old rifle. As the sun began to crest the opposite tree line, he pulled the rifle from its perch and placed it in his shoulder, peering through the magnified optic into the distance across the clearing.

"Right to left," he muttered into the gentle breeze, reminding himself of the old Marine Corps mantra that had been beaten into his head almost a decade before. He'd found the method to be a simple, yet effective tactic: reading causes the brain to become complacent when scanning left to right. Reversing the direction would, in theory, give the observer a heightened ability to pick out discrepancies.

Slowly he scanned, pausing only to wipe away the beads of sweat that began accumulating on his brow. He was heavily dressed. He had made the trek out to the position in the freezing darkness, but now, with the sun beginning its ascent, the temperature was escalating rapidly. As he contemplated shedding his outer layers, he caught a slight movement through his rifle scope. Across the field, a dark shape lumbered into the open.

Even at a great distance he could feel the ominous presence of the beast. Her hair was shaggy and long, swaying with each of her plodding strides. The color was off for a grizzly: dirty blond with darker patches encircling her belly and meaty paws. She ambled into the clearing toward the stinking mass of fetid flesh, stopping every so often to cautiously sniff at the air.

As the grizzly came within range, Stark placed the scope's crosshairs over her torso and considered his shot. He knew the steal-jacketed .303 round had to land in the beast's chest directly above her front legs. A hit anywhere outside of the heart or lungs and the animal would likely retreat back to the thick tree line from which she emerged. Slowly he worked the rifle's bolt, chambering a round, never letting the crosshairs leave his intended target.

The bear took her time approaching the carcass, glancing around the foggy tundra as if she could feel the old rifle's barrel pointed at her vital organs. Finally, she reached the staked bait. She hunched over to lap at the bloody slush beneath, then raised her head high to chew at the wet mess of meat and sinew. Her position couldn't have been more perfect. Her extended neck exposed a ten-inch-wide target of soft tissue, leaving nothing but four-hundred meters of chilly morning air between the chambered round and the beast's heart. Stark pulled the rifle in tight. His scruffy beard scratched against the wood stock. He took a deep breath and slowly squeezed the trigger as he exhaled.

The moment before the rifle kicked, the bear reared, spinning her head to look out over the lake. The recoil ground Stark's numb, wet elbows farther into the mud as the shot echoed out across the tundra. The beast shuddered violently as the .303 round struck her left thigh. With an enraged roar, the creature spun on her hind legs and bounded back in the direction she had come from. In a single deft motion, honed by a thousand repetitions, Stark threw back the rifle's bolt and chambered a second round. Steadying the rifle's wooden stock against the root in front of him, he placed his crosshair slightly above the bear's back and squeezed the trigger again, intent on letting the rifle's recoil surprise him when it went off.

The second shot never came though.

A faint mechanical thumping reverberated overhead, managing to rip his focus away from his retreating prey. In the distant sky to the south, a black speck appeared. It moved quickly, barreling along its northbound route until passing directly over the clearing. The sleek helicopter looked to be a newer model — private, Stark judged based on the lack of markings on the jet-black door panels. It coasted above the eastern tree line as the bear disappeared into the foliage beneath it. Continuing swiftly on its path over the frozen wilderness, the black craft sank behind a row of sun-framed pine silhouettes.

Stark cursed before rising from his concealed position. His knees popped and needles shot though his sleeping feet. He rotated his muscular frame in a violent semicircle, resulting in an incredibly satisfying string of cracks. He was cold, wet, sore, hungry, and his eight-hour expedition seemed to have been all for nothing. The man-eater that had taken Durrs' life escaped his grasp once again, and he doubted he would have another opportunity as clean as the one he just missed.

But it wasn't the escaping grizzly that sent a pang of anxiety deep into his gut as he gathered his gear. The clearing at the edge of which he stood marked the dead center of a hundred-square mile property of nearly inaccessible land. This valley, *his* valley, was cut off from the outside world by a colossal mountain range and an expansive lake. This put the helicopter well outside the flight path of any civilian tour group or hunting party. The only aircraft that came out this far into the wild were the ones that he chartered. Furthermore, he knew for a fact that there was nothing but sheer, uninhabited wilderness to the northeast for far longer than that flight had fuel for. Whoever was in that chopper was either lost… or looking for him.

Slinging his rifle over his shoulder and clipping his faded Nalgene to his belt, Stark turned his back to the clearing and made his way toward the trail that led back to the Homestead. It would be a solid four hours walk before he made it back. This was good. It gave him time to think.

That evening the Homesteaders put Jackson Durrs to rest.

At dusk Stark carried the canvas shroud containing what little they could recover of the mangled corpse up a step-ladder and laid it to rest atop a sedan-sized pile of crisscrossed, kerosene soaked logs. Every one of the community's thirty-two members watched in solemn anguish as the young widow Amy Durrs placed a torch at the pyre's base, and the bushels of pine branches at its center erupted.

Stark had to gently pull her back as the flames flared up and encompassed the body. She resisted at first, but after a few moments gave in, falling back to a safe distance and staring blankly at the burning mass. Stark wanted to comfort her, but he knew there was nothing he could say or do that could begin to ease the sickening despair that she felt in that moment.

The flames grew ever higher, licking at the cold air as they consumed the canvas shroud and emitted their warm glow around the open paddock. For nearly an hour the community stood silently until the pyre collapsed. Once there nothing more than a scorched pile of embers, Stark nodded to Andrew Russo, considered by many to be the Homestead's unofficial second in command. Russo ushered the rest of the Homesteaders away through the night to the Koutla, where they had prepared a feast in Jackson's honor.

Stark stayed back with Amy. He turned to her, clasping both her hands in his and looking into her puffy, red eyes.

"He was a good man," Stark said softly. Despite his regular poise and confidence, he always found that the right words were damn near impossible to find in situations like this.

She nodded, then cast a sad smile. "He would have wanted to go out like this. Ever since we came here... He loved this place. He loved what he was doing. Before all of this we were rotting on the inside, but the last two years were the happiest of his life." Her face screwed up and she began to weep for the first time. Stark pulled her close and whispered consoling words.

"I don't want to leave!" she gasped after a moment, pushing him away. "I know that's what everyone expects. I know they don't think this is the place for a widow, but this is my home. I can't go back by myself." Her voice broke.

"Nobody expects you to leave, Amy. You belong here with us. We're your family." He paused. "Why don't we go back to the Koutla? I know the boys are gonna have a few drinks for Jackson. I'm sure they'd love to regale you with some stories."

She cast a final, longing glance at the smoldering pyre, then together they made their way across the paddock to the Homestead's central building.

The Koutla was built in the style of a Viking longhouse. It was the second structure erected, immediately following the much smaller concrete clinic. Its walls were constructed from hewn tree trunks laid laterally atop each other like Lincoln Logs, while the angled roof was reinforced oak planking. Although the exterior was rather barren and more reminiscent of a log cabin than a community center, the inside was vibrant. Intricate carvings of mythological creatures spanned the walls and a long oak table ran the hall's length, engraved at the head with the words *In silvestre nihil corruptēlam est — There is no corruption in the wild*

Stark pulled open the thick door and ushered Amy into the hall. Russo stood near the head of the table, filling clay mugs with their homebrewed stout out of a cask and passing them down the table to the somber congregation. Amy took her seat and Stark slipped a fifth of whiskey into her hand. It was Jack Daniels, Jackson's favorite.

"This'll help a little," he whispered with a wink.

A hint of a smile crossed her face. She took a long sip as Donald Jameson walked up to the raised platform at the front of the room. He was a handsome man with an athletic build and his charisma made him a natural showman.

"Listen up!" Jameson yelled over the din. The call was echoed a few times by the already semi-inebriated crowd until the room was silent.

"Amy." Jameson looked at her and raised his mug. "Jackson was a great man. That goes without saying, and this one's for him!" He threw his head back and emptied the mug. The crowd followed suit.

"But he was also a clever bastard!" Jameson continued after wiping the froth away from his lips. "Now I know there are going to be a lot of stories told tonight of the man's good deeds, but I wanted to start this off with a little tale about the moment I knew ol' boy was really one of us."

Frank groaned from his seat nearby. Stark noticed the man slouching heavily to one side and had no doubt that he was already half-past shitfaced.

Jameson continued, regaling the Homesteaders with the dramatic tale of a prank gone wrong in which Jackson had managed to turn the tables on him and come out on top. By the end of it, the crowded table rose from their seats and applauded, raising their mugs high in Jackson's honor.

When Jameson stepped down from the stage to refill his mug Frank attempted to rise and take his place, but stumbled and fell face first onto the floor.

"Dave." Stark turned to the largest member of the community, a hulking man who could have made a career as an NFL nose-guard, and nodded toward Frank's blubbering, half-conscious form. "Do me a favor and take care of Frank, will you? The man's had a hard day, get him to bed. I'd help, but Hunt probably needs a relief from watching the barn."

Dave nodded and stood. "You got it buddy." His voice was a gravelly baritone.

Stark thanked him, gave a final, reassuring smile to Amy, then gathered a plate of food and a mug of beer and left the Koutla.

The barn had a rotating schedule of "fire watch" put in place after a black bear had broken in during their first spring and wreaked havoc on their livestock. The watch was intended to be split evenly among the thirty adult community members, but was more often than not tended to by the Homestead's animal caretaker, Tim Hunt.

Hunt was an Army Ranger years before the other veterans had even been old enough to join the service. He fought in Iraq and Afghanistan through the mid-2000s, finishing his career after he lost his left leg and most of his squad to an IED in Northern Afghanistan. After medically retiring at twenty-seven he spent three years attempting to become a veterinarian before deciding to join Stark and help create the Homestead.

Stark found Hunt sprawled out in the low hanging

hammock next to the sheep pen. The wooly animals radiated an incredible amount of heat, making their section of the barn a pleasantly warm napping area. One of Hunt's two large Akitas let out a low growl as Stark approached. Hunt jerked awake and slapped at the dog's rump.

"It's just Stark, you little shit," Hunt muttered as the dog gave him a pitiful look. He sat up, pulling his prosthetic leg off the hammock and regarded his old friend. "How's the funeral?"

"I don't know if I'd call it a funeral," Stark said as he handed Hunt the plate and beer, "but it's fine. Jameson told his goat head story. Seemed to brighten everyone up a bit."

"Good, good." Hunt picked at the food.

"I figured I'd relieve you for a bit so you could join them." Stark took a seat on a crate full of feed.

Hunt shook his head. "No, man, I'm good. Don't really do funerals."

"Like I said, not really a funeral. Just drinking and telling stories."

Hunt set his plate down and took a heavy drink from the mug before giving Stark a sorrowful look. "I can't, man. I… I, uh, I just can't do that shit."

Hunt was a man of few words. The rest of the community often considered him a bit of a curmudgeon. At thirty-four he was the second oldest Homesteader —after Alwan's ripe age of sixty-seven — and seemed to embrace the idea of being the community's grumpy old man. Even so, Stark could see that for once the man seemed to want to elaborate, so he waited.

"I was in a coma when my guys were buried," Hunt said after finishing the mug. Stark knew Hunt was referring to the men he'd lost in Afghanistan. "When I woke up and found out… I always wished I had been able to make their funerals.

I thought about their families, their parents, their kids… about how maybe I could've said something or done something that could have dulled their pain. I thought about that every day. I just felt guilty. One day, another war buddy snapped and killed himself. He'd been out for a while, was working on an oil rig after his old lady took the kids and left him. I dunno, I guess he got lost in it all. We've all been there…"

Hunt pulled out a bottle of bourbon from beneath the hammock and took a gulp before handing it to Stark.

"Anyways, I busted my ass to get to his funeral. Flew all the way up to West Virginia," Hunt continued, "got there, met his folks, his ex and the kids… Holy shit, man, it was rough. Like everyone I'd ever lost came crashing back down on me. I just, I couldn't handle it. Had to bail after the wake and almost drank myself to death. It's weird. It's like I'm fine with death and all, I've seen it enough and come to accept it. But when you see what it does to others… the fuckin' pain it leaves in the folks you leave behind…" His voice trailed off as he stared blankly at the floor by his foot.

Stark nodded. They sat in silence for a while, passing the bottle back and forth until it was nearly empty.

Finally, Stark cleared his throat and Hunt snapped back to the present. "Something happened today, out in the eastern clearing," Stark said.

Hunt raised an eyebrow when he saw a trace of anxiety pass over Stark's face.

"We had a visitor," Stark went on. "An unmarked helo passed over."

"You think it was them?"

"I don't know who else it would be."

"Jesus Christ." Hunt growled and ran his hands down his face. "How could they find us?"

"Maybe someone talked–"

"Who?"

"I don't know, Hunt. Someone, anyone who knew we were up here. They have a big net, we knew this day might come."

Hunt leaned forward and massaged his temples. Stark knew there were a hundred possibilities playing through the man's head.

"I'm going to town tomorrow. If it is them I have to deal with this before they make it out here."

"Fuck that," Hunt said without looking up. He paused for a long time. When he finally spoke, his voice was even. "We have to tell everyone."

"Absolutely not."

"What choice do we have? We were wrong in letting them come out here without telling them the danger—"

"I'll deal with it."

"At least tell Russo. He'll go with you. You can't take this on yourself," Hunt insisted.

"I can and I will," Stark returned. "These people are my responsibility."

"Just as much as you're ours," Hunt rasped angrily. "If you do this right now, it isn't about safety or protecting the community… You going out there alone screams to me that you're still on that fucking edge, man."

"It's not that."

"Then what is it?"

"I've come a long way since Mexico." Stark felt a bitterness leaking into his voice despite the truth in Hunt's words.

"Yeah, but don't forget, that *long way* began when you showed up at my goddamn doorstep with five bullet holes in you." Hunt stopped and tried to regain his composure.

"Look, what happened… it happened, and we've done right since that day. We built a family here, *a community*. But if you're still a cunt hair away from going off the deep end then we need to address that, because if we lose you, it'll hurt us just as bad as when you lost her."

Stark's face tensed. "Don't talk about her," he said darkly.

"I haven't," Hunt came back, a little more softly than before. "I haven't said a word about her for three long years. I haven't said a thing to the others about the money or the land… I swore my silence, and in return you swore you were done with that shit. *You* need to keep that in mind."

Stark nodded but he knew Hunt didn't believe he was actually agreeing.

"Either you tell Russo, or I'll tell everyone. It's that simple. If something happens to you, I can't be the only one here who knows the truth."

"I got you, boss," Stark said, rising from his seat and patting one of the nearly identical dogs on the head.

"…So you're going to tell him?"

"Yeah," Stark said. "Tomorrow morning, after the council meeting. We have to plan our first trip to Harkstaff anyways. Someone has to deliver Jackson's death certificate. We'll tell him, then you two will be in charge when I leave."

"Fuck," Hunt grumbled as he pulled his prosthetic back up onto the hammock and lay back down. "First Jackson, now this. For the love of god, what's next?"

"God's dead, Hunt," Stark called back. "Haven't you picked up on that yet?"

3

Stark woke with a dry mouth and a splitting headache. The funeral festivities had raged long into the night. As with every drinking binge since he'd crossed over into his mid-twenties, he immediately regretted every decision he'd made the night before as he cracked open his crusty eyes and the hangover hit him full force.

Ever so gently, so as not to disturb the sleeping woman beside him, he rose from his bed and crossed his quaint cabin to the mess of clothes heaped in the corner. He was the only Homesteader who didn't live primarily in the residence hall. While many of the men, especially those without spouses, spent a good portion of their summers in the other three hunting cabins that lay on the Homestead's outskirts, Stark had decided to make his own a permanent home.

It wasn't necessarily because he wanted to be secluded from the others; he considered all those who had chosen to join him in this endeavor to be close friends, even family. He simply enjoyed the solitude that the tiny, out-of-the-way cabin offered. There was no reason to worry about tidying up or keeping up appearances. He could live in all the filth and squalor that he damn well pleased.

Stephanie hated it though.

He looked over at the sleeping woman in his bed. If she had it her way, their secret rendezvous wouldn't primarily take place in his shithole cabin. On occasion, he would sneak into her beautifully decorated, anally tidy room in the residence hall for them to do their thing, but more often than not she would find herself waking up in his hodgepodge den, groggily searching for a bottle of water or any sort of palatable liquid that didn't have an alcohol percentage.

She let out a grumbling snore and rolled over. The unladylike noise brought a smile to his face.

Sometimes he wondered why they still kept their affair a secret. Up to this point Stephanie was the only single woman to have joined the Homestead. Within her first week they had begun fooling around. It happened almost as an accident — neither was interested in a serious relationship. For three years they had maintained a low-key, almost entirely sexual affair with a perfect lack of serious romance.

He pulled on a pair of faded blue jeans and a button up flannel. As his fingers maneuvered the buttons they brushed across one of the raised, quarter-sized scars on his stomach. He looked down, running a finger along the glossy tissue as his mind wandered over the events that had led to it.

No.

He cut off his own train of thought. There was no reason to ruin the day just yet. He was already fighting to subdue the anxiety lurking in the back of his mind over the impending conversation. He would put off those memories for a few hours, at least until it was time to reveal them to Russo. The thought of his best friend's reaction made him cringe. He expelled the whole topic from his mind, then pulled on a pair of old SWAT boots and silently snuck out the door.

The path to the main cluster of buildings was short, but Stark tried to take pleasure in the cool spring morning as he walked. He'd been raised in the country, and after spending the majority of his adult years bouncing around the world, he still found the refreshing beauty of the northern wilderness to be the one thing that put him most at ease.

As he emerged from the end of the path, a small shape darted into his peripheral.

"Bang! You're dead!" a high-pitched voice shouted as the four-year-old boy leapt out from behind a pine tree, pointing a stick at Stark and making a blubbering machine gun sound.

Stark feigned terror and collapsed, clutching his chest. "Why? Tommy, why?"

The boy froze and stared in disbelief, then looked down at the stick in his hands.

"I'm sorry!" he cried out, dropping his stick and running over to Stark. "Don't be dead! Wake up!"

Stark sprang to his feet and hoisted the boy in his arms, repeatedly tossing him high in the air and catching him. After a moment, Tommy managed to speak between gasping bouts of laughter. "Stop! No more!"

Stark set him down and the boy scampered off to his father who sat on a stack of firewood that lined the outside of the Koutla.

"You're late." Jameson's voice was still slurred. He ruffled his son's hair and gave Stark a cockeyed look. "Your girlfriend keep you for some morning delight?"

"I have no idea what you're talking about," Stark said as he walked by, shoving Jameson over the logs where he landed on his back and snickered.

"Don't hurt my daddy!" Tommy yelled after him as he desperately tried to help his father stand.

"It's ok, it's ok, buddy. Daddy's just a little dizzy." Jameson struggled to his feet.

"Tommy, what time did your daddy stop drinking?"

"An hour ago," Jameson said as Tommy stared intently down at his Mickey Mouse watch and tried to calculate the time.

Stark scoffed. "You're gonna regret that soon. Can you get someone to watch the kid? We need to have a council meeting."

"What about?"

"It's important. Is anyone else awake?"

"I saw Emma a few minutes ago. I think she was going to tend the animals." Jameson took a wobbly knee next to his son. "Hey Tommy, do you want to help Emma feed the horses?"

"No! You said we were going to build today!" The indignant toddler crossed his arms and huffed.

"We will later, I promise… Hey Emma!" Jameson called out.

Stark turned. Across the courtyard Emma emerged from the barn's side door.

"Yes?" she called back.

"Can Tommy help you?"

"Of course he can!" She beamed at the little boy.

"Thank you, Emma," Stark called with a wave. "Jameson, if you would be so kind as to grab the council…"

"Yeah, yeah… I'll rouse the drunks." Jameson nudged his son in Emma's direction. "Go on, boy, get."

Tommy stomped across the courtyard and joined Emma in the barn.

Jameson gave a sad smile as he watched the toddler go, and Stark couldn't help but mirror it. Tommy's story was a tragic one. Jameson had been a member of Stark's squad in Afghanistan. Shortly after rejoining civilian life, Jameson had fallen in love with a beautiful, albeit slightly unstable woman named Kara. When she became pregnant with Tommy,

Jameson had seen it as a blessing and a curse, knowing that her own fragile mental state, including a diagnosis of bipolar disorder, might be passed on to their child.

Kara was eight months pregnant when she was killed in a head on collision with a tractor trailer. In a bittersweet twist of fate, a passing doctor had pulled over at the scene of the accident and managed to deliver Tommy. Kara didn't make it. When questioned by police, the truck driver had sworn that she swerved into his lane on purpose at the last second. Months later, when Jameson cornered him in a bar bathroom, the truck driver still insisted that she committed suicide.

Jameson wasn't himself for a long time after that. He fell into a pit of despair following her death. It was only after accepting Stark's invitation to the Homestead that his jovial, quick-witted personality began to break through the cloud of darkness that had overtaken his life.

"Quit fuckin' smiling at me like that, you creep," Jameson taunted and shoved Stark as he walked by.

Stark laughed. "Tell them to hurry up. We have shit to do!"

"Reveille, reveille, reveille!" Jameson drunkenly sang as he gave Stark the finger over his shoulder.

****

Andrew Russo jerked awake violently. The room around him was ink black and silent. He scrambled out of the sweat-soaked sheets that clung to his legs and slapped his feet onto the hardwood floor. The faint taste of pennies soiled the back of his tongue as his heart pounded in his ears.

The floor.

He focused his mind on the smooth, cool wood beneath his feet.

There's the floor.
It's real.
Fuck.
It's real.
Please…

He straightened his back and took deep, slow breaths. Several moments later, he was able to unclench his hands from the side of the mattress and wipe the cold sweat from his face.

"It's nothing…" he whispered under his breath as he gathered his broken mind. He turned and reached his hand across the bed until he found the still sleeping form of his wife, Maya. Her chest rose and fell in a tranquil rhythm. Her gentle presence always managed to calm his frayed nerves.

Russo stood, feeling his way along the wall to the blackout shades that covered the long singular window of their room. Pulling back the edge to allow just enough sunlight to gather his bearings, he continued to pull in deep, rhythmic breaths.

He didn't remember the nightmare. He never did, but it always left the same sick feeling clawing through his gut — the feeling of witnessing something unnatural. Something so horribly wrong that it soured his mind. It was the same feeling he had the first time a demented middle school friend had shattered his innocence by showing him the video of a murder on Liveleak.

The same feeling he got when he discovered the torn body of a small child next to the impact mark of one of his M203 grenades in Afghanistan.

The same feeling that had suffocated him when he had found his brother sitting upright and pale in a pool of his own blood, staring blankly ahead at the kitchen wall, their father's old revolver half clasped beside him in rigor mortis.

He shook his head violently then glanced down at his

hands. They had stopped shaking. He knew he was fine. He knew that diving further down that rabbit hole of painful memories ran the risk of breaking him. Today he was lucky. Every day that dam of reason held he considered himself lucky.

A light rap on the door rescued him from the inner turmoil. *Distractions.* That was the key, the best solution to an unfixable problem. He pulled on a pair of frayed sweatpants and slipped out the door.

Jameson leaned against the opposite wall of the hallway that ran through the middle of the residence building.

"Hey, man. Big boss called a meeting," the tall, dark haired twenty-five-year-old said without looking up from the block of wood he was whittling. Russo could tell from the way he swayed back and forth that the man was still drunk.

"Yeah, ok." Russo paused, rubbing his sleep-swollen eyes and staring at the flakes of wood Jameson was absentmindedly flicking onto the floor. After a moment, Jameson took notice.

"Don't worry, *little boss*, I'll clean it up."

Russo flinched inwardly at the tease, which stung more than it necessarily should have. Russo was universally considered the second-in-command, but just like it had in the Marine Corps, the leadership role brought with it a regular flow of snide remarks.

"Tell them I'll be there in a minute."

Jameson grunted in response and started back down the hallway.

Russo gently shut the door so as not to disturb the still sleeping Maya, then crossed the room to the wardrobe he'd crafted two years before. A white hand-knit sweater caught his attention as he milled through the row of shirts left over from his previous life. It was his favorite sweater, a gift his grandmother had made for him shortly before he and his wife had followed his best friend to Alaska. He pulled it off the hanging rod and let his fingers pass over the soft, unmolested fabric.

His grandmother was an incredible woman; a true wolf in sheep's clothing. From an unknowing perspective, she would have appeared as just another kindly old Italian woman, but her Machiavellian nature and aggressive mannerisms made her one of the most compelling and powerful people Russo ever met. He looked up to her so much that when she had taken Stark under her wing, Russo had almost let his jealousy destroy their friendship.

Russo thought back to when the hardy old woman and his best friend had first met.

Russo and Stark were in different units in the Marine Corps, but after meeting during a fateful night of drinking they became instant friends. Stark was a loner, the type to spend leave blocks meandering around the barracks rather than traveling to visit his family. As often happens with Marines, Russo had taken Stark into his own family. During one Christmas leave Stark accompanied him on a trip to Boston. After all their drunken shenanigans at their duty station in North Carolina, Russo was amazed when Stark transitioned seamlessly into a civil, polite, even charming human being during that week.

Russo's grandmother had immediately taken a shine to Stark. The two were so similar. They connected in a way that he knew he could never replicate himself.

She had seen Russo's jealousy almost immediately and, as with any dispute within the family (or any dispute that she'd no doubt ever been involved in), she immediately nipped it in the bud.

"Don't worry, Andrew," she had told him, "you're still my

favorite."

He remembered the way her face creased with wrinkles like an over ripened pear when she winked at him.

"I need to make something clear to you. I understand that you might be a bit envious of my connection with your friend, but *you* must understand… this is a curse for him. There is a reason I didn't raise you to be like me. I raised you to be *good*. Stark isn't *good*. While you may fight your own demons, your *goodness* will fill a space in your heart that Stark will never fill. I look at the pain in that boy's eyes and it's like looking in a mirror. He has a broken soul. My own soul broke when that *diavolo* Mussolini killed my family, but I believe Stark was born that way. I mourn for his future because I know the struggles he will face trying to repair it."

Initially Russo had considered his grandmother's words to simply be kind lies told to sooth his anxious spirit, but as time went on and he watched Stark evolve over the next four years, he realized the truth in them. The man was in fact tortured.

By what? Perhaps simply his own existence. Stark seemed to be searching for something he could never find. It reminded Russo of the ancient Achillean mantra that claimed a good warrior searches only for a clean death. Russo found himself wondering if Stark was the embodiment of that idea. Perhaps the only thing that could give his best friend's soul rest was to be annihilated completely.

Russo had to remind himself of this from time to time in order to keep his own bruised ego in check. The way things had shaped up in the Homestead over the years left him as a strong authority figure, but sitting just under Stark in the perceived chain of command. When Jameson poked fun at him, calling him *little boss*, he had to make it a point to put his ego aside. Stark had earned his way into Russo's innermost circle, and if it meant putting up with childish quips in order to live as a family out here in their winter wonderland, then he was willing to do it.

Ten minutes later Russo adjusted the collar of his flannel jacket as he pushed through the side door of the Koutla. The hall was a mess. A dozen half-eaten platters of food were scattered haphazardly along the oak table, which was coated in a thick lacquer of stale beer. His boots made a *shtck* noise with each step as their soles clung to the sticky floor.

Stark sat at the head of the table. Next to him, Jameson sported a comically large pair of aviators. Apparently in the short time it had taken Russo to dress and cross the courtyard between the residence hall and the Koutla, Jameson's drunken state had morphed into a full-fledged hangover.

Just as Russo took his seat, the door at the opposite end of the Koutla banged open. Sam Oliver stomped in, yelling in a gravelly voice, "Aww shit!"

Jameson winced at the loud noise, looking for a second as if he was going to be sick before returning to his carving.

"Hair of the dog," Russo said, motioning to the keg at the table's head.

"Empty. Trust me, already checked," Jameson responded as Oliver came stomping toward them.

Sam Oliver was a very strange man by most standards. A casual conversation with him would often quickly devolve into a series of guttural swears and overly animated gestures imitating the internet sensation Tourrettes Guy.

Hunt was the last to arrive, calmly taking his seat opposite Oliver's dramatic entrance.

"Alright, let's start this shit," Stark said, pulling his chair closer to the table and taking on his usual air of authority. "We need to make arrangements for the first Harkstaff trip of the season. By now the mountain pass should be melted enough for us to get through. We're going to need to turn in a death certificate for Jackson as well as put in the first order for supplies. Do we have the list ready?"

Jameson opened a folder and sifted through its contents, pulling out three sheets of paper. He passed them to Stark.

At the beginning of every summer, the Homesteaders would put in an order through a specialty service that would deliver their products by helicopter, dropping a shipping container full of supplies in the paddock and taking the container from the previous shipment away with it.

"We can lump most of the new plumbing shit in with the secondary shipment, but I do want to order a few extra bundles of steel wire than we originally planned for," Hunt interjected as Stark browsed the list. "The paddock fence has too many gaps; I want to run a couple extra wires around to fill them in." Hunt was referring to the open grazing area alongside the barn that they had cleared and fenced in by wrapping thick steel cord in eight-inch rows around the surrounding trees.

"Got it," Stark mumbled, barely paying attention.

"Yo," Jameson pointed to the final paper once Stark reached it. "This satellite dish project is going to be a pain in the ass. I can't guarantee it'll work. Frank claims that if I make it to specs he can get us connected to the internet. It'll be expensive, not that that matters, but I want it to be known *now* that if it ends up being a waste of time, I'm not going be the one to blame."

"Yeah, ok," Stark muttered.

This wasn't the normal Stark, Russo noted. There was something off about him.

Apparently, he wasn't the only one to notice. Oliver slapped the table to get the group's attention. They all turned to him. "So, you're telling me that you're actually going to get us a porn machine?" he asked with a smirk in an obvious attempt to lighten the mood.

"I'm gonna put a child filter on your shit," Jameson retorted.

Knowing that the conversation could easily morph into Oliver and Jameson playfully throwing absurd, curse-riddled threats at each other, Russo tried to change the subject. "Is there anything else we need from Harkstaff? I know Frank made a list of a few thing he thinks might cheer up Amy, but other than that, this order seems pretty generic."

The table was silent. Stark stared blankly through the papers in front of him and didn't seem to register the question. Russo looked from face to face as the others shook their heads, finally settling his eyes on Oliver, who had his hand raised. "What?"

Oliver cleared his throat and took on a serious tone. "I, uh… I've been hearing some complaints from around the Homestead that a one-legged guy has been having sex with the sheep."

Jameson let out a wheezing laugh beside him and raised his hand for a high five. Oliver slapped it enthusiastically and both waited for a comeback from Hunt.

"Enough. We have shit to do," Stark said when Hunt refused to respond. "Oliver, Jameson, I need you guys to start getting shit together for the trip. It'll be the three of us and Irniq. Pack extra ammo. Now more than ever we can't underestimate the wildlife."

The duo agreed and rose, Jameson turning back as he reached the door and throwing Hunt a wink.

"My fucking dogs are better behaved than those two," Hunt muttered once they'd left.

"Yeah, I bet your dogs don't hump each other as much

either." Stark pushed the papers away and looked at Hunt. "Tell him."

"What?" Hunt was taken aback. "No! You fuckin' tell him."

Stark sighed.

"Tell me what?" Russo demanded. "What the hell is wrong with you two today?"

"I saw something yesterday morning... It's... there's something you need to know." Stark's demeanor throughout the meeting suddenly seemed chipper in comparison to the way he spoke now.

Russo wasn't used to being out of the loop. The fact that he couldn't imagine any secrets Stark would withhold from the other two council members brought with it a hint of worry. He glanced at Hunt, who sat stone-faced glaring at Stark.

"What? What are you talking about?" Russo prompted after Stark paused for too long.

Stark exhaled through his nose then met Russo's eyes. "There's something you don't know — something you don't *want* to know about... all of this," he said, motioning the room around them. "It's hard to—"

"He didn't inherit the land," Hunt interjected. "Well, he did, but not in the way we led everyone to believe."

Russo felt a knot forming in his stomach. "What the fuck are you talking about?"

Stark spoke in measured sentences. "Andrew, I consider you a brother. I didn't tell you this because I knew you wouldn't have come here, and you *needed* to come here. After what happened, you were already a potential target."

Stark pulled out a pack of Lucky Strikes and lit one, then tossed it across the table to Hunt, who took one for himself then handed the pack to Russo. Russo glanced at him sidelong with a raised eyebrow — they knew he hadn't smoked in nearly five years.

"You're gonna need one for this," Hunt said.

Russo waved him off, looking back to Stark.

"Ok… here we go," Stark muttered, leaning forward.

By the time the three men left the Koutla an hour later, Russo had smoked nearly the entire pack by himself.

4

May 7th

The next morning the party of four set off several hours before the sun crept over the tips of the distant fir trees that made up the horizon. The warm glow cut through the foliage, lighting up the well-trodden game trail that lead away from the Homestead and snaked up the neighboring mountain. The four men rode in single file along the winding path. Each of their steeds' labored grunts was accompanied by twin jets of vapor that cut through the cool morning air. The rugged quarter horses were laden with the bare essentials to make the two-and-a-half-day ride to Harkstaff.

Jameson and Oliver rode behind Stark. At the head of the group rode Irniq Locklear.

Despite having just turned nineteen, Irniq was a fantastic tracker. Born and bred in the Alaskan wilderness, he had spent his youth as a hunting guide alongside his father before joining the Homestead. Together he and his father had capitalized on what they half-jokingly referred to as "The White Man's Arrogance" to cater to wealthy wannabe big game hunters. When his older sister, Alasie, married Oliver, Irniq had taken it upon himself to join her in the Homestead. He had initially done so due to his fear that she might need his protection, but as months turned into years he found himself becoming an integral part of the community.

The party rode through the morning, traversing the forest at a moderate pace, careful not to wear their steeds too thin. By midday they had begun the gentle incline at the base of the mountain, which they had named the Fist. Their route led them along the edge of the thousand-foot behemoth, allowing them to circumnavigate its impassable peak, but still forcing them to take a treacherous path along sheer cliff ledges littered with megalithic boulders. By the time the sun's descent began casting long shadows along the muddy trail, their steeds had begun to show signs of fatigue.

"Hold up!" Stark shouted to Irniq, who had ridden a few hundred meters ahead of the group. When no response came from beyond the dense foliage, Stark called out again.

"He ain't stopping." Jameson pulled up to a halt next to Stark. "He was talking earlier about making the tundra before sundown. You know how he gets about this shit."

Stark sat silently and listened. It had only been minutes since he had lost sight of their Inuit companion and he knew Irniq hadn't made it beyond shouting distance. Behind them Oliver stopped and plucked his headphones out, making the tinny sound of the late 90's alt-rock music audible to the others.

"What is it?" Oliver asked wide-eyed, coming out of his riding trance like someone waking from a deep sleep.

"We need to break for the night, but apparently your brother-in-law doesn't agree," Jameson said, patting the glistening neck of his horse as it huffed at the rapidly chilling dusk air.

"Hey Tonto!" Oliver bellowed through the trees.

From deep in woods ahead came a high-pitched whistle. The three riders shared a puzzled look. There was no need for such means of communication this deep in the wilderness.

They goaded the horses on quietly.

Around the curving mountain path ahead, Irniq's horse stood alone, flanked on one side by a cliff wall and the other by a steep, wooded slope. The trio pulled their horses to a halt, scanning the surrounding forest for their friend.

"Here," Irniq called softly. He was halfway up one of the grand pines that bordered the path, signaling them to stop with one hand and holding a pair of binoculars in the other. "Do you smell that?"

Stark dismounted and made his way to the base of the tree. The remote scent of burnt motor oil lingered in the air.

"Quarter mile ahead, down at the base of the fist." Irniq pointed. "Definitely a vehicle, not moving though…" He paused and squinted harder into the binoculars. "Looks wrecked."

A wave of dread washed over Stark.

They've found me.

"We go in on foot," Stark ordered. "Jameson, I need you to stay with the horses. The last thing we need is predators taking out our ride. Oliver, Irniq, load up. Whoever thought it was a good idea to drive this far out did it with a purpose, and I'm guessing it involves us."

The tracker climbed down from his perch. Oliver moved to help Jameson secure the horses while Irniq addressed Stark. "Who is it?"

"That's what we're going to find out."

Irniq stepped closer, muttering in Stark's ear so the others couldn't hear. "No one from Harkstaff would try to bring vehicle out here. They know it'd be suicide. Is there something going on that I don't know about?"

Stark met Irniq's eyes and grasped his shoulder. "Brother, you know as much as I do," he lied through his teeth.

The teenager nodded anxiously and gripped Stark's

shoulder in return.

Irniq turned to Jameson. "There's a lot of predators on this mountain. Trust the horses. If they spook, you be ready to shoot."

"He's right," Stark said, pulling a shotgun from the back of his saddle. "Rifles and pistols, Oliver, don't try and bring that fucking bow. Just because you married an Inuit doesn't make you one. If it can't kill a bear, we don't need it."

They found the wreckage on the edge of the tree line that separated the mountain from the rolling tundra beyond. The pearl black SUV's hood was wrapped in a tangled embrace around a pine stump at the bottom of a gully.

As the three men cautiously approached the gully's edge, Irniq pointed to a tire strip of freshly turned dirt on the opposite bank. "It looks like they hit something on the other side and lost control."

Stark knew the old maps of the area that floated around the neighboring towns made it seem like there was a passable route for a vehicle to cut between the mountain's base and the massive lake that walled in the valley. On his first visit to the land years before, he made a similar mistake, and ended up shelling out thirty grand to replace the borrowed truck he'd sunk into the lake's shallows.

Irniq pointed to a dark mound protruding from the dirt a few yards behind the wrecked SUV. "Cub."

He was right. Flies buzzed around the corpse of the juvenile black bear that lay in a mangled heap beside the torn-up tracks.

They made their way down the gully's ledge to the twisted wreck. The driver's side rear door and front passenger door both stood ajar, and Stark could make out the driver in the front seat. Irniq and Oliver examined the bear cub's corpse while Stark approached the SUV, his short barreled 12-gauge centered on the vehicle's unmoving occupant. As he peered into the open cab he caught the stench of human shit and blood, and he forced a swift exhale to keep from gagging. The driver sat motionless, his head hanging from his shoulders by a thick flap of skin. His torso looked as if it had been hacked at with a dull chainsaw. Blood and innards carpeted the steering wheel and dashboard and his dismembered lower arm laid across the passenger seat.

Behind Stark, Oliver toed the cub. "Mama bear is not going to be happy," he said with genuine sadness — a rarity for the man.

"I think Mama bear already got hers," Stark muttered, stepping back from the SUV and motioning the others to look. He walked back to the dead cub. It was a black bear, unlike the grizzly that had killed Jackson.

Fucking bears.

"We've got two sets of human tracks leading into the forest. She followed them after she ate." Irniq fingered a deep paw print in the mud. He pulled his hand back and showed the others a red stain of blood. "Bitch wanted revenge."

It was half an hour before they found the first man. The two sets of tracks leading away from the crash site had split about two-hundred meters into the tree line. It was at the split that one set of prints, which Irniq had ascertained to belong to a very large man, was suddenly accompanied by an increasingly heavy blood trail.

They tracked the bloody trail and found what remained of the body at the base of an oak tree, lodged between the trunk and a rotting log. Irniq had indeed been right about the man's size. By Stark's estimate he had been well over six-feet-tall and probably close to three-hundred pounds before the bear had taken its fill. The mess of organs and flesh was held together by a soggy parka over a slim-fitting suit, which in life would probably have shown off an intimidating physique, but in death simply served as a wet bag to hold the remains together.

"We should move on," Oliver said as they spent the last moments of fading light examining the corpse.

Stark bent and rifled through the tattered suit pockets. He found no wallet or identification, only an empty shoulder holster tucked neatly under the left arm.

It's them.

It has to be.

"He had a gun," he said solemnly. "Keep a close eye out. If the other one's still alive, he might be armed."

"You think someone's gonna try and shoot us? We're their only chance of getting out of here alive," Oliver scoffed.

"They've been out here for at least a day, Oli. The cold and the forest can do strange things to a man," Irniq said.

"*The cold and the forest can do weird shit to a man,*" Oliver mocked in a nasally voice, drawing an eye roll from Irniq. "Motherfucker shoots at me, I'ma shoot him back."

"Yeah… you do that…" Stark surveyed the mountain slope. "We need to head back. It's too dark for Jameson to be up there alone."

As if on cue a lone wolf's howl drifted through the fresh darkness.

"What about the other tracks?"

"I'll take Jameson over any idiot who tries to bring a car this far into the wild. If he's still alive he'll have to wait until morning." Stark wiped the blood from his hands on the mossy log and stood. "Play stupid games, win stupid prizes."

As they pushed back through the semi-thawed forest, Stark couldn't help but glance around nervously. How could he explain to these men the danger they now faced without giving away the truth of his past?

It took them an hour to find their way back to Jameson, and another to lead the horses up the mountain's dark trails until they found a suitable campsite. The mood was somber as they sat around their modest fire. Orange flames licked the air as Oliver and Jameson sat upright in their sleeping bags and argued over a game of rummy.

Stark sat on a log beside Irniq. He knew something was bothering the tracker. Irniq was regularly stoic, but he seemed more distant than usual after finding the second corpse. After a brief period of staring at the flames in silence, Stark leaned in. "What is it? The bear attack?" Stark asked.

Irniq had been with him when they had discovered the half-eaten remains of Jackson drifting in the shallows. Stark considered that the scene today might have triggered some deep-seated emotions in the young man.

"No." Irniq turned to face Stark and leaned in close. "I'm worried about something out here far more dangerous than a bear. That blood trail, it started just as the tracks split. I think the man still out there, if he's even alive, attacked his buddy in order to get away from the bear."

Stark nodded. "Agreed. We should keep the fire low. No need to advertise our location." He stood up and spoke louder, including the other two in the conversation. "Gentlemen, we don't know who's out here. There was an empty holster on the big boy we found, so there's a good chance that the other is armed. I'll take the first shift, you all get some sleep. I want to start the search again as soon as dawn hits."

"Yessuh, boss-man," Oliver gave a dramatic salute before flopping backwards onto the ground. He and Jameson continued their hushed banter until they drifted off to sleep. Irniq laid his sleeping bag beside the fire, telling Stark to wake him for the second shift when he grew drowsy.

The night air was crisp and carried with it the wafting scents of pine and wood-smoke. Stark sat beside the dying fire, only adding the occasional log to keep the embers alive. Around him the ghostly sounds of the forest echoed off the trees: in the distance, a pack of wolves howled to each other, and somewhere down the mountain, in the flat tundra that laid beyond, an elk let out its long, shrill shriek.

Within an hour the thick wool socks and winter boots that encased Stark's feet lost their warmth and his toes began to numb. He stood up, pacing the edge of the encampment to restore circulation. His mind wandered over the events of the week: Jackson, the crashed SUV, the dead cub. What shit luck.

Or was it?

The Homestead never had any need for defenses or a sentry outside of the casual barn watch. What would have happened if these men had been able to reach the Homestead? How many people had been in danger of having their throats slit in the middle of the night by the giant suited man or his mysterious companion? Stark's mind wandered over the gut wrenching scenarios as he paced the edge of the camp.

Finally, he stopped himself. He had no idea who these intruders were or what they wanted. They could very well be from the IRS. Maybe his accountant, who was actually just an old Marine friend and investment banker, had fucked up his taxes. Maybe the Jew prick took the millions and ran off.

He grinned at the ludicrous thought. The man was an old friend, a master of finances and just as loyal as Stark.

No, whoever these people were they apparently traveled armed and without ID. The more he considered it, the more the idea solidified in his mind that his past was coming back to haunt him.

The sound of rustling foliage ripped him from his deliberations. Stark crouched and flicked off the shotgun's safety, pointing it out into the darkened columns of tree trunks. He knew the dwindling light of the embers silhouetted his figure and made his companions easy targets. Squinting to see past the glow of the fire on the nearby wall of trees, he lapped the camp, shaking each of the men awake and motioning from his ear toward the forest. They understood. Each one silently slipped from their sleeping bags and disappeared into the darkness of the surrounding trees.

The crunching footsteps grew louder. They were uneven, staggered, and shuffling like a B-rate zombie. Stark took a knee at the edge of the tree line behind the cover of a thick cottonwood and trained the twin barrels of his shotgun on the source of the sound. His finger drifted to the second trigger, the one that operated the bottom 12-gauge barrel filled with buck shot. The heavy deer slug in the upper barrel was useless without a visible target, but the buck shot would scatter quickly into the dark night and stood a far greater chance of hitting whoever, or whatever, was out there.

"Hello?" A cracking voice came from the darkness. "Please? Is there someone here?"

Stark glanced around to make sure the others weren't in his line of fire.

Like a battered ship emerging from the night a small man stumbled into the clearing. His features were hard to make out in the flickering light of the dying fire, but even beneath the layers of dirt and grime Stark could see that he was middle aged.

"H-h-help…" the dramatically shivering man whimpered, staring around with encampment with wide, terrified eyes. "Please… P-please, God, someone be here."

"Stop," Stark commanded, stepping out into the man's field of view with the gun leveled at his chest.

"Oh, God, thank you!" The stranger reached out toward Stark and stumbled forward.

"I said *STOP!*" Stark bellowed.

The man came to a sudden halt and the joy in his face morphed into a pitiful confusion.

"Do what he says, friend," Irniq said softly, emerging from the shadows behind the stranger with his revolver drawn.

"How many did they send?" Stark asked.

The man's panicked eyes darted from one to the other, finally focusing on Stark's face. "What? Th-there were just the three of us!" he insisted. A look of recognition flashed across his face. "You're Augustin Stark, right?"

Stark registered the motion as soon as it had started. The man's left hand grasped the outside of his jacket, pulling it back while the right hand darted inside. By the time his hand had disappeared under the thick parka, Stark had closed the ten-foot distance between them and arched the stock of his shotgun across the man's face. The strike drew a sickening thud and its victim fell limp to the forest floor. Stark hovered over the unconscious man for a moment, wondering if the impact had killed him.

"Jesus Christ, dude," Jameson said, materializing from behind a tree. "I haven't seen a hit like that since…" His voice drifted off as he stared at the limp form with bewilderment.

Oliver stepped out of the darkness. "A little harsh, eh?"

Stark ignored him and pulled the stranger's hands to his sides before reaching into the man's jacket. To his surprise he didn't find a gun, only a thin wallet with a laminated ID badge inside identifying him as Franklin Summerset, Senior Vice President of Lockstone Oil.

Maybe I was wrong.

Stark flipped through the wallet and found several corresponding IDs. He felt a hint of relief, but didn't relax yet. Just because the man carried a corporate ID didn't mean they were in the clear.

5

Stephanie Marza stood outside the Homestead's clinic. The radio call came in about an hour before. Starks's voice crackled through heavy static caused by the morning mist, alerting her that the party would be returning soon with a wounded stranger in tow.

She squeezed her hands under the arms of her puffy winter jacket and shivered. She wasn't a fan of the perpetual cold that lingered so long into the spring. Having grown up in a small Montana town, one might think she'd developed what most northerners called "thick blood," but her petite frame never seemed to be able hold onto the small amount of heat she managed to produce.

She looked back and considered returning to the warm building behind her. It was the only entirely concrete structure in the Homestead, and reminded her more of a nuclear fallout bunker than a medical clinic. Her eyes wandered to the plywood sign next to the main door. The letters B.A.S. were spray-painted haphazardly along its length.

Fucking Marines.

She had known what she was getting into when she had chosen to join her best friend, Maya Russo, in moving to this strange little community. She had prepared herself for stress, the harsh conditions, the lack of superfluous amenities. She had even come to terms with giving up the social media platforms she'd been so attached to.

But she hadn't prepared herself for all the fucking acronyms.

Who would have thought that one of the hardest things for a group of infantry veterans to let go of would be their incessant need to abbreviate everything? She knew the letters on the sign stood for *Battalion Aid Station*. She knew, and every day when she saw it, she wanted to spray-paint the words *Clinic* or *Hospital* or even *Fucking Doctor's Office* over it. It seemed like every day there would be a new phrase to learn: *CASEVAC*, *BCGs*, *COC*... The list went on and on, beginning with legitimate military jargon then devolving into things like the ever so popular *LMB* that was regularly scrawled on the whiteboard in the Koutla next to messages that Oliver didn't like. It took her a week to figure out what that one meant: *Lick My Butthole*.

Classy.

But she hadn't come to the Homestead for class. Sometimes she believed she'd come for the exact opposite. While all the other women with whom she now lived came to the Homestead alongside their husbands, she had come alone. When Maya first broached the idea, Stephanie had brushed it off as a joke. She had a life in Florida, a fantastic nursing job that she had somehow fallen into straight out of college and a social life so active it was hard to keep up with. She had only taken the subject seriously after a long night spent alone in her apartment with a bottle of merlot and deep personal confrontation.

Stephanie had always been a bit of a loner. Not in a social sense — she had never had trouble making friends or maintaining an active social life, but in a strange and ideological sense. During her freshman year at the University of Central Florida she had believed her desire for natural simplicity was rooted in her rural upbringing and would eventually pass. However, five years, tens of thousands of dollars of school debt, and the beginning of a promising career later she still had the nagging feeling tugging at the back of her mind urging her in a polar opposite direction.

She had begun to visualize herself as a marionette. The fine cords that controlled her led back to an ever-expanding series of outside forces: rent, bills, Facebook, Twitter, politics, taxes, student debt, credit cards, car payments, laws, social boundaries, prejudice, social justice, bureaucracy... The little strings that society embedded in her soul with painful little fishhooks had latched on one by one until she felt them controlling not only her actions, but her very character.

As a child, Stephanie was terrified of the dark, but as she developed into a woman, a greater fear loomed in her mind. The fear of stumbling, tripping up somewhere along the overly complicated route of life and being caught in the mess of these strings as they slowly pulled tighter, cutting off the feeling in her limbs, slowly constricting around her throat until she choked into a hellish oblivion.

That night, staring at the half empty bottle of California red, she began to seriously consider her best friend's proposition. Three years later, standing outside the harsh concrete clinic trying to warm her numb fingers, she was thankful she had.

In the distance, along the ATV-hewn path that led away from the BAS, four horses emerged from the trees. The colossal mountain looming behind them made for a picturesque view. *The Four Horsemen returneth,* she mused, watching them trot along the path toward her. She turned and banged three times on the thick steel door with her fist.

"They're here!" She knew the door would turn her words into an inaudible murmur to the doctor on the other side.

The door cracked open and Alwan's head squeezed through, his long, graying dreadlocks falling past the handle as he tried to let in as little of the cold as possible.

"Okay, get the newcomer in here. Stark says they found him across the mountain with hypothermia. No major wounds, but I been drawing him a hot bath and prepping a thoracic lavage just in case," the sixty-seven-year-old Jamaican said with a thick accent, then squeezed his head back through the opening and closed the door.

So many things fucked up about this.

Any stateside physician, or even first year medical student, knew the chances of putting a hypothermic patient in shock rose tenfold when warming them too quickly, which is exactly what she believed a hot bath would do. Had it not been for the incredible results of the man's often paradoxical healing methods she would have dismissed him as a kook years ago. However, she had witnessed on too many occasions the gentle older man care for and cure every patient that was brought to him, and had come to understand that his strange methods and insistence on the use of his beloved ganja were oftentimes more reliable than that of the doctors she worked with in Florida.

As the riders drew close she saw her new patient in a bundled mass straddling the back of Oliver's saddle. His entire upper body was stuffed inside a thick green sleeping bag with a hole cut out for him to breathe from.

Interesting blindfold.

She couldn't help but scoff at the weird ingenuity that erupted from the minds of men faced with unexpected challenges.

The newcomer appeared catatonic as Oliver rode up next

to her. The sleeping bag mask emitted a rambling, muffled murmur. Oliver pulled a knife from his belt and smiled, motioning to a series of cords that held the stranger to his back, making him a sort of horse-top human backpack. Stephanie understood, and before she could form a panicked shout, Oliver slid the knife under one of the cords.

"Catch!" he said with the gleeful tone of a deviant child holding a flame thrower and twisted the blade.

The cord snapped, unwinding rapidly as the slumped figure slid sidelong off the horse. While Oliver's intentions may have been humorous, his execution was poor. The semi-conscious man, entirely unaware of his surroundings, panicked as he began to fall and threw his weight to the left, which caused him to fall to the horse's side opposite Stephanie's waiting arms. His body hit the ground with a cringeworthy thump.

"Ahhh shit…" Oliver said in his gravelly voice, staring at the now entirely unconscious man.

"You fucking idiot!" Stephanie screamed, punching Oliver hard in his thigh. He let out a spout of curses and spurred his horse away from her, clutching the Charlie-horse in his leg.

"The fuck is wrong with you?" Stark shouted after him, stifling a laugh and dismounting to help Stephanie drag the limp body into the clinic.

The man was older: in his early-to-mid forties as best as Stephanie could tell. He was mostly bald and his face was marred with a thick coat of dirt that did little to disguise a swollen black eye. His slight frame and gaunt features reminded her of a wealthy Gollum. Under the makeshift warming layers, he wore expensive clothes, the type marketed to rich skiers and nature enthusiasts. They undressed him, then laid him on a gurney and Alwan chimneyed a series of ganja smoke breaths into the man's mouth, drawing a few weak coughs. They then slowly dipped him in the hot bath, feet first, gently sliding him down until only his head was unsubmerged. Alwan remained beside the bath, observing the man's breathing while Stephanie crossed the room and grasped Stark's arm.

He seemed not to notice her, maintaining a heated glare at the newcomer. She didn't expect any sort of affectionate gesture on his part. After all, that's how their relationship worked. She let go of Stark, then made her way back over to her new patient.

The stranger regained consciousness after a few minutes. Alwan helped him out of the stainless-steel tub and wrapped him in a robe before setting him down on the frayed leather recliner that occupied the corner of the room. Stephanie helped the doctor unpack a series of space heaters from the storage closet, where they had been stored the week before in preparation for the spring. They placed them in a tight semicircle around the shivering man.

"I think it's just about lunch time, Doc," Stark said evenly and nodded his head toward the door. Alwan understood but hesitated.

Alwan was a brilliant man, to say the least, having spent most of his life as a neurosurgeon in Boston. But it didn't take a neurosurgeon to read Stark's tone.

He stood slowly and gave Stark a knowing look. The doctor was a strict Rastafarian and did not condone violence or manipulation.

"Yeah, I guess you're right. Stephanie, please come get me when this is done. Augustin…" He paused in front of the much younger man and leaned in. "Whatever this man has done, you stay calm. He is fragile right now." With that, he pulled on his jacket and tri-colored Rasta cap and exited the building.

Stephanie knew the mentor-mentee dynamic that existed between the two, but was genuinely surprised to see Stark snap out of his agitated state and appear to reconsider his approach following the doctor's words.

"Stephanie," he turned to her, "maybe you should join him."

"Why?" She knew the answer but wanted to hear him say it before she told him off.

"Stephanie, just—"

"Did I stutter?"

He rolled his eyes. "Our friend here tried to drive in through the pass with two others, both are dead. I believe one of these men is dead because of him."

"Why were they trying to drive in?"

"Well that's what I'm going to find out."

"You're going to hurt him?"

Stark's brow furrowed in feigned offense. "What kind of person do you think I am?"

"You're starting to make me wonder." She paused. "Seriously, what are you going to do?"

"I just need to ask him a few questions, and I'd like the room if you don't mind."

"Don't patronize me. You and I both know I'm not going anywhere." She punctuated the sentence by leaning back against a cabinet of medical supplies.

Stark let out a resigned sigh and nodded. She was just as stubborn as he was, and she knew she'd won this battle. He crossed the room and knelt in front of the seated stranger, who stared past him with thin, bloodshot eyes. The doctor's magical ganja definitely had an effect on the man.

"Hey, buddy," Stark said, snapping his fingers directly in front of the stranger's face.

The snapping seemed to draw him from his daze. He met Stark's eyes then threw a bewildered look at Stephanie. She couldn't help but feel bad for the man. Besides the hypothermia and whatever-the-hell else happened on that mountain, she could hardly imagine how strange and terrifying this place must have seemed to him.

"What's your name?" Stark asked once he was sure he had the stranger's attention.

"My name... My name is Franklin... Franklin Summerset." He spoke slowly, clearly clawing through the THC-induced fog to find the right words.

"Yeah? And where are you from, Frankie?" Stark asked.

"I came to find a man named—"

Stark cut him off with a lightning fast slap across the face. Stephanie lurched forward instinctively but stopped when Stark raised his finger and gave her a stern look.

"Trust me," he mouthed before turning back to the stoned man. She did trust him. In truth she trusted him more than anyone else in her life. But she was afraid that she was witnessing the reemergence of the dark character she had heard hushed rumors about from the others.

"Frankie, if that is your name, I'm going to make this a very simple process. It'll be like a game, but very Pavlovian in nature. I'm going to ask you a question, then you are going to answer that question. If you stray from the answers, I'm going to set you back on the right path. Okay?"

Franklin took a moment to digest what he was being told. He nodded.

"Where are you from?"

"Err... Chicago," he said after a pause.

"Good. Now, Frankie, who sent you here?"

"The company I work for, Lockstone Oil."

"Good. Now tell me how you found me."

Franklin looked confused, as if the answer was obvious. "We're interested in acquiring your land. You *are* Mr. Stark, right?"

Stark nodded. Even though he wasn't facing her, Stephanie saw the tension melt from Stark's body.

His next action caught her completely off-guard. Without warning, he reared back and belted Franklin across the face with an open hand, immediately catching the stunned, pathetic face with his opposite hand and slamming it into the seatback.

Stephanie froze.

Stark's fingers dug deep into Franklin's cheeks as he leaned in close and growled in his face. She heard him say something, barely audible over Franklin's panicked, swine-like squeal. It echoed through her brain as she scrambled to understand what was happening: *Cartel.*

"What? No! Please! Stop! I have no idea! Please!" Franklin pleaded through Stark's hand.

Finally getting past her initial surprise, Stephanie lunged forward and seized Stark's shoulder. He spun to face her, his eyes feral slits and his face knotted like an attacking dog. She saw something in those eyes that made her forget the hardy, compassionate man she had come to know. It struck a primal cord of terror deep in her heart.

Then, in a heartbeat, it was gone. Stark's face melted back into his own.

"Sorry," he said, leaning back and releasing the panicked Franklin. "I just had to be sure of something."

Stephanie backed away. She didn't know exactly what she felt. A strange mix of confusion, fear, and disorientation as if something in her happy little world in the Arctic forest had suddenly changed dramatically. Some piece of the life she had built up here had just come unhinged and left her spinning off center.

Stark turned back to Franklin, who cowered in his seat sucking in short, choppy breaths.

"Sorry about that, boss, had to be sure." Stark smiled disarmingly, though it had little effect on his victim. "You're a businessman then, eh? Let's talk brass tacks."

It took a moment for Franklin to compose what was left of his scattered mind, but he eventually nodded.

"Okay, so, you want to buy this land?"

"We're willing to offer a substantial sum for the valley, well over asking price," Franklin was clearly still wary of his tormentor's capricious attitude and flinched as Stark stood.

"Why?" Stark asked, and began circling the chair like a shark. "I'm not going to hit you," he added casually as Franklin's eyes darted along with him.

"We, we believe the land would be a valuable asset."

"Clearly, but what are you planning on doing here?"

"I can't say."

"Of course… but it doesn't take a genius to figure it out." Stark stopped pacing and pointed a finger at Franklin. "You want to drill, don't you? The way I see it there's nowhere to fit a pipeline through these mountains, but you spotted a nice little lot of private land on some map that wasn't part of a national park and you thought 'why don't we frack it to hell?'"

"Mr. Stark, we're simply interested in purchasing the land. We've seen from your tax returns that you inherited this area along with a *very* substantial amount of money. We're interested in helping you expand your wealth for a mutual benefit." Franklin seemed to be coming down from his high. His voice was much more measured and his words more eloquently strung together.

"I'm pretty sure tax returns are supposed to be private." Stark raised an eyebrow.

Franklin paused. "We are a very large company, Mr. Stark, and we're willing to pay handsomely—"

"You keep repeating yourself... That's not the sign of a good negotiator. I'll save us both some time and make this excruciatingly simple: the land *is not*, nor *will it ever* be for sale."

Franklin opened his mouth to object, but Stark cut him off once again. "In the morning, we'll take you back to Harkstaff. The trip will take a couple days — we don't have any SUVs out here. When you get there, you're going to fly off back to Chicago or wherever you came from and tell your boss that he can fuck off. Then remind him that Alaska is a castle state, which means I can legally *kill* any intruders who trespass unannounced and armed on my property. Is that clear?"

Stephanie judged by the look on Franklin's face that he understood the sincerity of the threat. He nodded.

"Good. I'm going to get some food. Thanks to you I haven't had a chance to eat in the past day and a half. Maybe that's why I'm so grumpy." Stark turned and smiled at Stephanie. "All done."

She was still unsure of how to process the events that had just unfolded as Stark coasted across the room and out the door. As he left, Oliver entered, glancing from Franklin to Stephanie. After a moment, he sat down on a gurney.

"I have to watch you," he grumbled at Franklin, then turned to Stephanie. "Hey, can you help me win a bet?"

"What do you want?" she asked, still deep in thought.

"You and Stark... you guys are totally banging, right?"

"Fuck off, Oliver," she said, turning and leaving the BAS. She needed to be alone. The animalistic look on Stark's face burned in her mind.

Maybe it was time to go home.

Part 2

6

The summer months passed quickly. The people of the Homestead continued their regular routine: growing crops, raising livestock, and enhancing structures. Hunt's small-batch whiskey beat Russo's craft beer and Oliver's "toilet wine" at the Koutla solstice celebration. Jameson built the satellite dish, and Frank managed to get what he claimed to be an untraceable internet connection working, its speed comparable to a late-90s dial up service.

Much of the Homesteaders' free time during the month of July was committed to the annual "Olympics" where both men and women competed in a variety of events for the amusement of the community. Stark came in a close second to Dave in the strongman competition, but dominated in long range shooting. Russo took the gold in the crudely organized triathlon in which tree cutting with an axe replaced bicycling. Hunt's wife Natasha, a tattoo-covered princess warrior, took almost all of the women's trophies, adding a number of irreverent jokes to Oliver's repertoire. The games were wrapped up with a long night of heavy drinking and barbarian-esque celebration.

Every Sunday, the Homesteaders continued their ritual of gathering for a mandatory community meal at the Koutla, a tradition they affably referred to as "family dinner." At these gatherings, they passed around news and voted on major decisions that affected the community as a whole, such as upcoming construction projects, hunting excursions, and shipments to be delivered via helicopter.

By early August the sprawling garden released the bulk of its ripe bounty. Stephanie volunteered alongside Alwan to spend her days tending to the multi-acre oasis. Over the winter, her skin had taken on a ghostly pale hue, but after the summer months spent bathing in the sunshine, she'd managed to bring back a hint of the once perfectly tanned look she'd worked so hard to maintain in college.

She found a seat among the rows of tall tomato plants and pulled off her sunglasses, turning her face skyward to let her skin feast on the warm rays of light. When she first decided to take the chance alongside Maya and experience the Homestead, she'd been deathly afraid they were blindly stumbling into a year-round frozen wasteland. How wrong she had been.

The beautiful weather wasn't the only thing that had surprised her about the Homestead. It was a strange place, but it seemed to contain everything that her previous life had been missing. She had a family in this weird, Alaskan refuge. Not like the one she had been born into, (whom she still loved dearly) but rather a massive family of her peers. A *tribe*. The word still felt so strange, but stranger yet was the fact that such a thing was so alien back where she came from. She always had friends, but she'd never truly considered them family. Here in the Homestead, the people that she lived beside were just that, *family*. There was Maya, her best friend since college, the hopelessly lost young beauty queen who followed her sometimes neurotic warrior-turned-lawyer husband with steadfast loyalty. Oliver, the class clown who, despite his likely insanity (or perhaps because of it), always managed to keep even the tensest of moments light. Jameson, the roguish widower who devoted his life to his adorable son. Dave the giant, Frank the paranoid conspiracy theorist, Hunt the old curmudgeon and his Amazonian warrior of a wife Natasha. There was Stark, the man she lov—

Nope… Don't even think it…

These people, these weird, lost souls had flung themselves to the outer reaches of the world each to escape something different… and they meant more to her than anything she'd given up.

But why had she so easily considered leaving months ago after witnessing Stark's interrogation of Franklin Summerset? Was her devotion to this community really so flippant that she could be scared off after seeing a side of the man that she already *knew* existed?

Alwan dropped a basket of cucumbers beside her, derailing her train of thought.

"I guess those tomatoes *are* going to pick themselves." He smiled.

"Hush," she retorted and waved him off. "If I don't complain about you clam-baking the BAS, then you can't bitch about me enjoying the weather."

He chuckled and plopped down beside her. "This is true. I might as well join you."

They sat in silence for a few moments. It wasn't an uncomfortable silence; the doctor was typically a man of few words.

"Why did you come here, Stephanie?"

His question surprised her, but not as much as the entirely neutral tone he delivered it in. She slid the sunglasses back over her eyes and regarded him.

"I, uh…" she paused. It'd been so long since someone had

asked her that. She'd honestly forgotten the frail explanation she'd given her family.

He waited patiently, staring into her with his soft, intuitive brown eyes.

She took a breath and considered her answer. She remembered what she'd told the others when she first arrived, about how she just wanted a break, about how life back home wasn't really going too well, how bills were piling up and things were just getting out of hand. But none of that was true. Before all of this she had a fantastic job, and money had never been an issue. Something in Alwan's eyes made her *want* to be honest.

"I don't really know. I guess it just kind of came up and it seemed like a natural next step."

"And what will your *next* step be?"

"What? I don't know…"

"Will you live here forever?"

"I haven't really thought about—"

"How about five years from now?"

She stopped. The doctor wasn't a rude person. He was interrupting her for a reason. She didn't enjoy being psychoanalyzed.

"Why are you asking me this now?" she asked, annoyed.

Alwan shrugged like it was nothing. "We spend so much time together, you and I, but we don't really talk much."

"Bullshit."

Alwan laughed. "Yeah, ok, ok, you caught me…"

Stephanie waited for him to continue, but he just gazed across the field with a grin.

"So why did *you* come here?" she demanded.

"Oh, that's a long story. Maybe another time—"

"Dude. I swear I will hide every one of your beloved ganja plants if you don't spill it, so help me god…"

He let out a barking laugh. "Alright, very well. I'll tell you."

He pulled the basket of cucumbers behind him and leaned against it, then produced a joint from his pocket and lit it. After a drag, he offered it to her. She shook her head.

"Ah, where to start?" He took another deep inhale and closed his eyes. "Are you familiar with Jamaica, Stephanie? It's a beautiful land. Most people, they vacation there; they see the beaches and resorts and the cities, but that's not *Jamaica*. The Jamaica I know is built upon rolling green mountains and nestled deep in the vast jungles, the tiny villages that no tourists can find. I was born in one of these villages.

"I was sixteen when I came to America. A boy genius, they called me. Hard to believe now, eh? They gave me a place to live while I attended a prestigious university then medical school. I spent the next thirty years forgetting everything my father had taught me about how to live. Instead I became a real *rude boy*. You know what that term means in Jamaica, Stephanie?"

She shrugged.

"It means I let this country corrupt me, and I basked in its money and lavish pleasures much like you bask in the sun today. For thirty years I lived like this, a renowned neurosurgeon hoarding away my money and fame like it actually meant something."

"I'm picking up on the fact that you regret it," Stephanie muttered as he took another long drag from the joint.

"No, no not at all actually. I had a *fucking blast*." They both laughed. "But one day I was walking down the street in Manhattan, after giving a seminar at Columbia, and a beggar stopped me asking for change…"

"Let me guess, you ignored him, then regretted it later?" The annoyance in her voice faded as she became more wrapped up in the story.

"To the contrary, I gave him everything. What I couldn't give him on the spot, I donated. My cars, my houses, my savings, all gone in twenty-four hours. Do you know why I did this, Stephanie?"

She shook her head.

"When I walked out of that seminar I saw a giant poster on the wall of that school. An ad for a class they were offering on ancient civilizations. In big red print across its top it read 'Welcome to Babylon.'"

He stopped.

"That's it? You gave up everything because you saw a poster for a class on an ancient city in Iraq..?" She felt underwhelmed.

"Yes. I gave it all up over that poster. My father — God rest his soul — was a devoted Rastafarian. Despite what you may think, Rastafarianism is a bit more than a group of pot-smoking outcasts. To us, Babylon isn't just an ancient city in Mesopotamia. It's an ideology. An evil force behind the mindsets of today's most affluent societies. Babylon is the oppression by money, by power, by men and women who would seek to control you and take away your ability to govern your own happiness. I saw that poster and I realized that I had spent my life as not only a victim of Babylon, but as a contributing member goose-stepping among its ranks. All of a sudden, looking at that poster, it clicked. The emptiness I felt inside made sense.

"This place is my fresh start. When I asked you why you came here, you couldn't answer me. I hope that you stay long enough to find that answer." He stood slowly, his knees crackling.

"What is that even supposed to mean?" she asked indignantly, climbing to her feet and brushing the dirt off her pants.

"It means exactly what I said. I think maybe you came here for the same reasons as me, but I have yet to see you fully embrace this place. You're still tense, Stephanie, ready to flee at a moment's notice. Maybe that's what brought you here. I just hope that you don't run before the time comes."

She watched him as he picked up the basket of cucumbers and walked away toward the Koutla. "Alwan!" He looked back, but kept walking. "Do you think you escaped? Babylon, that is."

He laughed. "It's a tricky game, Stephanie, even after you think you've escaped, Babylon always comes to find you."

****

Stark and Russo lay hidden along the outskirts of the same field in which Stark wounded the grizzly three months before. They had concealed themselves along the tree line, just far enough in the open to observe their prey. A hundred yards before them, two sleek, black helicopters sat in stark contrast to the bright green grass and clumps of dark shrubbery that now coated the sun-soaked field. Both helicopters appeared to be the same make and model as the one that passed over the clearing earlier that spring. It had been sheer luck that Stark had spotted the two faint dots in the distant sky from his cabin that morning.

Stark peered through the magnified scope of Russo's AR-10, letting the crosshairs dance along the half dozen figures as they moved to and fro beside the farther of the two helicopters. They were unloading what appeared to be advanced surveying equipment.

The nearest helicopter only had three occupants. The tallest, whom Stark decided was the pilot based on the oversized headset and the cliché, fur-rimmed bomber jacket, leaned against the helicopter's flank, casually surveying the land around him. The second man, an elderly fellow far too heavily clothed for the sixty-five-degree afternoon, paced around the nearside of the giant metal beast, eyeing the phone in his hand and occasionally barking orders to the others. The last of the three sat inside the helicopter, barely discernible through the darkened windows, but Stark immediately recognized him as Franklin Summerset.

Stark pulled his eye away from the scope, his thumb instinctively brushing the safety toggle to check its position as he handed the rifle back to his companion.

"Our boy Franklin is in the near bird." Stark rolled on his side to fish a crumpled pack of Lucky Strikes from one of his cargo pockets. "I guess he didn't get the message last time."

Russo reached deep into the neck of his white wool knit sweater to scratch his upper arm. He threw a disgruntled sidelong look at Stark before peering through the scope himself.

Earlier that afternoon Russo had been sipping a gin and tonic as he helped his wife Maya prepare the weekly "family dinner." Now, three hours after Stark had surreptitiously ushered him away from the long oak table laden with vegetable stews, roasted lamb, and honey scones, Russo lay on a pile of mushy bright green moss. His bodyweight squeezed the cold, dirty juice out of the plant which soaked through the immaculately kept bright white sweater his grandmother made him years before.

"A bottle of Glenlivet says the old guy's the boss," Stark muttered, cupping a Zippo to his mouth and lighting one of the bent cigarettes.

"I hate scotch," Russo responded vehemently, continuing to glare through the scope.

Stark chuckled, but in truth he was slightly worried. He couldn't tell if Russo's irritated disposition was simply the result of being torn away from helping his wife, or if it was an extension of the dissenting attitude he'd taken on months before, following their revealing conversation with Hunt.

Russo's beak-like Italian nose flared as a string of smoke wafted across his face. "You're fucking serious right now?"

Stark smiled mischievously back at him, the short cigarette spewing long trails of smoke skyward as it hung loosely from his lips.

"You really are." He paused, clearly contemplating slapping his friend. "So much for recon... Why don't you just send up a flare, make *completely sure* they know we're watching them?"

"I thought about it, but the flare gun's back with the horses." Stark stood up, brushing twigs and bits of moss off his shirt and knees. "Plus, subtlety isn't really my thing."

With that, Stark turned and strolled back toward the tree line where their horses were hidden.

"Let's go say hi!" he shouted over his shoulder. He could feel Russo's furious glare burning into the back of his head. Stark knew that whatever was about to happen with the stubborn oil men, Russo's day was only going to get worse.

Even from a distance, and with the rhythmic bouncing atop the trotting quarter horse, Stark was able to discern that the pacing boss-man was well into his golden years. The way he stood gave it away: tense and hunched like a cramped, arthritic fist. His taut black pea coat did little to conceal the puff of multiple layers underneath.

Thin-blooded southerner.

Stark chuckled inwardly

I wonder if thin blood drains quicker...

He pondered the question for a moment, then another arose that took precedence:

What the fuck is wrong with me?

"I think your buddy Franklin missed you." Russo interrupted Stark's inner diagnostic and shifted his focus back to the helicopter. Franklin had opened the helicopter door just a sliver to point out the approaching duo to the boss-man. He motioned specifically in Stark's direction like a child tattling on a bully.

"Eyes on the pilot," Stark muttered through still lips. "If anyone's armed, it's him."

"Just let me know if you're going to do anything stupid," Russo hissed back as they pulled their horses to a halt just outside the overhang of the helicopter blades.

Stark grinned and winked at his friend as he dismounted, then turned to the slight, hatchet-faced old man.

"Mr. Stark, my name is Edward Masterson, CEO and founder of Lockstone Oil. I've traveled a long way to meet you," the man said, extending his gloved hand.

Masterson was clearly the type of man who was far more at home in an office than his current environment, with a perfectly maintained quaff of salt-and-pepper hair and glaringly white teeth. Despite his twisted frame, he had a strong air of confidence — almost arrogance — which Stark immediately found repellant. The elderly man reminded him of every scumbag congressman and billionaire he'd ever seen on TV, emanating an aura of patronizing maliciousness.

"Mr. Masterson, welcome to my land. I see you've brought along my old friend Franklin. I'll be honest, that's one face I never thought I'd see again." Stark fixed a tight grip around the outstretched hand and nodded to the man cowering in the helicopter.

"Yes, Franklin here told me how you saved his life. I cannot express my gratitude, or that of my company."

Stark saw clean through the too-polite smile on the old man's face: there was no gratitude there.

"Well, while your thanks is duly noted, I'm not sure he gave you the right impression. I explained very clearly that my property is not the place to be trespassing."

"Indeed, I heard about your, err… line of questioning." Masterson glanced quickly over at Russo, then the rifle balanced across the front of his saddle. "We tried to reach out to you in several ways, Mr. Stark, however it seems our message never made its way to you."

"I already turned down your offer, and I believe I made it abundantly clear that I have no interest in selling. So, beyond that, how can I help you? I'd venture a guess that you're looking to charter a bear hunt, but something tells me you're more of a *most dangerous game* type."

As long as your quarry isn't armed, you slimy little bitch.

Masterson cracked a smile. "I'm going to cut to the chase. Have you ever heard of the supreme court case Kelo v. the City of New London?"

Stark glanced at Russo, whose face suddenly darkened.

"Eminent domain," Russo muttered.

"Precisely." Masterson cast an approving glance at Russo. "You see, Mr. Stark, the federal government reserves the right to procure private land for public use. After your *aggressive* little run-in with Mr. Summerset, I reached out to some old friends in Washington and told them about all the wonderful things Lockstone can do for the great state of Alaska. Of course, due entirely to the seasonal constraints of the area, I've had to get the process streamlined. As of next week, this land will become property of the federal government, and by next month the deed will be signed to Lockstone Oil."

Stark couldn't help but scoff at the arrogant old prick. "I'm pretty sure that's not how that works. Lockstone isn't the—"

"It is how it works," Russo cut in sullenly. "Kelo v. New London. The Supreme Court decided that the fed can steal any land it wants and redistribute it to other private buyers if it's 'for the greater good.'"

The gravity of the situation began to take hold. Stark felt a rush of hot blood course to his cheeks.

"Very good!" Masterson crowed with a surprised grin. "You're a lawyer?"

"Yeah," Russo murmured. He was clearly as absorbed in the crushing news as Stark.

"Stanford Law, class of '67. You?"

"Suffolk."

Masterson didn't even bother to suppress a hearty laugh. "Good for you, son. Everyone's got to go somewhere."

The taunt snapped Stark back to the present. "You're a mouthy little shit, aren't you?"

"Excuse me?" Masterson recoiled, clearly taken aback by the insult. His demeanor morphed from a condescending grandfather to an indignant child-king. Stark guessed it had been a long time since someone had spoken to him in such a way.

"Why wasn't I notified of this shit?" Stark demanded.

Masterson's lips pulled taut, revealing the row of sharkish, pearly whites. "We sent you many letters. I'm not sure what they put on them for an address. Most landowners maintain an address, you know. Maybe they tied them to *pigeons.*"

Stark considered picking the old man up and smashing his head against the steel door of the helicopter until his skull collapsed. Something in his eyes must have betrayed him, as Masterson's attitude shifted as suddenly as it had before, this time from bitter back to pleasant.

"I apologize: I'll admit I've put you in a difficult situation… maybe more so than you can currently comprehend. Either way, I would be more than happy to fly you back to Harkstaff to collect your compensation and make arrangements to vacate my land, which you have until next week to be clear of."

Stark had already begun formulating a plan in his head. This was as good an opportunity as any to make a lasting impression. Russo wouldn't particularly enjoy it. No, Russo was going to be *very* upset, but he was always butt-hurt about something or other.

Stark turned to the pilot. "When you flew in, it was over the big lake to the south, right?" The pilot nodded. "Yeah, you kind of have to, huh? The wind off those mountains will tear this thing to pieces. One way in, one way out." Stark then addressed Masterson. "Have you ever seen a helicopter go down in water?"

"Is that supposed to be some kind of threat, *son*?" The bitterness was leaking back into Masterson's voice.

"No, no, not really." Stark began pacing the length of the helicopter. "I just don't like flying over water in these things. Brings back bad memories."

"Well then I guess you won't be joining us." Masterson gave a flippant wave. "It was nice to meet you, Mr. Stark. I suggest you get back to civilization sooner rather than later. I would hate to evict you in a less pleasant way."

Stark stopped pacing and leaned against the helicopter door, blocking Masterson's way. He could hear Franklin's fingers anxiously drumming through the cool steel.

"I was in an infantry battalion in the Corps, but I'm guessing you already knew that. A man like you always does his homework, right?" Stark asked.

Masterson gave an exasperated sigh. Clearly, he thought their business had concluded.

"On my first deployment, we were part of a Marine Expeditionary Unit. In a MEU, each company gets its own mode of transportation. One company gets 'tracs, another gets trucks, we got helicopters. Wherever we needed to go, we flew there."

"Mr. Stark, I am a very busy man—"

"Humor me. You *did* fly all the way out here just to tell me how you're going to take my land." Stark waited patiently until Masterson nodded his consent before continuing. "Thank you. As I was saying, during our work-up we flew everywhere. On one of those little trips our bird ran into some technical difficulties. You know, it's really hard to tell if something's gone wrong when you're a passenger in one of those things. You're already disoriented, it's loud as hell, you're half asleep strapped in a seat that's way too fucking small with a five-point harness. You've got your flak jacket, Kevlar, eye pro, gloves, rifle, countless little straps and metal pieces jutting out, ready to catch on the seat or either of the two motherfuckers you're jammed between. I was listening to good 'ol Johnny Cash when we hit the water. *'I hurt myself today… To see if I still feel…'* "Stark sang poorly, *"'I focus on the—'* BAM!"

Stark took a sudden step toward Masterson. In the corner of his eye he saw the pilot's hand twitch toward the opening in his jacket.

"We bounced once," Stark whispered, his voice suddenly dark. "That was the wakeup, that was our warning. One life shattering, teeth jarring *thud*. Then we were under.

"When a helo hits the water, it flips on its head. All her weight is up top, the engine, the rotors, so as you sink you find yourself being ripped along in this death spiral as cold water just slams into you like a Mac truck, forcing its way up your nose and down your throat.

"They train you for the escape, only during the simulation, you're being dunked in a warm pool, and everyone knows when you're about to go under. When it happens for real, you get the guys who panic, who aren't prepared. The guys who forget the steps to getting out of the eighty pounds of gear. The guys who *lose their fucking minds*. It's a terrifying thing, to be in a position like that, not knowing if you'll live or die. It's not like the threat of being killed by a man… There's no one to fight. No one to reason with. No one to plead to. It's just you caught in a flurry of limbs and silent screams, that cold, black ocean surging into your lungs as she drags you deeper and deeper down into her freezing belly."

Stark stepped back then turned to Russo and winked. Russo responded with a wary look and shook his head. He knew something bad was about to happen.

"Russo, remember what old Tomahawk Dick used to say back in the day, about how the best way to take down a chopper was the rotor housing? You think he was full of shit?" Stark asked.

"Stop!" Russo belted out.

Too late.

With lightning speed, Stark yanked his .45 from its holster and fired three rounds into the exposed machining between the helicopter's rotors. Masterson thrust his hands out in alarm and shrieked. By the time the pilot got a hand inside his bomber jacket to draw his own weapon, both Stark and Russo had him in their sights.

"Throw it!" Stark barked. "Far!"

The pilot grunted and obeyed, tossing the pistol into the field. The onlooking surveyors were silent behind the cover of the large boxes of gear they had been hauling out of the second helicopter.

Stark holstered his weapon and stepped close to Masterson. He could feel the nervous hatred resonating off the old man's face.

"I'm going to do you a favor, *son,*" Stark growled. "I'm going to give you the satisfaction of knowing that a man is going to decide whether or not you die today. Now, are you going to fight, reason, or plead?"

Masterson froze in place. Stark couldn't tell if he was paralyzed with fear or simply unfazed by the show. He waited a few seconds then leaned in closer to Masterson.

"Speak up," Stark whispered.

"You won't do a damn thing," Masterson challenged through gritted teeth. Stark smiled, then jerked forward violently as if he was going to strike. Masterson flinched hard, stumbling and falling to the ground.

Stark crouched over him, snarling his words directly in the man's ear. "The only thing that will save your life today is my *apathy*. I've killed enough men to know that the only pleasure in the act comes from killing a *worthy* adversary. Someone who has the *ability* to kill you back. You're a fucking cockroach. A weak, pompous, miserable old insect whose only power lies in the imaginary value of a piece of paper. A twerp like you *can't touch* a man like me. I want you to remember that when I send you scuttling back to your soft little world with your tail between your legs. If you want this land, you send someone out here that's man enough to take it. I'll be waiting."

With that, Stark stood back and yanked open the helicopter door, signaling a terrified Franklin to get out. The pilot pulled Masterson to his feet, and together the three men retreated to the second helicopter. Stark reached deep into his saddlebag and retrieved a bright orange flare gun.

"Maybe if you dump that gear you'll have enough fuel to get all of you back!" he yelled after them.

Masterson cast Stark a final, loathing glance as he screamed for the last of the surveyors to climb aboard.

Fuck you too.

Stark climbed atop his steed and fired the flare into the lame helicopter's open door. It took only a moment for the blinding ball of fire to ignite the leather seats inside.

Within minutes, the helicopter was fully engulfed in flame. Stark rode toward the tree line, Russo following silently. The second helicopter hummed over the crackling flames as it rose into the air, leaving tens of thousands of dollars' worth of discarded gear underneath.

"Sorry about that," Stark called behind him nonchalantly, hoping to gauge Russo's anger by his response.

But Russo simply shook his head and remained silent.

Stark believed he had witnessed the man's entire spectrum of negative emotion, but the look on Russo's face in that moment expressed something new.

It had taken three long years, but Russo had finally reached his breaking point.

****

Stephanie wasn't particularly hungry. A mound of roasted lamb smothered in onion and mushroom gravy sat on her plate nearly untouched. She picked at it occasionally, taking a bite here and there as she listened to the varied conversations that erupted around her.

She looked at Maya seated halfway down the long table next to Russo's empty seat, angrily poking at her own plate. She had a good reason to be upset: Russo's sudden disappearance beside Stark had left her alone to juggle the couple's responsibilities in catering this week's family dinner. Had it not been for Stephanie jumping in to help, the meal would likely have been ruined. Furthermore, Maya had no idea where her husband and Stark had gone, and judging by their secretive demeanor as they rode off together, there was a good chance she would never find out.

Maya was a wonderful young woman, but not the hardiest or most understanding.

She and Stephanie met their freshman year in college and quickly became inseparable. Over the four years they spent in the nursing program, they each filled in the gaps in the other's personality perfectly. Stephanie was the smart, mild-mannered girl-next-door, while Maya embodied the typical ultra-positive, ultra-emotional, gorgeous ditz. Together they navigated the complexities of college life flawlessly. After graduation, Maya returned to Boston and married Russo, while Stephanie remained in Florida. It was barely a year later that Stephanie reluctantly accepted Maya's invitation to join the Homestead.

The cold winters had not been kind to Maya. While her outward beauty had not faded, her bubbly personality seemed to gradually go flatter with each passing year. Every so often, she would wonder aloud to Stephanie whether she made the right choice, or what life would be like if she had stayed in Boston.

Next to Stephanie, Oliver flicked a piece of cucumber across the table at Hunt. The little green projectile missed, instead bouncing off Natasha's tattooed chest and falling between her breasts, which had begun to engorge due to her pregnancy. Natasha laughed and Alasie reached over the three-year-old between her and her husband and smacked him over the head.

"I'm going to take the bat off that wall and use it on you

someday, Oliver," Hunt growled. He was referring to the crossed clubs hung over the head of the table with the inscription *Trial by Combat* bellow it. The plaque had been hung almost as a joke, but stood as a central reminder to the ultimate right of any individual in the Homestead.

"You'll have to catch me first." Oliver winked and gave Hunt's prosthetic a playful kick under the table.

"Boys, stop," Stephanie cut in. "Why don't you just go out back and get rid of this sexual tension?"

Natasha and Alasie laughed.

"Speaking of sexual tension, where's Stark?" Hunt asked with a *fuck you* look.

You sassy bitch.

She considered striking back with a cruel retort, but thought better of it. This wasn't the place or time for her to show off her ability to destroy a man's ego with only a few words.

"No idea."

"Sure you d—" Oliver was cut off by another slap from Alasie.

"Don't fuck with her, Oli," she said, then turned to Stephanie. "He's an idiot. They both are."

Hunt looked as if he was going to say something then flinched — Natasha clearly pinched him under the table.

Stephanie knew the situation was just as awkward for the other two women as it was for her. On one hand, she appreciated their looking out for her, but on the other, she hated their pity. She knew that, in their eyes, her poorly concealed relationship with Stark was an embarrassing topic.

Dinner continued uneventfully. Jameson started a group discussion over whether or not the Homestead could survive a winter with a deadly influenza outbreak brought in from the outside. Oliver quickly shifted the conversation's wheels in the direction of a zombie apocalypse. After an hour-long argument, it was agreed that the safest way to withstand the zombie hoards would be to seal the narrow avenue between the southern lake and the Fist with explosives. After Natasha sarcastically pointed out they didn't have any of said explosives, Frank proudly exhibited his technical skills by pulling out his tablet and using the Homestead's newly configured Wi-Fi to dive deep into the dark web and pull up a recipe for a fertilizer-based homemade explosive. The plan was solidified: should a zombie apocalypse ever strike their neck of Alaska, they would seal the valley and the Homestead would indeed survive.

Stephanie had been so absorbed in listening to the fantastic theories of the cold climate's potential effects on the undead that she hadn't seen Stark take his place at the head of the table, or that Maya had slipped away. Oliver noticed Stark first.

"Where the fuck did you come from?" Oliver shouted over the row of jabbering heads. There was no answer. Stark leaned over an empty plate, entirely detached. Oliver stood up and yelled louder.

The hall fell silent and all eyes turned on Stark. He continued to stare through the table in front of him for a moment before the sudden silence struck him. His head snapped up as if he had just woken from a dream. Stephanie looked at Oliver and saw his face turn from jovial to serious. It was incredibly uncharacteristic for Stark to be this openly frazzled. Something was very wrong.

After a long pause Stark spoke. "Dinner's over. Clear the hall."

The community members glanced at each other with a mix of confusion, worry, and even a hint of outrage. This was not a place where orders were given; they had come here to escape that type of governance. But the gravity with which Stark spoke resonated through the crowd, and they rose to leave. Stephanie began toward Stark, but as they locked eyes he quickly shook his head once. She turned toward the door. Whatever it was that had inspired this shift in his demeanor, she knew she would have to find out later.

She milled through the crowd to the residences. As she shuffled through the central hall and made her way to her room, Jameson brushed by her.

"Jamie, what the hell is going on?" she asked as he hurried by.

"Don't know yet. Stark called a council meeting though. Is Russo in there?" he asked, pointing at the Russos' door.

"No idea," she said as he banged on it. His question was answered a second later when the door swung opened and Russo emerged. His face appeared determined, but she could see through to the nervousness beneath. Without a word, he and Jameson headed back down the hallway toward the Koutla. From beyond the cracked door Stephanie heard her best friend sobbing.

"Maya?" she called softly as she approached. "Maya, can I come in?"

Maya was huddled on the corner of the bed, her head in her hands. Her shoulders shook violently as she hiccupped between whimpers.

"What is it, honey?" Stephanie cooed as she sat down and gently took Maya in her arms. She had been in similar situations a hundred times before and knew exactly how to calm her friend.

After a period of gasping sobs, Maya spoke. "I don't know what they did out there. I don't know what's happening, but Andrew told me we're leaving. He told me to pack but he wouldn't say anything else."

"The boys probably just got in a fight. It'll be okay. Plus, I thought you *wanted* to go home?"

"I *do!* It's not that…" Maya looked up at Stephanie with pleading eyes. "He's scared, Steph. I've never seen him like this, like… *really* scared."

"Oh, come on, yes you have," Stephanie said reassuringly. "Andrew's a strong guy, but it's not like you've never seen him a little afraid. What about when we first came out here? He was *literally* shaking next to you on the plane."

Maya wrung her hands. "I know he can get nervous, he's kind of a nervous man, I get that. But that's not what I'm talking about. He's *scared.*"

Stephanie paused, not knowing whether Maya was simply nervous over the prospect of change or if she was right, if something happened that had actually frightened the battle-hardened man. She thought back over Stark's strange behavior at the Koutla, and tried to ignore the anxiety that begun seeping into her own thoughts.

"I just want this all to be over. I just want to be back home where it's warm and there are regular people and I don't have to live like a goddamn barbarian. I love him so much, Steph, but I don't think I can take any more of this. I need him to be serious this time. I'd never abandon him, but I don't know if I can keep this up." She collapsed into tears once more.

Stephanie had noticed Maya becoming increasingly despondent as of late, but apparently hadn't realized the extent of it. There was something else at work here.

"What's really going on, Maya?" Stephanie asked, pulling her friend's bright red face up to meet her gaze.

Maya paused and swallowed hard. "We can't get pregnant, Steph. We've been trying so hard, at least *I* have… You know I've always wanted a family, but — I mean we were only supposed to come here for a year! It's been *three!* I thought it was time, and that maybe a baby would make Andrew come back to his senses and we could go home…"

Stephanie hugged Maya tighter and rubbed her back.

"I mean, I look at Tommy and Oki and I *know* that I'm ready!" she went on, a hint hysteria leaking into her voice. "Natasha, Emma, everyone here is getting fucking pregnant except *me!*"

"Wait, what?" Stephanie stopped her friend and gave her a puzzled look.

"Everyone's getting pregnan—"

"No, did you say Emma is pregnant?" Stephanie pulled Maya to arm's length, surveying her face to tell if she was lying.

Maya, realizing she'd given up a secret, refused to meet Stephanie's eyes.

"Maya… Maya, answer me."

"You can't tell anyone, not yet at least…" Maya whispered. She continued to look down like a puppy caught peeing on the rug.

"Why?"

"Frank's impotent. It's not his."

"Wait, they can't have sex?"

"No, I meant sterile. Frank is sterile… they have sex, but his… swimmers don't… swim…" Maya said haltingly, weirdly uncomfortable with the subject considering her role as a nurse.

"But there's a chance—"

"Zero percent chance. He was diagnosed years ago. They just don't work. Emma's pregnant with someone else's kid, and she won't tell anyone whose it is."

Stephanie sat back and scrolled through the catalogue of potential fathers in her mind. There were a handful of single men among the Homesteaders who, under normal circumstances, would likely jump at the chance to sleep with Emma. However, even with the knowledge of her pregnancy, Stephanie couldn't imagine any of them risking banishment, or worse, tribal justice, to do so.

"I think it's Jameson's." Maya's blubbering had come to an end with the introduction of the dramatic topic and her voice held a bit of venom. "He's already got one, so we know his... *you know*... works."

"No," Stephanie disagreed. "It wouldn't be Jameson. He wouldn't risk it for something so trivial. It has to be someone stupid."

"Whoever it is isn't going to last long when she starts showing. You know Frank is going to go ape shit and try and use those *stupid* baseball bats in the Koutla. I can't imagine many people he'd beat in that fight though..."

"Stark would stand in for Frank." Stephanie turned back to Maya. "You know he would. And if this mystery father accepted a trial by combat, Stark would kill him."

Maya rolled her eyes. "And the fact that *that* seems normal to us means it's time to leave."

Stephanie snorted in feigned agreement. "Don't worry, Maya. If Andrew is serious this time, then by the beginning of the winter you'll be back in Boston, eating fancy dinners at the Harp and wiping geriatric butts at Mass Gen."

The reminder that Maya's escape from the Alaskan wilderness might be imminent prompted a paltry smile. "You mean *we*."

Do I?

It wasn't like Stephanie hadn't considered it, but in that moment the sudden thought of rejoining society left a sour taste in her mouth. For the sake of Maya's flippant emotions, Stephanie squeezed her and agreed. "Yeah honey, I meant we."

Three hours later, Stephanie left the residence hall and made her way around the Koutla, past the BAS and along a thin dirt trail into the forest. After a hundred yards, she reached the river that ran north to south along the Homestead's outskirts and opened the door to Stark's cabin. It was cold and empty. A small piece of paper was nailed to the log wall directly across from the entrance.

Dealing with it, be back soon.
DO NOT FOLLOW

7

Stark rode through the night. The rugged mountain trails passed far quicker atop the Honda xr650 motorcycle than on horseback. He had just enough fuel lashed to the motorcycle's rear to make the one-way trip to Harkstaff, and knew that as long as he could avoid wrecking the bike on the rough trails and rocky passes he would be able make the tundra by the following morning, then Harkstaff by that afternoon.

His plan in sneaking away from the Homestead had been simple: he knew the council would immediately reject the idea of him traveling to town by himself to deal with the impending legal issues, so he had cleared the Koutla mid-family dinner and sent the council members to find Russo before quietly slipping away to his cabin and gathering the dirt bike and necessary gear for the trip. He had circumvented the Homestead using a hunting trail and doubted the distracted community would even realize he was gone until he was already halfway to the mountain's pass.

He was very aware that he had overreacted when dealing with Masterson.

It was one thing to get the message across, but emasculating the arrogant prick and destroying the helicopter had been going overboard, even for him. There was just something about the old man that Stark found so utterly revolting that he hadn't been able to help himself. In Stark's mind, it was men like Masterson who had corrupted the world and created the need for an escape like the Homestead.

Men who valued money and power above human decency.

Men who logged rainforests and denied global warming and built sneaker sweatshops.

Men who profited off war and the death of young men and innocents.

Masterson had immediately grown to represent all of these things in Stark's mind the moment he opened his mouth. He was a cocky, fragile, weak little man with nothing to offer the world except his shrewd manipulations and willingness to destroy anything or anyone to turn a profit.

Not this time though. There was no way in hell Stark would let the creep destroy what he and the Homesteaders had worked so hard to build. Stark knew it would be an uphill battle to have the eminent domain claim overruled, but he was willing to do whatever it took, even if it meant drowning the bastards in their own blood.

He hoped it wouldn't come to that.

Kind of.

But there was something else eating away at his mind as he rode through the forest: the threat of losing something he valued more than any land or money or even ideology. He was afraid that the standoff had been Russo's last straw. Ever since earlier that summer, when he revealed to Russo the events that led up to his inheritance, Russo had become increasingly distant and irritable. Stark worried that his best friend had been battling with the idea that Stark had created the Homestead as more a literal escape than an ideological one. While Stark knew the fallacy in this, he worried that Russo's growing impatience was the result of that idea taking hold. Attacking an oil man and destroying his helicopter probably didn't help.

He had a feeling that he would return to find his friend with packed bags and a ticket back to Boston.

By mid-morning, Stark approached the edge of the tundra that marked the end of the mountain. He walked the motorcycle through the thick forest to the gully where he found the wrecked SUV three months before. The Homesteaders had already casually examined the wreck on their periodic trips to Harkstaff over the summer, but he had too many unanswered questions left in his head to just ride by.

Aside from the small spots of bright orange rust that showed through the chipped paint of the crumpled hood, the outside of the vehicle looked relatively unscathed. Its plush leather seats had almost entirely rotted away and the torn body of the driver had become nothing more than a pile of chewed bones. What was left of the blood stains that had coated the vehicles interior were now dark brown smudges smeared into the crevices of the windshield where scavengers' eager tongues had been unable to reach.

Stark flipped through the mush of waterlogged paperwork in the glove compartment. The SUV was a rental from Fairbanks signed over to Franklin Summerset with a corporate credit card from Lockstone Oil. He pocketed the few legible bits and continued to investigate the SUV's compartment.

Lodged deep under the passenger seat he found the missing pistol, a rusted Sig Sauer 9mm with a full magazine and round in the chamber. The bodyguard must have fumbled it in the wreck and not had time to retrieve it in the ensuing bear-wrought chaos.

Stark used the GPS strapped to his wrist to mark the vehicle's location before following the path that had led them to the bodyguard's corpse, operating purely on memory in a terrain that had dramatically changed over the summer months. It took him over an hour to find the meager pile of remaining bones and cloth lodged at the tree's base.

He felt confident from the blood trail that Franklin was complicit in the death of the larger man, and knew that if he could find some sort of evidence of the Lockstone employee's crime, it may go a long way in the upcoming legal battle. As much sway as Masterson claimed to have with the government, the murder of one employee by another would surely throw a wrench in their legal team's gears. Stark knew he needed as much help as he could get.

He bent and sifted through the dull white bones and tattered cloth. As he shifted one of the gnawed femurs, he noticed the glint of metal from the soil beneath. Digging his hand into the moist dirt, he felt the edge of a blade.

He fished the knife out and examined it closely. It was clearly expensive. Stark guessed it to be Italian-made by the look of the intricately carved ivory handle — the type of knife a wealthy man might receive as a gift from a loved one. He turned it over in his hand and noticed an inscription on the four-inch folding blade:

FRS, with love

F.R.S.

Franklin R. Summerset.

Stark grinned ear to ear. He couldn't have been luckier. Carefully folding the stainless-steel blade back into the ornate handle, he turned to continue the last leg of his journey over the seventy miles of picturesque sun-soaked grasslands to Harkstaff.

The town of Harkstaff was tiny even for Alaska. With just over six hundred inhabitants, the quaint municipality might remind a casual visitor more of a frontier camp from the times of Lewis and Clark than a modern town. Its infrastructure was lackluster, the only paved road was the crumbling main street that ran north to south through its center for less than a mile and was bordered by the vast majority of the town's businesses. The single stoplight in front of the schoolhouse had quit working years before Stark first touched down on the town's airstrip. It had remained broken for years, as the four employee sheriff's department had given up on enforcing traffic laws ages before.

Harkstaff itself stood well off the beaten path. It was only accessible by a single passing highway and the miniscule private airfield that dominated the town's northern edge. The buildings were hardy, but more often than not poorly maintained. The people who had been drawn to live in the failing town weren't exactly the type to care about outward appearances. As long as a house was warm, it would do.

Most of the town's service centers sat in a cluster halfway down Main Street. There was a clinic that doubled as a dentist's office, a humble church with a haphazardly leaning steeple that had been condemned since the 90s, a sheriff's station (which also served as the county jail with its two holding cells), a poorly stocked grocery, and a general store.

The general store belonged to Alasie and Irniq's uncle, Tulimak Locklear. His family had owned the business since the town was little more than a hamlet, and in his 65 years,

Tulimak had turned it into the most, perhaps only, successful operation in Harkstaff.

This was Stark's first stop. He had a good relationship with the old man, and knew that if anyone in the area would fill him in on the circumstances of Masterson's return, it would be Tulimak.

Stark putted down the worn, cracked pavement of the main street and pulled to a stop under the red, white, and blue sign that read *Locklear's Goods*. The town drunk looked up from his perch on the weathered wooden stairs leading up to the store's porch. Stark caught something in the man's face that put him on edge.

Fear.

The bum stood quickly. The pint-sized bottle of cheap vodka he was holding slipped out of his hands and bounced off the wooden step. Without hesitation, the bum turned and shuffled away.

A pang of adrenaline surged through Stark's blood.

Something was wrong.

During his many visits to the town it had never been a very lively place, but looking around now he realized that the streets were completely abandoned. While he couldn't see the frightened faces staring at him through the drawn blinds of the surrounding buildings, he could *feel* them.

What the fuck is going on?

He considered swinging the bike around and bolting back to the wilderness, but immediately abandoned the idea. The fuel light had been on since before he entered the town, and the two gas jugs attached to the bike's rear were completely empty.

He leaned the motorcycle against the side of the porch and instinctively brushed his hand against the pistol at his side. The revolver's cold steel was comforting against the butt of his hand. There was no way Masterson intended on somehow ambushing him here — that would be legal suicide. No, something else was at work.

He climbed the stairs to the porch and glanced through the dirt-stained window. Aside from Tulimak, who stood at his regular position behind the counter, the store appeared to be empty.

"Fuck it," he muttered and pulled the door open.

Tulimak was staring down intently as he scrawled at a yellow order form. He looked up as the bell attached to the door rang and Stark saw that his face was pale and sunken.

Something was *definitely* wrong.

Even from across the room, Stark could see the old Inuit's eyes were full of remorse.

"Mr. Locklear, nice to see you're still in business." Stark attempted to sound casual as he cast a wary look around him. "If I didn't know any better I'd think the town had been abandoned since my last visit."

Tulimak swallowed hard and nodded. As Stark approached the counter, the old man flicked his head toward the back door. "Augustin, it's good to have you back. I see you have another order form for me?"

He motioned down to the folded paper he had been scrawling on when Stark entered.

"Yeah," Stark said, slowly reaching over and pulling the paper toward him.

FBI

Go peacefully, for both our sakes

Stark nodded, trying not to show the swirl of confusion that had overtaken his mind.

The FBI? What did the FBI want with him? He hadn't broken any federal laws… had he?

Sure, he'd threatened a man's life and destroyed a helicopter, but that was on his own land. Surely that wouldn't bring the FBI all the way out here…

A much more ominous possibility clawed its way to the front of his mind. Could Masterson have figured out his past? Could the old bastard have learned the true story behind his fortune and sicced the Bureau on him?

Tulimak cleared his throat, snapping Stark back to the present.

He had to give himself up. Despite the seemingly endless capacity for violence that he'd discovered in himself, he wasn't, nor would he ever be, a cop killer.

"I, uh… I'm having a problem with this pistol on my side." Stark spoke loudly and clearly in the direction of the back door. "Could you please remove it for me and place it behind the counter?"

"Yes," Tulimak said with equal volume. "I will take that. Are you otherwise armed?"

He raised his hands and Tulimak reached across the counter and pulled the pistol from its holster.

"No, I am no longer armed," Stark nearly yelled, staring into Tulimak's grateful eyes and mouthing "thank you."

Tulimak nodded, then stepped back far behind the counter and raised his own hands.

The back door burst open. Five men in blue jackets with the yellow FBI lettering emblazoned across the back poured into the room and surrounded Stark with guns drawn.

"Down on the ground!" they all shouted in various volumes and timing. Stark complied, laying forward on his stomach. He had no intention of giving them an excuse to shoot him. He let them wrench his arms behind his back as he breathed in the thick coat of dust on the time-worn wood panels.

Through an ear pressed hard against the floor, Stark heard the thump of footsteps approaching from the store's entrance. As the agents patted him down, he caught a snippet of conversation between one of the agents and a crackling voice that he recognized as Masterson's.

"Yeah, that's him," Masterson said with pleasure. "Be careful, the man is certifiably insane."

Before Stark could turn to look at the old bastard, one of the agents pulled a rough sack over his head.

"What the fuck is thi—" he tried to yell, but was cut off when a foot jabbed into his ribs. He winced as they pulled him to his feet.

"You're being detained under the US Patriot Act of 2001 for conspiring to commit domestic terrorism. Due to this, your rights as a US citizen do not apply to this arrest," a man's voice commanded. "Did you travel here with anyone else?"

Terrorism?

"What the fuck are yo—" Again, Stark's muffled speech was cut off by a swift punch to the ribs. This time he lashed out himself, lunging headfirst in the direction of the blow. His blind head-butt connected, drawing a sick thud and one of the agents cried out in pain. In an instant, Stark was lateral again, face-down on the ground with a hand crushing his face into the thick black hood and the floor beneath.

"Motherfucker!" another voice shouted. "He broke my nose!"

"What did you expect?" the initial voice asked sarcastically. "It's never a fuckin' easy day with these fringe right militia freaks. Taze him."

Stark felt his body seize violently as 50,000 volts of electricity shot through his skin, up his spine, and into his still swirling brain.

8

Andrew Russo hunched over a bowl of elk stew. The Koutla was eerily quiet for this Sunday's family dinner; tensions had been running high since Stark's disappearance a week before. Almost all of the community's questions had been left unanswered. Russo had told only his wife, the council, and Stephanie about Masterson and the eminent domain claim. He kept the story of the burning helicopter to himself, feeling that there was no need to raise unnecessary alarm among the people. If Jameson, Oliver, or *any* of the Homestead's founders found out about Stark's temper tantrum, Russo was sure they'd ride off into the night and follow their beloved chieftain through the gates of hell. Russo would doubtlessly be left to deal with the fallout… as usual.

The others didn't know Stark like he did. Sure, most of them had considered Stark a close friend even before joining him on this crazy experiment. A few of them, namely Jameson and Oliver, had even fought alongside him in Afghanistan. They trusted him. Completely. Just as Russo had. But what they didn't realize was that Stark was flying by the seat of his pants — just making shit up as he went along.

Russo knew the truth.

Russo had learned the dire secret buried beneath the

foundation of their community.

The first time Russo landed in Harkstaff, Stark had been his best friend. Even then he knew that Stark was a mad genius, an agent of chaos whose greatest gift was the uncanny ability to convince others to bend to his will without them even knowing. He played people with the same elegance with which Clapton jammed on the guitar or Shakespeare penned his verse. But Russo never thought Stark would play him.

Now, after three long years, the arrogant son of a bitch had finally revealed that he'd done just that. That the whole community was built on a lie.

Furthermore, Stark's stupid and childish attack on Masterson solidified Russo's belief that the man he had trusted with his life had officially slid into the chasm of insanity.

Maybe Stark had been there from the start.

Within an hour of realizing that Stark had disappeared, Russo had already mapped out the impending events in his head. The asshole would ride day and night to Harkstaff, where he would rent a room at the dingy inn and call up his money guy to assemble a team of big-wig lawyers in an attempt to drive the eminent domain case into the ground. Then when the smoke cleared, he would show up back at the Homestead before the first snow, trying to sweep everything cleanly back under the rug where it belonged.

But this was it for Russo.

He finally realized his position in the grand scheme of things: he was just another patsy that Stark had used on this little misadventure. A sidekick. A right hand man. *A supporting character.*

Over the years, Stark had somehow managed to convince him that they were equals in the community, but even *that* was a lie. Another in a long list of manipulations.

"Little boss" Jameson called him.

The community mother.

The guy people went to with their bullshit problems or when they couldn't find Stark because he'd gone gallivanting off into the forest for days or even weeks at a time as he so loved to do.

Russo had tolerated it when he actually believed in the path they were on. But now, realizing it was all a lie spouted by a delusional maniac, he suddenly couldn't stomach it.

As soon as Stark returned from dealing with his latest blunder, Russo would turn in his two weeks' notice. He and Maya had already packed their belongings. They would get the three years of monetary compensation from Stark's dirty little piggy bank, then settle down back in Boston far away from all of this frontier bullshit.

"Russo!" Dave Johnson's giant voice boomed from far down the table. Russo glanced up from his brooding. "These guys won't answer us. They keep saying to ask you. Where the hell is Stark?"

Again, pawning the bullshit off on me.

"He's gone to town," Russo yelled back.

"No shit, but why? Are you going to tell us what the hell happened last Sunday?"

Russo didn't respond this time. As much as he still loved the people of the community, he had already mentally checked out.

Let someone else deal with this shitshow.

The awkward silence loomed for a moment as the entire community looked to Russo for an answer.

When it was clear he wasn't about to give one, Hunt spoke up. "The government is taking our land."

The people crowded around the table shared confused looks. Frank spoke up first. "What do you mean, *taking our land?*"

Russo knew the conversation would quickly get out of hand if he left Hunt to try to explain the complexities of the legal issue. He caved, turning to Frank and speaking loud enough for the entire room to hear. "Apparently the federal government has declared eminent domain. It means they're forcibly buying the land off Stark and giving it to an oil company."

The hall rang with irate cries.

"There is *absolutely no way* that is legal," Natasha stated assuredly, crossing her arms as if her attitude could somehow affect the truth of the statement.

"It's very legal," Russo said matter-of-factly. "The simplest way I can break it down for you is that the government can grab up any private land it wants as long as it does so for the good of the public. In this case, their argument is that the oil company will have a positive effect on the community and bring job opportunities to Harkstaff... but it's all about tax revenue and dirty dealings."

"Hold on!" Dave shouted, quieting the murmuring crowd. "Why are we just hearing about this now if you've known for a week?"

"The man who came here claimed that the process had been streamlined in the three months since they last approached us. There's a good chance rules were bent and laws were broken. If that's the case, the whole thing will likely be thrown out. I'm sure that's what Stark's checking on now."

"Wait, you're *sure* that's what he's doing? He didn't tell you?" Frank asked. "Aren't you the lawyer?"

Russo gave him a dirty look.

"Stark snuck off to do it himself," Hunt cut in.

"Why?" The crowd began to mutter amongst themselves.

Russo knew it was time to tell them the truth. Well, some

of it. Concealing it would only serve to create more lies and confusion. "I assume he didn't want to drag anyone else down with him if things went south. He... well, he threatened the oil exec that came out here last week."

Even the council members leaned in at the new information. Up until now they had believed themselves to be completely in the loop.

"What do you mean, *threatened?*" Jameson demanded.

Cat's out of the bag now.

"He burned one of their helicopters." The table erupted in angry shouts. Russo felt a wave of validation flow through him. "I know, he's lost his fucking mind."

Jameson stood up from his seat, alarmed. "You let him do *what?*"

Russo recoiled. "*Let* him? You think I can control him?"

"Yes! That's what you do!" Jameson came back and then paused. Russo could see a darker revelation overtake him. "And you let him go to town after that, by himself?"

"He needs to do this on his own." Russo turned back to his plate.

"What the fuck does that mean?" Jameson demanded, his voice rapidly becoming more antagonistic.

"There's more to it than you know."

"Really? More goddamn secrets? What now?"

Russo fell silent and looked at Hunt, who shook his head. He knew he could not reveal to the group, or even the other council members the information he'd learned that spring — the story that had entirely eroded his trust and loyalty to his best friend.

"You slimy fuck! Don't pretend there's more to it than there is. You've already packed your shit and you're bailing on us. You don't give a fuck about how this goes," Jameson hissed through gritted teeth.

Russo felt an intense wave of indignant rage. He stood up fast, sending his chair skittering across the floor.

"Fuck you, you prick!" he shouted, pointing his finger down the table at Jameson. "Since when am I in charge of that crazy bastard's decisions? You think I have some God-given power over any of this? I can't even get *you* to listen to me half the time, how am I supposed to get *him* to? This is *Stark's* town! I'm done playing mommy to that psychopath's absentee daddy! I'm not your fucking leader! *HE IS!*"

The room fell silent. Thirty angry faces glared back at Russo with a mixture of confusion, pain, and anger. He could hear the three-year-old Oki whimpering into his mother's arms from down the table.

Alwan was the one to break the silence. "You're a fool."

Russo wheeled on him.

The doctor didn't shy away from Russo's furious gaze. "What do you think your role here is, Andrew? After all these years do you really think we're all just pawns in Augustin's game? He may have financed this, but *we* built it… together. You came here for a reason, Andrew. Do you *really* believe that because people treat you the way they do that they don't respect you? Is that what this is? An ego bruised by brotherly resentment? You just let your best friend, a man you called your *brother*, walk a very dangerous path alone, all because you were jealous?

"Do you really want to know why people joke about you being the town mom? I'll tell you: it's because you're the one who's always been there for them when Stark wasn't. You say this is Stark's town, and that he's our leader. Some of that may be true, but before this evening, it was just as much yours as it ever was his."

The softly spoken words crushed down on Russo's soul harder than a million furious accusations from Jameson ever could. Russo wanted nothing more than to reveal the truth to Alwan, that the root cause of his rage wasn't really the insecurities about his role in the society.

It was Stark's *betrayal.*

But as he scanned the faces around the table, he recognized that same feeling of betrayal being thrown back at him by the people he had just moments before been so eager to abandon.

Jameson addressed the crowd. "I'm leaving for Harkstaff in ten. Oliver, I expect you'll come with. Irniq, the invite's open. Hunt, you're in charge." He stared directly at Russo. "That is, if you can check your ego and not turn into some power hungry, psychopathic, teenage cunt like your predecessor."

"Oh Jesus, what the fuck are you gonna to do?" Russo spit back. "I guarantee he's shacked up at the inn watching reruns and playing rummy with the sheriff and waiting on a call back from his lawyers."

"You would assume that. He blows up a goddamn helicopter then disappears to town for a week without contacting us. Yeah, I'm sure *everything is fucking fine!*" Jameson roared back as he headed for the door, then paused and turned to Russo. "Why don't you grab your wife and all that shit you packed. We'll drop you off at the airstrip."

"So, you're afraid he got arrested? What are you going to do if he did? Break him out? Think about this!"

"Yeah," Oliver broke his silence and stood to follow Jameson. "That's exactly what we're gonna to do."

With that, the duo left the Koutla. Irniq followed close behind them.

"Goddamn it!" Russo screamed, spiking his mug on the ground and following them out. When he reached the door, he swung back and pointed at Hunt. "Radio watch twenty-four seven. If anything stupid happens, you have the BAS ready for us!"

He met Maya's teary eyes from across the hall.

What the fuck did I get you into, girl?

9

Special Agent John Leonardo jerked awake to the alarm blaring from his cellphone. He sat up immediately, knowing that if he didn't force himself out from under the warm sheets, he would be tempted to hit snooze. He hoisted himself up from the stiff hotel mattress and pulled on the cheap robe that lay at the foot of the bed, snorting at the childish calligraphy of the black letters scrawled across its back in sharpie:

PROPERTY OF HARKSTAFF INN

He couldn't imagine what type of person would want to steal the frayed cotton garment. Well, actually he could. To the rugged inhabitants of the failing town, even a threadbare rag as this one might seem appealing.

He made his way across the cramped hotel room into its musty bathroom and leaned against the sink, staring into his own disheveled reflection in the stained mirror.

What the fuck am I doing here?

He leaned close to examine the ever-growing crows' feet that bordered his eyes. Fifteen years in the Bureau had taken their toll. This Alaska case was just the latest in a string of shit assignments he and his anti-terror team had been forced into, and it surely wouldn't be the last.

He pulled a razor from the meticulously kept toiletry bag by the sink and began his morning ritual. Ten minutes later, he climbed out of the lukewarm shower, dressed in the same cheap suit he wore the day before, and left the dingy inn.

Two weeks earlier, Leonardo and his team had been knee deep in investigating a street gang in Nevada with suspected ties to Boko Haram. After wasting three months on the case, his superiors pulled them from the arid American southwest and shipped them out to the brisk wilderness of eastern Alaska. The deputy director to whom he reported, a plump little Q-ball of a man named Hirsh, had seemed irregularly anxious as he described this new assignment over the phone, stating that the Director of the FBI himself had requested to be kept in the loop every step of the way. At the time, Leonardo thought whatever it was that was happening up here in Alaska *had* to be important. However, over the past week Leonardo had found himself befuddled as to why the Director was so personally involved.

Leonardo had flown into Fairbanks with a team of seven agents then spent nearly a day traversing the poorly kept roads to Harkstaff in order to locate and arrest a wealthy lunatic who had secluded himself deep out in the forest. A man who Leonardo's superiors in the FBI insisted was a home-grown terrorist. His chain of command seemed confident that the case was open and shut, and at this point he found himself eager to believe them. With this Stark character now in custody, Leonardo hoped the regional office in Fairbanks would assign a long-term SAC (Special Agent in Charge) to replace him and his team.

The morning air was thick with the scent of the previous night's rain as he made his way to the sheriff's station. Inside he found one of his agents, a hulking Asian man named Chen, sitting behind the sheriff's desk listening to a tale from one of the town's less-than-brilliant deputies.

"I swear to you, it's true!" the deputy insisted as Leonardo stepped through the door.

"Morning, Leo," Chen greeted him with a nod, wincing a little as the motion contorted the reinforced bandage that covered his broken nose.

"Chen," Leonardo said curtly.

Chen was a new addition to his team, and so far, Leonardo was not impressed.

Leonardo turned to regard the baby-faced deputy. "Please, don't stop on my account."

"I was just telling your man over there how the sheriff one-shotted a grizzly with that rifle up there." He pointed to a large caliber hunting rifle that hung over the door. "Killed it with one shot. I can prove it!"

"What, do you have it on video or something?" Chen was doing little to conceal his condescending grin.

"Nah man, he was by his'self. But the rest of the bullets are still in it. Like I said, he just used the one. I'd say take her down and check for yourself but I don't know if the sheriff'd like you messing with his prize rifle."

Leonardo didn't feel like crushing the simple young man's dreams by pointing out that the sheriff, who was the boy's uncle, could have simply reloaded the rifle afterwards.

"So, you keep a loaded rifle over the entrance of your station? Where anyone you bring in here can grab it?" Chen asked.

"Well… I guess no one's ever thought about it like that. Most we ever really bring people in for is drinkin' too much." The deputy narrowed his eyes at Chen. "You got a devious mind, don't you?"

"What's your name, son?" Leonardo interjected.

"Matthew Carr," the deputy responded proudly, coming

to an awkward form of attention. "But my friends call me Matty."

"Ok, Carr, we need somewhere to interrogate the prisoner."

"I've been waiting all week for that! Mind if I watch?"

Leonardo sighed. The deputy couldn't have been older than twenty, and clearly didn't have much — if any —real world experience. "Yes, Carr, I mind quite a bit. This man is a suspected terrorist. You have neither the clearance nor the professional experience to join us."

"Oh..." Carr slouched for a moment, then his chipper spirit came rushing back. "Uncle Mi— I mean the Sheriff, had me clean out the old evidence locker for you guys to use to interrogate Mr. Stark. I got a table and a couple chairs in there, but I couldn't find one of them cool heat lamps like in the movies. If you want one, you're gonna have to order it from Tulimak over at the general store, but it'll probably take a couple weeks to get here."

"That's fine, Carr," Leonardo said.

There was a knock at the door. Leonardo opened it to see a small, ghoulish man waiting.

"Hello, Agent Leonardo," Franklin Summerset greeted him, holding out a satellite phone. "Mr. Masterson was hoping to have a word."

"Yeah, uh, hold on." Leonardo shut the door and turned to Chen. "Go ahead and get Stark all set up. I don't think I need to remind you to make sure he's secure."

Chen grunted and instinctively brushed a hand over his bandaged nose.

Leonardo left the building and took the phone from Franklin.

"Hello?"

"Hello. Is this Special Agent in Charge John Leonardo?"

"Yes. Mr. Masterson, I'm glad to hear from you. I have some more questions regarding Mr. Stark's assault on you and exactly what you witnessed up there."

"Yes, another time, I'm currently very busy," the crackling old voice responded. *"I just wanted to let you know that I have heard wonderful things about your work, and I trust that you will do what's right regarding that savage outlaw."*

"Mr. Masterson, this is an investigation by the Federal Bur—"

"Yes, yes, I am well aware, young man. Who do you think had you assigned to this case? Your Director is a very old friend of mine; he assured me that he would have his best conducting this investigation. You should be honored. I myself had to depart from that hellhole shortly after our meeting, but I assure you I will be returning soon. I just wanted to call and let you know once again that the full assets of Lockstone Oil are at your disposal. Should you have any issues, just let Franklin know."

"Mr. Masterson, this is very abnormal," Leonardo said before realizing that the old man had already hung up. He handed the phone back to Franklin. "Real nice boss you've got there."

Franklin nodded and gave a wide grin.

...creep.

"So, you're the guy in charge?" Stark asked across the plastic folding table, breaking a long and uncomfortable silence in the cramped interrogation room.

Leonardo leaned back in his chair. He always felt a sense of accomplishment when his quarry spoke first. "Yeah, that would be me."

"You like taking your time, don't you?"

Leonardo had chosen to let Stark simmer in his own

misery while he spent the week gathering intel on the outlying community the locals called "The Homestead." After coming up with little more than a few barely discernable satellite images and a spotted internet history from the village's illegal hook-up, as well as seeing Stark's nonchalant, almost bored demeanor, Leonardo realized that the past week might have been a waste of time.

Stark sighed and crossed his arms — at least as far as the handcuffs would allow him. "Look, pal, I see this going one of two ways: you're either going to listen to what I have to say and figure out what's really going on, *or* you're going to act like a dick and be a patsy to that conniving bitch Masterson. How about we skip the witty banter and you just tell me now: are you looking for the truth? Or are you looking for an excuse to keep me locked up?"

Leonardo was intrigued. It wasn't often that he dealt with suspects this confident, but then again, the truly crazy ones weren't often shy.

"I'm a sworn agent of the federal government, Mr. Stark. Despite the feeling I get that you aren't going to believe me, I promise you that my goal here is to get to the truth behind this situation. I do have to say though, there is a lot of condemning evidence here."

"Ok, well, I'm going to have a hard time defending myself if I don't even know what you're charging me with."

"Let's dig right into it then." Leo opened the folder in front of him. "I see that you did four years in the Marine Corps. Two tours overseas in leadership billets, a Navy Marine Corps Achievement medal with a valor device, and a relatively clean record despite what your First Sergeant described as 'a rebellious personality' and 'often egregious disregard of orders.'"

"I know that quote's not on any official record," Stark

interjected.

"No, it isn't. I spoke to him a few days ago. Part of the whole *investigating* thing. I'll be honest, he doesn't think very highly of you."

"The feeling's mutual." Stark smirked. "The man was a POG bureaucrat and a coward. He once put himself in for a medal after hiding in the back of a truck during a raid. But now isn't really the time to be rehashing old war stories, is it?"

"No, it isn't. I'd much rather talk about what happened after you came home. We have on record that you used your GI Bill for two years at Northeastern before dropping out. Philosophy major? How was that?"

Stark leaned forward. "Can we cut to the chase? I get it, you want to get me talking, see if I slip up somewhere and give something away. I've seen enough cop dramas to know what you're going for, but frankly, it's far more obnoxious in person." He stared hard into Leonardo's eyes. *"I want to know what you're charging me with."*

"Answer the fucking questions shithead," Chen piped up from where he was leaning in the opposite corner of the room.

"Hush," Stark came back. "The adults are talking."

Leonardo held up a hand for Chen to be silent. He couldn't see the man behind him but he had a feeling the towering agent was wringing his hands furiously.

"Mr. Stark—"

"Just call me Stark."

"Ok, Stark, I get the feeling that you don't fully comprehend the severity of this investigation. We apprehended you under the suspicion of plotting to commit domestic terrorism. Under the Patriot Act, we don't have to reveal *anything* to you. *But* in order to keep this conversation amiable, I will tell you that we have enough evidence to put you and your friends in that encampment away for a very long time."

"Bullshit."

"No, not bullshit." Leonardo was growing annoyed with Stark's attitude. What he had initially taken as confidence now seemed more like simple denial. "You went off the grid for a year and a half between when you dropped out of school and when you first showed up here. Where were you?"

"Traveling."

"Traveling where?"

"All over."

"Alright buddy, I can't help you if you aren't willing to help yourself." Leonardo snapped the folder shut and stood.

Stark let out sigh and held a hand up for Leonardo to stop. "Ok… ok… give and take. I get it. I met a girl in school. We decided to take a year off, traveled around Europe for a while then backpacked through South America. What else do you want?"

Leonardo sat back down. "This girl, her name was Paige Muller? Daughter of wealthy banker Anders Muller?"

Stark's face darkened at the mention of her name. "Yes."

"When she disappeared four years ago, were you questioned?"

"I spent a week getting smacked around by the Mexican Federales."

"But were you questioned by the FBI?"

"Your people refused to be involved in the investigation. I thought you said you did your homework?"

"I did, and I saw that a month after your girlfriend went missing while in *your company,* her very wealthy father was found with a self-inflicted gunshot wound to the head, only one day after signing his estate over to you. You get how that looks, right?"

"Why don't you tell me how it fuckin' looks."

"Well, to be frank, it looks like you were complicit in her disappearance."

Stark's demeanor transformed dramatically. The sarcastic annoyance was gone. His eyes cut through Leonardo. He couldn't help but feel an uncharacteristic chill shoot up his spine.

"But that's not what we're here for." Leonardo cleared his throat. "We're here to find out exactly what you're using that land and that money you inherited from Muller for. Agent Chen here thinks you're just a hapless anti-government wackjob. But I think you're smarter than that. You seem to me like the type of man that could really do some damage if he wanted to, especially with all that cash. Since you're so eager to get this over with, I'm going to ask you flat out: what are you planning up there, and who else is involved?"

"Alright." The spark of levity returned to Stark's eyes and he leaned forward on the table. "Give me a smoke, this might take a while."

Leonardo snapped his fingers at Chen without looking back. Chen grunted and handed him a cigarette, which he rolled across the table to Stark.

"Fuegos?" Stark made the signal for a lighter and Chen begrudgingly threw one on the table in front of him.

"Thanks, little guy," Stark muttered and lit the smoke before tossing the lighter back. "Where do you want me to start?"

"Anywhere you like."

"Ok, my plans…" Stark took a deep drag and pondered the ceiling. "Well, after I sort out this whole mess, I plan on heading back to my cozy little cabin. I'll probably make some dinner when I get there. Maybe a nice stew, or some salted pork…"

He clearly noticed Leonardo's annoyance.

"Sorry, that's not what you're looking for, I'm getting off track. What I'm *really* looking forward to is spending the night working on a painting of your little buddy over there getting butt-raped by an elk while his mother—"

Chen lunged forward and Leonardo was forced to grab him by the collar before he made it over the table. Stark forced a laugh and flicked the lit cigarette into Chen's face, sending it bouncing off his bandaged nose in a tiny explosion of embers.

"You motherfucker!" Chen roared.

Leonardo had to use all his strength to hold the hulk of a man back.

"Out! Now!" he screamed at his subordinate.

Chen regained a semblance of his composure and stomped out the door, slamming it behind him. Leonardo turned back to Stark. "You want to play fucking games? Is that what you think this is? You're about to spend the rest of your life in solitary confinement and you're acting like a goddamn child!"

Stark's laughter subsided. He spoke deliberately. "Listen to me, Agent Leonardo. Listen closely. You're on a witch hunt. I've broken no laws, and have absolutely no intention of harming any Americans or committing any sort of terrorism. You're here because a man named Edward Masterson is attempting to abuse the law and steal my land for his oil company to drill on. He has illegally racketeered within the government to claim eminent domain on my property and I'm sure he put your bosses up to this terrorism nonsense in order to stall me until the decision is final. *Any* so-called evidence that you have is a fabrication created to ensure this whole thing goes down in his favor. If you actually *are* looking for the truth, that is exactly what you'll find."

Leonardo was tired of the games. "How do you explain this then?"

He pulled a sheet from the folder and slammed it on the desk in front of Stark.

"What is it?" Stark asked, glancing over the document.

"We've been monitoring traffic on that illegal satellite you set up. That right there is a recipe for homemade explosives pulled off a 'how-to' website set up on the dark web for ISIS sympathizers. It was downloaded the day before we arrested you. Tell me, how did Masterson 'fabricate' that?"

Stark gave the paper a perplexed look and Leonardo waited for a witty retort.

"Nothing?" Leonardo finally asked. "That's what I thought. I hope you're prepared for a long stay here, Mr. Stark, because aside from this, we have a witness who claims you tortured him in your bunker out there. He saw a lot more than you think he did. We know you're manufacturing explosives, and until you wisen the fuck up and tell us what you're planning on using them for, you won't see the light of day."

"I can't explain this," Stark muttered, staring the sheet of paper. "But I can assure you that Franklin is lying."

"Your word doesn't carry much weight right now. Tell me: who else is up there?"

Stark looked up, all of the humor disappeared from his face. "You *need* to heed my words very carefully, Agent Leonardo. You're on the wrong side of history with this one. Do not, I can't say this with enough emphasis, do *not* try to go up there without me."

Leonardo rose and walked to the door. "You're going back in that cell. If you come to your senses, let me know."

"Leonardo," Stark called after him. "If anything happens, you have to understand. *You're* the bad guy here."

10

Russo crouched in the long shadows cast by Tulimak's house. He held his AR-10 rifle tight against his chest, nervously brushing his thumb against the safety toggle as he stared out across the moonlit main street of Harkstaff. Beside him, Irniq and Jameson leaned against the building's shingled siding and waited patiently for the old man to return home.

The party had hung to the outskirts of town, stashing their ATVs far down the street and sneaking house to house to their current position. Oliver was happy to put on the skills he'd garnered growing up as an underprivileged miscreant in Philadelphia by deftly breaking into the old church that sat across the street from the sheriff's station. He climbed to the top of the crooked steeple to provide them with a bird's eye view of the clustered buildings.

They all knew something had changed in the small town. Three blacked-out SUVs stood out like sore thumbs, one parked beside the sheriff station and the other two outside the inn. Russo had suspected they might run into trouble with the local sheriffs if Stark had in fact been arrested. But the presence of the oversized Suburbans with government plates made him consider for the first time that this might be bigger than he anticipated.

Now, more than ever, Russo worried that they were in over their heads, that the long blood trail Stark had left behind had led all the way up into the frozen wilderness.

Jameson had remained indignant throughout their trip over the mountain and across the rolling grasslands to Harkstaff. He no doubt held Russo personally responsible for whatever had befallen Stark. Russo was tempted to quell this by divulging the true reason behind his supposed betrayal, but for some reason allowed the remnant feeling of loyalty — especially after swearing secrecy to his old friend — to control him.

Irniq cupped his hands over his mouth and sounded an owl call. Across the dark street, a figure materialized and approached the house. A moment later, the call was echoed. Tulimak trudged into the flickering light of his front porch, up the rickety stairs, and took a seat in the wooden rocking chair at its end directly around the corner from the hidden trio.

"Irniq, what the hell have you gotten yourself into boy?" the older man muttered discreetly as he pulled a corncob pipe from his pocket and lit it. Irniq leaned toward the railing, but Tulimak held out a foreboding hand. "Stay in the shadows. I don't know if we're being watched."

Russo instinctively squeezed tighter to the building.

"What's going on, Uncle?" Irniq whispered. "Why are there government vehicles here? Where's Stark?"

Tulimak took a puff of his pipe and shifted nervously in his seat. "The FBI are here. They say he's a terrorist. They're holding him in the station."

Russo shared a worried glance with the others. His fears about Stark's bloody past in Mexico being exposed were suddenly overcome with the confusion of the federal government deeming Stark a terrorist.

"Do you know anything else?" Irniq asked.

"No."

"Thank you, Uncle. Stay here and keep quiet. We have to figure this out," Irniq said, then turned to leave.

"Wait!" Tulimak said a little too loudly, drawing a hiss from Jameson. "What the hell have you boys been up to out there? What have they gotten Alasie into?"

"They're liars, Uncle. They're trying to steal the land. I swear she is not in danger. Please, *please* stay quiet. We need to deal with this and you can't interfere."

Tulimak leaned over the porch's railing, staring directly at his nephew and speaking in a somber, yet commanding tone. "Be smart, boy. This is a tinder box. For the love of God, do not throw a match on it."

Irniq nodded and the three men cut around the back of the house. They huddled together inside Tulimak's standalone shed. Irniq sat atop a rusted snow blower while Jameson leaned between the shovels and rakes that hung along the wall and shook his head.

"Terrorism?" Jameson couldn't seem to wrap his mind around it. "What is this? It's gotta be a mistake."

"If I had to venture a guess, this is Masterson's doing," Russo said.

He knew that Masterson had alluded to having contacts in the government, and didn't put it past the man to use them to cook up false charges.

"Yeah," Jameson nodded. "Well, we're *fucked.*"

The Motorola clipped to Jameson's side chirped once. He pulled it from his belt and spoke into it. "Oliver, we've got a big problem."

"Yeah, no shit!" Oliver's hushed voice came from the speaker. *"Agents Mulder and Scully just came out of the grocery store.*

Headed your way."

Russo leaned out of the shed and squinted down the road toward the illuminated sheriff's station. Two faint figures meandered away from the grocery and toward the inn. He raised his rifle and peered through the scope. They both wore matching blue jackets with the signature yellow shield imprinted on the chest.

"What the hell is going on?" Oliver demanded over the radio.

"There's no time to explain," Jameson responded. "Stark's in the station. We've got to get him out. You need to be our guardian angel."

Russo wheeled around in protest. "You have got to be fucking kidding me! You can't break him out — this is the *FBI!"*

Jameson cracked his neck. "You can help, or you can stay here, Andrew. Just don't get in the fucking way."

They bided their time until the FBI agents disappeared into the inn before darting through the shadowy lane behind the houses. Russo wanted to scream at Jameson to stop, to lay the man out with a butt stroke, to do anything to force the hot-headed fool to reexamine the situation, but he knew Jameson was beyond reason at this point. All Russo could do was tag along and try to ensure things didn't get out of hand.

But they were breaking a man out of jail... things were already well out of hand.

The trio bounded from shadow to shadow, using Oliver as an eye in the sky to guide them along the edge of the road, across it, and to the backside of the sheriff's station, where they crouched under one of the open windows. Russo motioned the others to stay low while he peeked inside.

There were two men sitting opposite each other at a card table. The man facing the window wore the same deep blue jacket as the other FBI agents and had a bandage covering his nose.

"Your turn, piggy," the FBI agent said. "High or low?"

"I told you not to call me that!" complained the man in the sheriff's uniform sitting opposite him.

Russo recognized the sluggish voice as Matty Carr, the halfwit deputy.

"High or low, kid," the agent asked impatiently.

"High."

The agent flipped a card on the table in front of him and let out a hearty laugh. "Drink, *little piggy!*"

Carr groaned and took a swig from a bottle of Bacardi 151, slamming it back down on the table and coughing.

"Oh man." The agent continued to laugh. "How do you hillbillies drink this shit?"

"It's cheaper to ship a bottle of this out here than a case of vodka, and this'll do the same job."

"Whatever you say, kid. Alright, my turn." The agent regarded the bottle and shivered. "High."

"Ok, ok, hold your horses. Let me get these cards in order."

Russo crouched back down and signaled for Jameson to retreat around the corner of the building so they could figure out their next move. Jameson shook his head and motioned to the side door, waving his open hand to signify a column.

He wants to bum rush it.

Please don't be this stupid.

"Stack up," Jameson whispered, raising his rifle as Irniq fell in behind him. They silently glided around the corner to the station's side entrance.

"Irniq, door," Jameson ordered under his breath. Irniq circled around him and grasped the door handle. Both men nodded to each other in unison.

3... 2... 1...

Irniq turned the handle and pushed hard. The heavy door budged in its frame but didn't open. Irniq flashed the others a panicked expression. Inside the building, Russo heard the FBI agent call out.

"Who is that? Leonardo?"

Russo knew this was the type of hellish situation where the only way out was to dive in headfirst, deeper into the rabbit hole. He shoved Jameson against the wall under the window as a shadow grew along the alley. Russo could feel the man's presence above them as he peered into the night. After a second, the footsteps moved to the door and the lock clicked.

"Leo?" the agent asked nervously as he cracked the door. "I just had a little drink to ease the pai—"

Jameson charged inside, knocking the agent to the ground. Russo followed on his tail.

The room was empty aside from the two occupants. The agent was sprawled out across the floor, Jameson's rifle pressed firmly to his temple. Matty Carr sat at the foldout table with the bottle of liquor, a thermos of coffee, and a mess of cards strewn in front of him. He met Russo's eyes with dumb panic and whipped his hands into the air.

"Stay down, bitch," Jameson hissed at the FBI agent.

Russo plucked the pistol and pepper spray from Carr's duty belt. As Irniq entered and relocked the door behind him, Russo secured Carr in his own handcuffs, throwing him down on the room's singular couch.

"Draw the blinds!" Russo commanded. Irniq complied.

Jameson had disarmed the FBI agent, who remained spread eagle on the floor. He turned to Carr. "Where do you keep the extra cuffs?"

Carr let out a whimper and a dark stain spread around his crotch.

"Goddamnit kid, where do yo—"

The prone agent swiped Jameson's leg, toppling him. Russo and Irniq both leveled their rifles as the agent scrambled on top of Jameson, but neither had a clean shot. Before they could intervene, Jameson flipped the larger man onto his back and pummeled him with heavy rights until he went limp.

"Is this your first—"

"Shut the fuck up!" Jameson spit back at Russo through bared teeth. "Go get Stark!"

Russo crossed through the door that lead to the two meager cells. The room was dimly lit, but he immediately recognized his old friend attempting to poke his head through the bars of the closest cell.

"What the *hell* are you doing here?"

"We're here for you; I couldn't stop these morons from rescuing their fearless leader." Russo scoured the cell door for the lock.

"It's operated by a pin pad on the wall," Stark told him.

Russo leaned back into the main office. "Jameson, get the door code from the deputy."

Jameson took a threatening step toward Carr, who lurched backwards in terror and squealed. "I don't have it! The FBI didn't trust us. That guy knows! You gotta wake him up!"

Oh God.

"Jameson." Russo tried to convey a calm tone. "You better pray that you didn't kill him. Get that code before one of his buddies comes wandering over here and this nightmare turns into a gunfight.

As if on cue, the radio atop the sheriff's desk crackled to life. "*Chen, radio check. Over.*"

All three men stopped cold, dead in their tracks. Time stood still, then a light beeping sounded from Carr's watch.

Russo looked at the clock on the wall.

11:00

Hourly radio checks.

Fuck...

All three men burst into action: Jameson and Irniq hunted desperately for something to revive the unconscious FBI agent while Russo ran his hands over the outside of the cell's lock, praying that there was a backup keyhole.

"Stop." Stark grabbed Russo's hand through the bars. "You need to listen to me. They've got me for domestic terrorism."

"I know," Russo growled, pulling his hand away and turning to examine the pin pad.

Stark grabbed him by the shirt and pulled him to the bars. *"Listen to me!"*

Russo stopped and met his eyes.

"This little rescue is *exactly* what they need to fry us all. I'm already fucked. But they don't know who's at the Homestead. As far as they know, there could be as few as five people up there. This gives you and the others a chance. You need to get everyone out before they raid it. They have a satellite watching the area, but if you get the majority out at night, they won't be able to tell. Someone will have to stay behind to make it look like it's still inhabited. When these fuckers come, burn it all. Use the fire as cover and bail. Leave no trace. Don't let Masterson take anyone else down with his lies."

In the neighboring room, Jameson splashed the Bacardi on the unresponsive agent's face and shook him violently.

"Listen," Stark continued, "there's a small pass going through the Fist into Canada. Follow the game trail where you got your first elk. About five hundred yards east you'll find where it starts. It's rough, but you can make it through."

"Do you even realize what you've gotten us into?" Russo

spat.

"Of course I do! But the bastard had this set up before I even fucked with him. He had Franklin lie to the feds and say we were planning a terrorist attack or some shit. There was no stopping it, and I'm sorry you have to deal with the fallout. But it's on *you* now to get our people to safety."

The radio on the desk crackled again, the voice more persistent this time. *"Chen, answer the damn radio. If I find you passed out drunk, I swear I'll write you up this time."*

Stark looked desperate, gripping the front of Russo's shirt with white knuckles. "Destroy the satellite dish right away; they're watching everything that passes through it. If anyone tries to log onto any sort of personalized website, their identities will be compromised. If everything goes to shit, I need you to contact a man named Enrique Espuezeto. He's the mayor of a town in Mexico just over the border. Tell him where I am, and that this is the last chance he'll have to get me or the money. If those Mexican fucks hold a grudge like I think they do, then they'll show up and burn this town to the ground. That should give you the cover to get out safe."

"Cut the martyr shit. You're coming with us." Russo spun back to Jameson. "Wake him the fuck up!"

Stark shook Russo, pleading now. "I'm not going to see everyone I care about locked up for the rest of their lives without trial because the greed of one slimy asshole. Contact the Mexicans, Russo. Do it for Maya. Do it for Oki and Tommy. Those kids need their parents. Don't make me spend the rest of my life chained up like a dog knowing that I destroyed the lives of all the people I love. For fuck's sake, do it for *me*."

Russo saw the anguish behind Stark's eyes and felt his heart sink.

"Go," Stark ordered as he released Russo and retreated to

the back of the cell. "Now."

Just then something inside Russo broke. The wall of resentment that had built up over that summer came crumbling down as he saw his friend withdraw into the darkness. All the rage melted and he realized that he had horribly misjudged Stark. This *was* his best friend, a man who would sacrifice anything for the safety and happiness of his friends. Suddenly, more than anything in the world, he wished he could tear the bars off the cell and have Stark back at his side. Glancing over at Jameson furiously shaking the unconscious agent, Russo realized this might very well be the last time he saw Stark.

"Uh... hey dickheads..." Oliver's voice came over the radio at Jameson's side. *"You're about to have company. Mulder's coming in hot, I'm uh... I'm not trying to smoke a fed, but let me know what's up."*

****

"Goddamn drunk," Leonardo grumbled to himself as he ambled along the broken pavement toward the po-dunk sheriff's station.

He'd suffered through plenty of shit assignments before — it came with the job. But one thing he couldn't stand to suffer was incompetence. When Chen had first been assigned to him, Leonardo had taken it as a challenge from his superiors. But now it felt more like a punishment. Chen had a long list of red marks on his file and a reputation as an insufferable alcoholic. Now the incompetent prick had stopped answering his radio. While Leonardo knew there was a chance the battery had died, he almost hoped he would find Chen passed out drunk alongside the deputy so he would have an excuse to get the man reassigned. Or just fired once and for all.

The night air was cool and a light breeze brushed against Leonardo's face. Halfway to the station a shiver ran up his spine.

He paused.

It wasn't from the cold.

It started as almost nothing, but gradually he was overcome with an eerie feeling as if he was being watched... But he wasn't just being observed... No... It was a more primal feeling. An uncanny awareness of some ominous presence in the surrounding night. His eyes darted from building to building. The small town basked in the light of the full moon and appeared to be entirely void of life. Squinting at the sheriff's station ahead, he could see through the dimly lit windows that the blinds had been drawn.

Why?

He continued forward, slowing his pace as he fished his cell phone from his pocket. He opened up the group chat that included all seven of his agents; he knew none of them would have their radios on while they slept.

Everyone to the sheriff station
High alert

He finished typing the message and hit send. The text appeared to send, then a small exclamation popped up: message failed, no service.

Shit.

The anxious feeling multiplied. He had never felt anything this eerily intense in his life, and wondered for a moment if he was slipping into the grip of his first panic attack. Knowing that his phone would connect to the sheriff station's Wi-Fi if he got close enough, Leonardo picked his pace back up and attempted to look casual as he fluttered his thumb over the send button. He stared intently into the yellow glow of the windows as he closed the last twenty feet to the station. A sliver of blinds broke apart the tiniest bit. Someone glanced out at him.

The lights cut off.

Without a second's hesitation, he bolted into the alley that separated the sheriff's station and the grocery. He felt the rush of adrenaline and fully expected to hear the clap of gunfire with every heavy footfall. He ducked behind a hulking steel dumpster and leaned hard into it. His heart pounded in his ears as he peeked back out at the now pitch-black windows of the sheriff's station. They were silent and still.

Seconds passed that felt like an eternity. He glanced down at his phone and saw that the message had gone through — two of the recipients were marked *read*. He squeezed tighter against the dumpster and drew his pistol. Backup was on the way. Now all he had to do was wait.

The window nearest to the dumpster exploded as a folding chair crashed through it, sending splinters of glass cascading over the earth at Leonardo's feet. Before he could bring his pistol up to bear, an orange blur flew out of the dark room and erupted in a plume of flames against the wall above the dumpster. Liquid fire rained down on Leonardo's neck and jacket as he curled into a tight ball.

"What the hell was that?" A half-awake agent's voice came over the radio.

He scrambled to find the transmit button. "Molotov cocktail! They've taken the station!"

From inside the blacked-out sheriff's station, a man's voice called out. "Throw out your weapons! We don't want to hurt you!"

Leonardo swatted at his burnt jacket then pulled his pistol

tight to his chest as he had practiced so many times in training. He crouched low and leaned out from behind the dumpster to see into the smashed window. The flickering yellow light of the flaming dumpster beside him illuminated a figure inside. He snapped the pistol forward and fired three quick rounds at the silhouette. The handgun bucked violently and greenish-orange flames erupted from its barrel. The heavy flash from his pistol seemed alien to him — the whole action seemed slowed, almost unreal. In that split second, Leonardo came to the startling realization that he'd never fired his weapon at night before.

The adrenaline-fueled thoughts were torn from his mind as the silhouette returned fire. Bullets snapped by, thudding against the wooden wall of the grocery store behind him. He threw himself back behind cover and crawled as deep as he could into the corner of the wall and the hot dumpster.

"Cease fire!" he heard a voice shouting over the crackling flames.

The dense cloud of stinking smoke that spewed from the now fully engulfed dumpster rolled over Leonardo, filling his nose with the thick stench of burnt refuse and charred wood. He glanced upward through watering eyes and saw that the wall above him had begun to blacken and burn.

From down the street in the direction of the inn, he heard his team yelling and a cacophony of small arms fire. The sporadic popping of handguns was offset by the methodic boom of a not-too-distant high-powered rifle. Above the chaotic din he heard the repetitive screams of the agents: *Sniper.*

Leonardo knew he had to think fast. He couldn't just hide here behind cover while his agents were pinned down in the street. He drew in a deep breath and forced himself to listen to their panicked cries and used them as motivation.

"Geronimo," he muttered to himself, then leapt out from behind the dumpster and charged at the station's side entrance.

He threw every ounce of his two-hundred-pound frame against the heavy door. The wood around the lock splintered and it swung inward. He stumbled over the threshold and fell face first on the floor. Recovering quickly, he swung his pistol in a wide arc around the room from the ground. It was empty aside from the hog-tied deputy and Chen's limp form draped over the couch. Leonardo scrambled to his feet and pulled open the door to the cells. The room was almost completely black, the only light coming from the flames behind him. He could see that the cell that housed Stark was still securely closed.

"Where are they?" Leonardo demanded from the pitch-black cell.

There was no reply. He leaned forward and scanned the darkness for Stark's shape. A heavy fist exploded through the bars and connected with his face. He saw stars as meaty hands grabbed him and hauled him against the cell door, clawing at the arm that held his pistol.

"I won't let you hurt them," Stark growled into his ear.

Desperately, Leonardo grappled against his attacker's overwhelming strength. Stark slammed Leonardo's back against the steel bars repeatedly, then looped a thick arm around his neck and squeezed hard. Leonardo felt the disorientation from the punch amplified by the blood supply being cut from his brain. His mind grew foggy and the world swam around him. In a desperate last resort, he flipped the pistol over his left shoulder and fired.

The arm released and flopped limply off Leonardo's shoulder. He collapsed on the jail floor. The dark room spun as the blood rushed back into his head. A thin line of warm liquid ran down the side of his face and a piercing ring emanated from his left ear.

The desperate voice of his senior agent squawking through the radio cut through the fog. *"They're getting away!"*

Leonardo lurched to his feet and stumbled to the front door. He watched half a dozen ultra-bright flashlights illuminate the leaning church steeple as his agents emptied countless rounds into its frail sides. The old steeple shuttered as the impacting bullets smashed away chunks of wood. Then with a final, creaking death-wail, it leaned perilously and collapsed.

Leonardo had heard all the stories from his old man about combat, about how the mind plays tricks on a man in dire circumstances, but in that moment, he could have sworn he heard a drawn out, almost garbled cry echoing from across the town, "Aw shit!"

The steeple crashed through the roof of the church with a deafening crunch. In an instant, the town was silent. Out of the corner of his eye, Leonardo caught sight of what looked to be three ATVs bolting behind the houses toward the toppled wreckage. He leveled his pistol, but immediately pulled it back, knowing that he couldn't risk firing through the small gaps between the buildings. The ATVs swerved up to the church and a figure limped from the wreckage and leapt aboard one of them before they turned and sped away to the north.

Leonardo's radio squawked with the frenzied calls of his team, but he could barely make out their words after the deafening point blank gunshot. He looked down at his pistol and had no doubt that it wouldn't reach the retreating targets.

The bear rifle will.

He grabbed the hunting rifle from its plaque above the door, hoping desperately the halfwit deputy hadn't been exaggerating his claims and that the gun was still loaded. Running out to the middle of the street where he had a clear view of the retreating ATVs, Leonardo took a knee, rested the rifle in his shoulder, and centered the scope's crosshairs on the closest moonlit figure.

He fired. The ATV jerked violently to the left and the rider toppled off of it. The other two vehicles continued for a moment before realizing that their companion was down, then came to a sudden halt. Leonardo worked the lever action and took aim once more. His target rose and sprinted toward the others. He placed the crosshairs just over the figure's back and squeezed the trigger. The rifle kicked hard and as the barrel came back down, he saw his target drop limp to the earth.

An enraged scream echoed through the night air, but was cut short as a handful of agents swarmed around Leonardo and opened fire on the distant targets. The ATVs roared back to life and jetted off across the airfield and into the forest beyond.

Leonardo lowered the rifle and felt a hand grasp his shoulder.

"Jesus... you good?" Agent Amanda Ferrara, his second in command, asked.

"Yeah." Leonardo wiped at the quickly coagulating blood that leaked from his ear. He looked down at it and saw that his hands were shaking.

"Did they get Stark?"

"No, I... I think I killed him though," Leonardo told her as he stood. His legs were wobbly but he did his best to act in control. "Did anyone get hit?"

Ferrara shook her head. "We're all good. If I didn't know better, I'd say they were missing us on purpose."

Leonardo smacked himself on the cheek; he still felt

detached from reality. "Get a car, we need to recover that body."

Ferrara sprinted across the street and leapt into an SUV.

As she pulled up next to him, Leonardo yelled to the other agents. "Chen is down in the station. He needs immediate medical attention. Get the doctor, then do a sweep of the town and find out exactly how the *fuck* this happened! And put out that fucking dumpster!"

He climbed in the SUV and they drove between the houses that skirted the road and out across the open landscape, pulling to a halt twenty feet from the motionless figure.

The body lay in a twisted heap. Aside from a dark, red entry wound on the back of the head, which shone bright in the beam of Ferrara's flashlight, the body seemed relatively intact. Leonardo cautiously flipped the corpse over, revealing an exploded mess of brains and skull where the face had been.

"Oh, sweet Jesus!" Ferrara recoiled with a coughing gag.

Leonardo tried to maintain his focus as he rifled through the dead man's pockets. "We, uh, we need to get a forensics kit from the station. The sheriff should have one."

He pulled out a worn wallet, inside an endearing photo of a handsome young man holding a small boy opposite a laminated South Carolina ID.

Donald Jameson, what the hell made you think all this was a good idea?

"*Hey Leo,*" the voice of an agent came through the radio. "*We've got the old man from the shop going ballistic here. He's demanding to see the body. Thinks it might be his nephew or something.*"

Leonardo knew the old Inuit was more involved than he had initially let on. "Lock him up. He's obviously got something he's not telling us. Get me all of the sheriffs and a forensics kit out here, then send up a quick brief to HQ in

Fairbanks. Tell them I'll get them a detailed report as soon as I've got this all sorted out."

"*You got it, boss. Hey… Great shot, Leo. That was some real medal worthy shit back there.*"

The image of a valor medal pinned to his chest flashed through Leonardo's mind, but the brief moment of gratification was cut short when he glanced back down at the body heaped at his feet.

He had just killed a man. In his fifteen years on the force he had never had to use his service pistol. Now, as he stood over the hunk of meat and bone that minutes before had been a twenty-five-year-old man, Leonardo felt an overwhelming awareness of his own power over life and death. A complex and terrifying understanding of the fragility of human existence and his own ability to destroy it. This was followed by a gut-curdling cognizance of his own mortality.

He didn't quite know how to process it.

All he knew was that he didn't like it one bit.

****

Tommy shifted anxiously in Stephanie's arms. She scooted him farther onto her lap and clicked pause on the cartoon playing on the computer in front of them.

"You ok, hun?" she asked, plucking one of the headphones from his ear.

"Where's my daddy?" The little boy looked at her with his big, opulent eyes.

"He had to go to town for some things. Don't worry, he'll be home in a couple days," she cooed, squeezing the plump little boy tight. "Do you like the movie?"

"The rabbit's funny," Tommy responded with a smile. She replaced the headphone and clicked play.

Tommy always had difficulty sleeping when Jameson made the trip to Harkstaff. Since the boy had arrived at the Homestead as an infant Stephanie had taken it upon herself to care for him when his father wasn't around. This evening was no different than most; the boy had tossed and turned and whimpered throughout the night until she finally carried him to the BAS where she could ease his separation anxiety with a hard drive full of children's movies.

Her mind wandered as the CGI rabbit on the screen continued its colorful song and dance routine.

What a strange place to raise a child. Jameson no doubt had the best intentions when he had brought his infant son with him to the Homestead, but had it been the best decision for the boy? At what point would the devoted father realize that Tommy needed a more traditional upbringing? A social life with others his own age? A real school? A future of his own choosing?

Whenever that happened, Jameson would leave. She had heard the heart-wrenching story behind Tommy's birth and knew that Jameson poured his entire heart and soul into providing the best life he could for his beloved son. There was no question in her mind that once the time came they would depart and reenter the real world together.

Across the table, the boxy shortwave radio crackled to life.

"-an you hear me?" a tinny, desperate voice came through the speaker.

She stood, placing the boy back into the chair alone despite his frustrated moaning, and grabbed the handset.

"Russo?" she asked.

"Yeah! Listen—" The signal was weak and the voice melted into indistinguishable garbling.

She keyed the headset a half dozen times in order to break through his transmission and relay that his words weren't getting through. The transmission cut out. She turned up the speaker's volume and keyed the mic. "Russo, I can't understand you. Speak slowly."

There was a second of silence, then Russo's voice cut clear as day through the BAS.

"Jameson is dead!"

The statement echoed through the inside of her skull several times before she was able to fully grasp its meaning. Slowly, she looked back at Tommy. The toddler had pulled the headphones from his ears. He stared at her with a mask of terrified confusion.

"Listen to me Stephanie! You need to—"

She keyed the mic furiously to cut him off; the child had already heard too much. She needed to get him away from the radio. "Stop, hold on, I'll be right back."

Before she released the transmit button Tommy shouted across the room. "Where's my daddy?"

"Jesus Christ!" Russo's furious voice followed her as she rushed back to the little boy. *"Why the fuck is the kid with you? Did he hear me?"*

"Put your headphones in, sweetheart," she urged the toddler, plugging them into his ears. "Everything's ok, watch the rabbit now."

"Stephanie, answer this goddamn radio!"

"Jesus Christ, Andrew! What the fuck are you talking about?" she hissed, turning the radio down low.

"Listen to me! Something very bad has happened. The FBI arrested Stark, and they're going to raid the Homestead. I need you to get Hunt and destroy the satellite dish."

"What? Why?"

"Because fucking do it, that's why!"

The ATV roared in the background of his frenzied orders and she knew he was speeding back. Even in the best-case scenario, the trip would take them at least a day.

"Tell me *exactly* what's going on."

"The FBI thinks we're terrorists, but they don't know who's up there. They're watching that connection, and if they can get into our computers and data, they can figure out exactly who we are. Stephanie, stop trying to figure shit out and listen to me." Russo stopped yelling and spoke gravely. *"Burn that fucking satellite dish to the ground."*

"Ok…" A swelling panic threatened to overwhelm her, but she wrestled it back.

She needed to destroy the satellite dish.

She rushed over and snatched Tommy up, forgetting to pull out his earphones. The laptop clattered to the ground and, in an instant, was accompanied by Tommy's furious bawling.

"It's ok. It's ok," she repeated over and over, almost as much to herself as him. She jogged along the small courtyard to the barn.

Inside, Hunt and Natasha lay intertwined in their hammock.

"Wake up!" she screamed, kicking the underside of the taut canvas. Both of them bolted upright, teetering for a moment and almost capsizing.

"Stephanie? What the fu—" Natasha began, but cut herself short when Stephanie thrust a weeping Tommy into her arms.

Without another word, Stephanie sprinted out the barn door, grabbing one of the wood axes that leaned against the wall as she passed. The satellite stood in the center of the courtyard that divided the Koutla and the barn. She brought the heavy metal axe head slamming down on its steel base. It bounced back, leaving little more than a dent. She was going to need something far more destructive.

"Stephanie! What the *hell* is going on?" Hunt shouted from

deep inside the barn.

She dropped the axe and ran back inside. "Gun! Give me a gun!"

"Stephanie!" Hunt wrestled to attach his prosthetic leg.

"There's no time to explain!" she insisted, eyeing the rifle propped against the support beam by Hunt's hammock.

"Stephanie, stop!" he barked, snatching the rifle and flashing her an alarmed look. "Tell me right now, what the fuck is going on?"

"Jameson's been ki—" She stopped. Tommy was staring at her in terror. "Something happened, it's *really bad*. We have to destroy the satellite dish!"

"Stephanie, you're not making sense." Hunt finally secured his stump in the socket of the metal leg and stood.

"Trust me! Please!" she begged. Her voice cracked and she realized there were tears streaming down her cheeks.

Hunt gave Natasha an anxious look, then nodded. "Ok, I trust you. Get some gas."

She searched desperately among the ATV equipment for a gas can small enough to carry outside. Finally, she found one half-buried between a bale of hay and a bag of feed.

"Hell of a way to wake everyone up..." Hunt was muttering when she stumbled outside to join him. He pulled the rifle to his shoulder and blasted it repeatedly into the steel-encased base of the satellite dish.

"Pour it on." Hunt motioned to the gas can clutched in her shaking hands.

"What?"

We're really going to burn it?

"You said to break it, this is how we break it. Pour the fucking gas, Stephanie."

She complied, splashing the stinking fuel through the holes and into the circuitry beneath. Hunt seized a dry pine branch from the nearby tree line, lit it, and threw it. With a heavy *poof*, the satellite dish erupted in a plume of flames that licked the overhanging tree branches.

She took a deep breath for what felt like the first time since the radio call, and was assaulted with the stench of burning wire and bubbling plastic. Beyond the flames, confused and terrified faces pressed themselves against the residence hall's windows. They had no idea. She had no idea.

All she knew was that her time at the Homestead was over.

It was time to run.

11

Stark leaned against the cold concrete wall of his cell. The faint glimmer of dawn cast thin beams of sunlight through the steel bars. He ran his hands over his face, pausing on the rough scab that had formed along his left cheek. He'd been lucky. Leonardo's bullet had almost killed him, glancing at an angle off his cheekbone and knocking him out cold. Now a deep, two-inch long gouge cut laterally below his left eye.

He had no idea what had happened following the jarring gunshot the night before. He'd been woken up at gunpoint by several agents, but Leonardo hadn't been among them.

The door to the station's office creaked open, wafting the stench of burnt garbage from the smoldering remains of the grocery store next door. If the people of Harkstaff had ever been on the Homestead's side, they definitely weren't now.

Edward Masterson sauntered into the room, his fingers flicking across the screen of a smart phone. He stood for a moment outside the cell's door with his eyes fixed on the device before it made a *whoosh*.

"Sorry about that — replying to an old friend." He looked up. "You may have heard of him: John Chism."

Stark did indeed recognize the name of the Attorney General.

"Anyways, I thought I'd stop by and check up on how things are going in your little winter wonderland up here. I heard you lost a friend last night... Sad."

Stark had no idea what Masterson was on about, but the evil smirk that creased the man's face made his heart drop.

"Oh, you didn't know?" Masterson went on, reading Stark like a book. "Yes, our mutual friend, Agent Leonardo, gunned down one of your lackeys as they tried to escape." He formed a gun with his gnarled fingers and pointed at Stark. "I haven't seen the body myself, but based on the description, I believe it may be your lawyer friend."

"Why are you still here?" It took every fiber of Stark's being not to let the rage leak into his voice; he couldn't give Masterson the satisfaction.

"Again, straight to the point. I like that about you." Masterson paused. "Well, I don't. I think it's rude, but it is one of your *less* antagonizing qualities... I'm wise enough to recognize when I've adequately disciplined a cur for shitting on the rug. I'm here to cut you a break, you *terrorist,* you." A smirk accompanied the word. "I believe it's the easiest way for everyone here to come out on top."

"You're offering a deal?"

"Indeed. Call it a show of pity. I don't want to put these government men in any more danger of being attacked by your mountain people, and I don't think you want to die in jail having your friends' blood on your hands. I'm offering you the opportunity to simply die in jail with a clean conscience."

For a moment, as he stared at the wrinkled old fossil of a man that stood before him, Stark questioned his own lack of faith. Maybe there was a devil.

"You want me to kill myself?"

"No, no of course not. That would be a mess. I only want

you to admit what you've *done*." He used air quotes around the word. "And then I want you to serve your time — life in prison. In exchange, I will use my influence to have your followers charged with far lesser crimes. I'm sure many of them will get off scot-free: unknowing accomplices in a cult-like terror organization. How does that sound?"

"You want me to help you shore up this investigation as quickly as possible so that you can get to drilling. I get it." Stark rose to his feet but remained leaning with his back against the wall. "Tell you what. I'll do it, but under one condition: you come into this cage for just five seconds…"

Masterson laughed. "Goddamn brute to the end. I looked into you some more, boy, and honestly, I'm surprised how easy this has been. Everyone we asked said you were brilliant. A lunatic, yes, but brilliant. I guess they were just being nice, eh? Take the deal; it's the best one you'll get."

"Why do you want this land so badly? You don't even know if there's oil here."

"There may be, there may not be. It doesn't matter. I'll take this land because I *can,* and you *cannot* stop me. That's the point, son. There's nothing you can do but wallow in here like a beaten dog and lament over the damage already done. Make it easier on yourself, come over here and lick my hand like a good boy." The amount of sheer pleasure in Masterson's tone was disgusting.

"Fuck off, you little rat coward." Stark had had enough of this conversation even before it begun. It was time to end it.

Masterson grimaced at the last word, but recovered with a dry, lipless smile. "They said your friend, the one who they killed… They said he died slowly." Masterson's eyes narrowed as he went on. "A real *coward's* death. They hit him in the spine while he fled, tail between his legs. I heard he took a good hour to bleed out, wailing and crying like a baby the whole time, cursing your name…"

Stark launched off the wall and took a single charging step toward the bars. Masterson let out a choking gasp and recoiled, slamming the opposite wall with a thud and clutching at his pigeoned chest. Stark laughed for the first time in days.

"I'll watch you take the needle, you son of a bitch," Masterson growled once he regained his composure, then stormed out of the room, slamming the door behind him.

Stark settled back down onto the cement floor. He hoped beyond hope that Masterson was full of shit, but in his gut, he knew that at least some of what the man told him was true.

In the next cell over, somebody coughed.

"Who's there?" Stark called out.

"Tulimak," the old native responded.

"Jesus, you heard all of that?"

"Yeah, I don't think your friend knew I was here," Tulimak chuckled lightly.

"Why *are* you here?"

"I heard they killed one of your guys. I had to make sure it wasn't Irniq. When I insisted on seeing the body, they knew I had to be connected."

Goddamnit. Masterson wasn't lying.

"Who'd they get?"

"The man with the scar. Handsome fella. I'm sorry, Augustin. I don't remember his name."

"Jameson," Stark muttered, a pit forming in his gut.

"Yeah, that's the one. I'm sorry, son. But I can tell you that bastard was lying. Your man died quickly; I don't believe he suffered at all."

Stark heard the words but didn't entirely process them.

Jameson is dead.

The thought bounced around the inside of his skull. It

didn't feel real. He knew it was true but it reverberated more like an empty mantra than a statement of fact. Jameson's face flashed across his mind, his voice, his hearty laugh echoing after one of their ridiculous endeavors. Then the thought of Tommy rushed in.

Squeezing his eyes shut, Stark willed away the memories, embracing the numbness that he had come to know so well and shoving the snippets of memory deep down into the unexplored dungeon of his mind.

Not now...

He commanded himself to repress it; he'd process it later. But after all this time, he knew there would never be a moment where he would willingly open that door and explore that pain. He'd keep it barred, fighting to keep it closed, living in terror of the moment when the memories inevitably came crashing through the mental barrier like a horde of demons in the night.

"You need to make this right," Tulimak said from across the wall that separated their cells.

Stark scoffed.

What the fuck do you think I'm trying to do?

"And what *right* can come from this, Tulimak?"

"You have to find a way to make the FBI realize they're being manipulated by that asshole. All those people you lead, they need you."

"And how do you suggest I do that?"

"I don't know. *You* need to figure that out."

"Aren't you old Inuits supposed to be wise?" Stark's voice was sharp. He didn't need some old man reiterating what his mind had already been screaming for days.

"I'll consider myself wise when I understand why a rich white boy like you is off playing Lord of the Flies in the damn mountains." Tulimak's tone shifted to match Stark's. "And what's more, I'll consider myself content when I know my niece and nephew aren't going to be murdered by the government because you have a fucking chip on your shoulder, son."

"Fuck off..." Stark knew Tulimak was right. He leaned back and stared at the scars on the backs of his hands.

For minutes, the gentle ticking of the clock that hung outside the cells filled the room. "It... it wasn't ever supposed to be like this..." Stark fumbled for the right words. "We just wanted to escape."

"Escape what?"

"Everything. The world we lived in. The greed. The toxic society. Living day to day with the singular goal of scraping together enough cash to give our lives value. Living in a state of indentured servitude to a society that couldn't give a shit about us... The talking heads on TV that vomited up nothing but the most malicious events of the day, pushing agendas and giving misleading commentary on things they didn't understand just to appeal to a brainwashed populace... Living in a world where the concept of individuality has raped communities into submission, where nobody realized that expressing their 'glorious self' was a bullshit ploy to sell them more trends and steal power from people...

"We just wanted to escape, to go back to something fundamentally human. To do away with screens and lies and egos and corporate overlords. Just to escape...."

Tulimak sighed and Stark could almost feel the old man's eyes roll from across the wall.

Stark snorted. "Yeah, well it's easy to dismiss someone as a nut these days. We didn't want to change the world, just to carve out a little piece of it for ourselves."

"Well, what do you want me to say, Augustin? You're talking about wanting to get out from under the thumb of the government and corporations like they're some evil institution of villains out of a Bond movie. Those things you describe, they're the product of society, of people like you and me. It's just the way of the world."

"Exactly!" Stark almost shouted. "It's the product of fucking *people*. A cultural disease. A million powerful individuals who spend their lives trying to find new ways to take what *you* have for themselves, and once they have it, they want your submission. I'm not an idiot. I don't imagine there's some evil organization out there like the Illuminati. No, the enemy of humanity isn't a single sentient force, but a million sentient beings, all fighting for power and wealth." Stark sighed and shook his head.

"The America that exists today is a sick society, developed in a fashion that has taken away any concept of personal responsibility. Look at the government, look at congress: people don't have to answer for their crimes or their shitty deeds if they're above a certain rung on the ladder. You want a successful society? Create one that's small enough to where the individual's vote *actually* matters. Where the laws exist on a communal level and if a leader betrays his people, he can be hanged on the spot."

"And that's what you founded in that valley? The perfect society?"

"No. We weren't anywhere near perfect. But we were a community, and we had each other. That's all we needed."

The door to the sheriff's office swung open, punctuating their conversation. A female FBI agent walked in alongside two deputies. Stark couldn't help but let his eyes run down her slight frame. She was attractive, with olive skin and almond brown eyes. The puffy blue FBI jacket concealed her figure but he could tell that she was in good shape. She noticed his wandering eyes and snorted. He could see her forming the word *pig* in her mind.

"Mr. Stark. Please stand and place your hands against the wall," one of the deputies ordered.

Stark complied, but maintained eye contact with the woman. "Where's Leonardo?"

"Don't worry about it." The twinge of resentment in her voice made him wonder how much damage his would-be-rescuers had inflicted the night before.

The cell door slid open and the deputies snapped handcuffs over Stark's wrists. Together, they hauled him out of the cell.

****

Stephanie jabbed at the embers in the Koutla's main hearth with a cast-iron poker. The cacophony of frenzied voices that echoed through the hall did little to drown out Tommy's incessant sobbing. Her ears seemed attuned to it, cutting through the mess of curses and shouts and grasping onto the hiccupy, choking whimper of the three-year-old boy.

"I don't know!" Irniq yelled over the din, not aiming his voice at anyone in particular but rather addressing the teaming crowd of upset Homesteaders that surrounded him. Stephanie turned to regard him. He was standing beside the table with his hands raised as if he was trying to prove he wasn't hiding anything. The entire community was demanding answers, but the frayed, exhausted nineteen-year-old seemed to have none.

Only two people in the hall were seated. Oliver gently rocked Tommy back and forth in the corner of the hall, his own face mirroring the toddler's pain. Russo sat in his regular position close to the table's head. He appeared to be deep in thought, staring down at the space between his hands and moving his mouth silently. Maya cowered behind him, wringing her hands and casting frightened glances at Stephanie.

"*I don't fucking know!*" Irniq screamed, his voice now hoarse and cracking. "Ask Russo! He talked to Stark! Ask fucking Russo!"

The crowd's attention shifted to the seated man. Maya's eyes grew wide with panic and she pinched Russo. He snapped back to the present.

"Well?" Dave boomed.

"I... uh... ok." Russo stumbled over his words. He took a breath, then stood, leaned forward on the table, and addressed the group. "Shit's gone downhill. I'm not sure how to soften the blow, but it's over. This, all of this, is over. Everyone needs to pack what they can carry—"

Dave slammed his fist into the table. "What happened to Jameson?" he roared.

Russo shut his eyes and took another deep breath. "He's dead. The FBI shot him in the back."

The room went silent. All eyes shifted to Tommy. Oliver glared back at them, a hand cupped over one of the boy's ears while he whispered soothing words into the other. He rose and left the Koutla with the whimpering child held close.

Russo cleared his throat and went on. "Jameson tried... *We* tried to break Stark out. It went to shit, we couldn't get into his cell. The FBI is holding him on charges of terrorism. The oil exec that came here to buy the land set it up. As of right now, *we are all fugitives*, and with the laws the way they are, we won't even get a trial... Stark told me about a pass that cuts through the Fist and into Canada. We need to gather what we can carry and leave as soon as possible. The one good thing we have going for us is that the FBI has no idea who exactly is up here. If we can make it into Canada, we have a good chance of getting out of here before they fuck us."

"This is ridiculous," Frank argued. "We've done nothing wrong. Let them come here, they'll see that. They can't arrest us for nothing!"

"They can and they will," Russo countered. "There's a lot at stake here, even for them. The oil company has the FBI in their pocket and they're out for blood. Tomorrow night you're all going to leave. Take the day to pack any necessities, and when we have the cover of night, Hunt will lead you across the mountain. Make sure you destroy *any evidence* of your identities. I won't lie, it's going to be a hard journey, and you have to be sneaky, but I *know* everyone here is up for the challenge."

Maya flinched every time he referred to the group leaving but not himself. Frank seemed to notice his wording as well. "What do you mean Hunt will lead us? What are you gonna do?"

Russo stood up straight. "Irniq and I will wait them out. It's stupid to imagine that they don't have satellites watching us. We need to make this place look lived in or else they'll realize we left. The forest canopy will cover your egress, and if we can pull it off, they won't suspect anything until it's too late. Nobody outside of Stark, and now us, knows about the mountain trail. As far as the FBI is concerned, our only way out is through Harkstaff."

Irate murmuring erupted through the group once more. Emma hesitantly came forward and addressed Russo. "I don't think this is a good idea."

Russo raised an eyebrow, and Stephanie noticed Emma's hands drift to her stomach.

"I don't think I should try and make it over the mountain on foot. What if something happens?"

"You'll be fine," Russo insisted. "Everyone here is in good enough shape and we have plenty of provisions and experience to make this work."

"I,,," Emma was lost for words. Stephanie suddenly knew exactly what she was leading to.

"Now's not the time," Stephanie blurted out, stepping forward and grasping Emma's arm.

"Not the time for what?" Frank asked, his tone still indignant.

"I'm pregnant," Emma said, casting a terrified glance at her husband. "I don't want to risk losing it."

The news took the room by surprise, especially Frank, but as his face morphed from confusion to anger, Stephanie knew that he put two and two together.

"You fucking whore," He growled.

"Frank, please!" she whimpered, but in an instant, he was beyond reason.

"Whose is it?" He seized her by the shoulders and shook her. Dave made a move to subdue him, but Irniq got there first, shoving Frank and sending him toppling over a chair.

Frank leapt back to his feet and glared at his wife. "Who?" he demanded again, but she didn't respond, instead burying her face in her hands and cowering behind Irniq. Frank scanned the faces around him before settling back on the young Inuit.

Even in the strained silence, it became abundantly clear that Irniq was the father.

"Him?" Frank aimed an accusatory finger at Irniq. His pain was audible in his cracking voice. "Emma? Him? The fucking kid?" He bowed forward, grasping the table with white knuckles and looking like he might vomit.

"I'm sorry, Frank," Emma said softy. "I'm so sorry…"

Silence. The tension had sealed the lips of the on-looking

crowd. Dave attempted to place a reassuring hand on the betrayed husband's shoulder, but Frank jerked away and righted himself. "You fucked my wife." He jabbed a finger at Irniq. "You fucked my wife, and you put a little piece of shit in her stomach. I'm going to fucking kill you."

"Enough!" Russo yelled from his seat, but Frank ignored him and crossed the room to the two wooden clubs that hung on the wall. He pulled them off their plaque and sent one skittering across the floor to Irniq's feet.

"It's *your* law, Russo," Frank stated in an eerily detached voice. Stephanie almost didn't recognize it as his. "You wrote our fucking laws, didn't you? Infidelity results in banishment, but this little piece of shit can demand trial by combat. Go ahead, you little shit, be a man."

Irniq looked from Frank to the club and then to Russo, who shook his head.

"We're not doing this Frank." Irniq kicked the club away. "There's too much going on right now. We'll deal with this when we've got everyone out of here."

"Bullshit!" The rage rushed back to Frank's voice and he brandished the club in front of him. "Pick up the club, you backstabbing coward."

Irniq's hand crept to the pistol at his side as he matched Frank's glare.

"Enough!" Russo roared. Suddenly he was in between the two. He motioned to Irniq to take his hand away from the gun. The young man complied.

"This is horse shit!" A burst of spittle spewed out of Frank's mouth as he screamed. "We live by our fucking laws! That's how we've always done! What? Stark leaves and suddenly the laws don't mean anything! Who the fuck are *you,* Russo, you fuck!"

Russo slowly bent and picked up the club from the floor,

then squared up with Frank.

"You're right," Russo said evenly. "We live by our laws. Stark is gone, Jameson is dead, and we're on the verge of oblivion. If you want Irniq to face you in a trial by combat, then so be it. But I stand as his proxy."

Frank snarled and shook his club at Russo. "You can't fucking do this. You can't bail him out, you shit. You're the reason we're in this mess. You fucked up, and now you're screwing all of us! *And he screwed my fucking wife!*"

Russo stood tall. He held the club at his side and remained uncannily calm in the face of the enraged man. "You're right. That doesn't change where we are now though, does it?"

Frank made a disgusted face. His shoulders slumped, and for a second he made as if to turn away, but then lunged forward and swung hard at Russo's head. With the deftness of a boxer, Russo ducked the attack, coming back up behind Frank and swinging his own club crosswise like a Louisville Slugger. It connected with the back of Frank's head with a startlingly loud crack. He crumpled to the ground and lay still.

Russo stepped back as Stephanie rushed forward to Frank's limp form. Blood had already begun to pool under his face, dribbling from his nose and ears. She felt for a pulse, careful not to shift his neck. It was faint, but he was alive.

The room was dead silent.

Russo stepped onto the table and addressed the mortified crowd. "Listen to me, because I'm going to make this very clear." His voice boomed as he pointed the stained hardwood club in an arc around the room like a scepter. Stephanie felt a strange nostalgia; it was almost as if he was channeling Stark's spirit. "You will pack the bare essentials. Come nightfall tomorrow, everyone besides myself and Irniq will follow Hunt across the mountain. It will take a couple days, and you can only travel after dusk, but if you follow his commands everything *will* work out. I know this is shocking, but if there was ever a group of people who could persevere through what you're about to do, it's you. Go now, get ready, and leave nothing behind that they can use to identify you."

"Fuck off," Oliver called out, startling the group. Nobody had noticed him reenter the Koutla. He limped forward, his exposed left leg swollen and splinted from his tumble off the steeple the night before. "I'm staying too. Doing stupid shit was me and Jameson's thing. Like hell am I gonna let you two dumb fucks stay here without me."

Stephanie saw a hint of grateful smile cross Russo's otherwise stern expression. He nodded.

"So be it. The three of us stay, and the rest of you leave tomorrow at dusk. It's been a privilege and an honor building this place alongside all of you. I promise we'll make it through this."

Russo stepped down from the table and looked at Frank's limp form. Around him, the crowd shuffled but didn't immediately disperse.

"Get the fuck out of here, dickheads!" Oliver yelled. "You heard the man, pack your shit!"

The Koutla cleared. Russo took a knee next to Stephanie. "Will he live?"

"He's alive now," she said. "I don't know if he'll make it over the mountain though. He definitely has brain damage. I need Alwan to help me move him and figure out if there is any spinal damage or a cranial fracture."

"Fuck," Russo muttered. The dominating aura that had surrounded him moments before melted to reveal a mass of anxious regret. "Irniq, get the doctor and take over his radio watch."

He placed a gentle hand on Frank's shoulder and spoke. "I need him to live, Stephanie."

Maybe you shouldn't have fucking hit him then.

She almost said it out loud, but she knew the words would do no good now. Russo had been forced into a tight spot, and had done the only thing these men seemed to know how to do when confronted: he fought his way out.

****

Stark was once again in the makeshift interrogation room. The off-white plastic table in front of him was marked with countless nicks and a handful of crayon smudges. The sheriffs had obviously pulled it from one of their homes when they had converted the small evidence locker. Leonardo sat across from him, shuffling through a folder and appearing to make a conscious effort to avoid eye contact. The female agent had replaced Chen in the corner.

"I want to get off on the right foot," Leonardo finally said, looking up from the folder. Stark noted that while the agent's tone was stern, there was a marked degree of sympathy hidden behind it. "Last night, four men assaulted this station in an attempt to break you out. They attacked my agents, and we ended up killing one of them, a man named Donald Jameson."

"I heard you killed him yourself." Stark's eyes fixed in an unblinking stare into Leonardo's.

"I did," Leonardo said. "I imagine he was a friend of yours, and I assure you I took no pleasure in it. However, I do not regret my actions. Your people attacked us, and we fought back."

"You shot him in the back."

"It doesn't matter now. What's done is done. All we can do is move forward from here and try to ensure that no more blood is shed over this. I believe it goes without saying that neither side wants any more violence."

Stark was silent.

"We need to go to your compound. If what you claimed is true, about Masterson and Lockstone Oil, then we need you to give us entry to see it for ourselves. After last night's events, this is already a far more serious matter than it was. The Director is involved, and I imagine that, unless I start producing results, I'll be replaced with someone who might not go about this as… calmly… as I intend to."

Stark snorted. "You want to go up there and see them, get a list of names and faces so you can make sure they won't escape your grasp. Don't try to convince me you suddenly changed your mind and believe me."

Leonardo shifted uncomfortably in his seat, then motioned to the female agent. "Ferrara, I could use a coffee please."

She nodded and left the room.

"I looked into the man that I killed," Leonardo said. "He was a single father. I know he brought his son with him up into the mountains. I also know he was the opposite of the profile we typically see in cases like this. I'm willing to give this another chance. To give *you* another chance."

"He was the first person you've ever killed. You don't have the stomach to do it again, do you?"

Leonardo nodded. "He was the first, but if we continue on this path, I don't believe he will be the last. I will not hesitate to put down *anyone* who threatens the safety and wellbeing of my team. However, I want to believe that will not be necessary. I admit, I came into this investigation with the assumption that you and your people were guilty. But the longer I'm here, and the more I learn, the more I'm willing to consider that there are outside forces at play. I am offering you an olive branch, Stark. I want you to get in contact with your people and tell them to let us into the Homestead. I need to see this place for myself."

Leonardo seemed genuine. Stark had the creeping suspicion that Jameson's death had rattled the agent's cage far more than he was letting on. "Put me in front of a radio."

Five minutes later, Stark sat at the sheriff's desk in front of a shortwave radio. Leonardo stood in front of him and two other agents at his flanks, their hands anxiously flittering next to their holsters.

Leonardo had outlined his plan: Stark was to tell the Homesteaders to allow the FBI team to land a helicopter in the garden clearing that bordered the Homestead. They would make no arrests, nor would they take anything with them. They would simply observe the compound and speak to the people in order to ascertain a greater understanding of both the previous night's events and the community as a whole.

Stark plucked the radio's handset from the table. The correct frequency had already been dialed in.

"BAS, BAS, this is Stark, how copy?" He waited for a response.

Seconds passed, and just when he was about repeat the call, a voice came through the speaker.

"Stark?" He recognized Stephanie's gentle voice. *"Is that you?"*

"Yeah."

"What's going on? Are you still with the FBI?"

"Yeah, they're here. I need you to get the Italian stallion."

"You mean Ru—"

Stark keyed the headset furiously, drowning out the name. Leonardo shot him a disapproving look.

"No names, doll face." Stark took pleasure in knowing that on the other end of the transmission Stephanie would be fuming over the misogynistic nickname.

"Ok," she responded shortly.

It took a moment, but Russo's voice came through the speaker. *"Hey."*

"Hey."

"Good to hear from you, buddy. We're missing ya here." Russo's voice held a hint of sarcasm.

"It's good to be missed," Stark responded. Leonardo spun his hand, signaling Stark to get on with it. "I'm here with some friends. They want to come out and visit our little palace."

"Yeah, I was expecting they would. What's their plan?"

"They want to fly in tomorrow at noon, land in the garden, and get a tour. No arrests, no taking shit back with them... The guy in charge here, an agent named Leonardo, he's trying to convince me that he's not part of this whole bullshit frame job. Says he thinks this is an opportunity to learn the truth."

"And what truth is that?"

"That we're not crazy, right-wing terrorists intent on destroying the world."

There was a pause, and when Russo came back through the speaker he was laughing. *"Ok... You think it's a good plan?"*

"I think it's a chance we have to take."

"Are they making you say that? Blink twice if you're under duress."

Stark chuckled, and even Leonardo grinned.

"Seriously though," Stark spoke into the handset. "If this guy's legit, this could be our only chance at proving we're not the monsters that Masterson claims."

"Yeah." Russo's voice lost its jovial tone and became sullen. *"I agree... You really think they can be trusted not to fuck with us if we let them in?"*

Stark met Leonardo's eyes and nodded. "Insha'Allah."

Leonardo threw him an alarmed look and one of the agents snatched the handset away from him.

The other end of the radio fell silent.

"What the fuck was that?" Leonardo demanded.

"It's a vet thing. It means 'God willing.'"

****

Russo placed the handset back on the BAS's counter. He glanced over at Stephanie, who gave him a cockeyed look.

"What did that mean?" she asked.

"Insha'Allah... God willing. It's something the Afghans used to say when they weren't feeling very committed to following an order... It means 'probably not.'"

He strummed his fingers on the table while she considered the implications of conversation.

"What now?" she asked.

"We move up the timeline. Everyone leaves tonight."

12

Leonardo could feel the hum of the Bell 429 helicopter reverberate through his teeth as he leaned over in his seat and stared out the window. The tumultuous white caps that rolled across the lake beneath them were visible even from his lofty perspective. In the rapidly approaching distance, the mottled green of the clearing at the lake's head gave way to a sprawling canopy of trees that stretched for miles toward the distant mountain range.

Beside him, Agent Ferrara crouched and stared over his shoulder. "Beautiful…" she whispered under her breath as they sped over the clearing. Below, a bull elk flipped his antlers before fleeing into the foliage.

It was strange, but Leonardo was starting to understand the magical allure of the Alaskan bush. Never before had he seen such unmolested natural beauty. The valley below him touched something in his soul, and he couldn't help but get a sick feeling as he conjured the image of a drilling operation tainting its purity.

"Five minutes!" the pilot called out, poking at the GPS attached to the control panel. Leonardo settled back in his seat and turned to his six-man team.

"Remember," he yelled over the din of the engine above

them. "We're here to observe. Stay on your toes. There's a fifty-fifty chance these people are whack jobs, but we have their leader. Just don't give them an excuse to do something stupid."

The agents all nodded.

"Good thing Chen's not here," Ferrara quipped, drawing a hearty laugh from the others. Chen was on bed rest for the time being as the result of the beating he'd received during the Homesteaders' attempted rescue. He'd chosen to remain in Harkstaff as a limited duty, but active, member of the team.

The five minutes passed quickly, and soon Leonardo saw two small clearings amongst the bristling pines and leafy birches. They flew low over the nearest, and he picked out a handful of animals grazing in the open field. A flock of sheep gathered around a singular Connex box that sat in paddock's center.

"The other one," Leonardo called out to the pilot, who nodded and deftly maneuvered the helicopter to the next clearing. It was sectioned off into separate segments by a canal system and covered in a diverse array of crops that had just reached the peak of their seasonal growth.

Hell of a garden.

The pilot put the helicopter down in the center of the field atop a crudely painted X in a barren patch of earth. Leonardo assumed the Homesteaders had marked this as their landing zone. He was apprehensive about playing directly into his quarry's hands, but landing directly among their crops would be a less than amiable way to kick things off.

The team waited for the rotors to slow to a gentle swing before exiting the craft. Leonardo was the first out, cautiously eyeing the surrounding tree line for onlookers.

"Oy!" a voice echoed from across the field in the direction of the other clearing. Two men emerged from the trees. A series of structures were barely visible through the filter of tree trunks behind them.

"Remember," Leonardo said over his shoulder. "Play it cool. Don't think for a second we aren't outgunned here."

Ferrara let out a shaky breath. Leonardo patted her on the shoulder and tried to conceal his own worry.

"Stay there!" the taller of the approaching men commanded. As they came closer, Leonardo saw he was almost painfully Italian, with a wiry physique built around a boxy frame that reminded him of a 19th century iron worker. The shorter man walked with a heavy limp, and Leonardo couldn't help but grimace as he saw the array of swollen bruises that covered his round face.

"Which one of you is Leonardo?" the taller man asked as he closed the last few yards.

Leonardo spoke up. "I am."

"I considered using an alias, but in the spirit of keeping things honest..." The man extended his hand. Leonardo grasped it and shook. "My name is Andrew Russo."

The shorter character made an arc around the group, placing himself between them and the helicopter.

"That's just Oliver," Russo said. "Don't worry about him. He was in a helicopter crash a long time ago. Somehow he's still always perplexed by them."

Oliver ran a hand over the craft's nose, then patted it fondly.

"Mr. Russo, I'd like to begin with learning how many others you have out here." Leonardo used his most official tone.

"Yeah, I figured you would." Russo motioned to the forest surrounding the clearing. "If you look *really hard,* I bet you can spot one or two of them."

Leonardo's stomach twisted into a knot.

"Yeah, sorry, but obviously we're going to cover our bases." Russo shrugged, then held his hands up submissively. "I need everyone to stay completely still, and I promise that nothing bad will happen. I just need to prove a point before we start."

He pointed to a Mason jar duct-taped to a gardening stake twenty yards away. On cue, it shattered and a distant gunshot echoed across the clearing.

The group of agents instinctively twitched, a few raising their rifles ever so slightly. As a unit, their eyes darted from distant tree to distant tree like meerkats caught in the open. Leonardo cursed himself for ever believing that these mountain people might have a semblance of honor.

"Ok, let's remain calm. You brought guns, we have guns. Even playing field. Let's talk." Russo's facetious attitude dissipated as he continued. "Agent Leonardo, I understand the rules are simple: I allow you to see our home, and in return, you won't try to grab any of us, or any of our shit. Are we on the same page?"

"Yeah…" Leonardo didn't like the way this man was talking to him, like he was a child.

"Ok. There's one small tweak… I need your team to stay here. As a show of good faith, I'll let you hold onto your pistol, but it can only be the two of us."

"Absolutely not!" Ferrara protested.

Leonardo held up his hand to silence her. "I don't think that will work out, Mr. Russo. Either we all go in, or we leave."

Russo nodded solemnly and looked over Leonardo's shoulder. "I was afraid you'd say that."

From behind him, Leonardo heard a gravelly, hauntingly familiar voice mutter a drawn out "aw shit."

He turned, along with the rest of the team, to see Oliver

leaning against the helicopter. His hands were extended at his sides, an M27 hand grenade clasped in one and the pin dangling from the other.

"Don't be stupid," Russo said. "If you shoot him, he lets that spoon flip. Then there's no more helicopter, and you're all stuck in a big ass, booby trapped field with a dozen rifles zeroed in on your dome-pieces."

"You fuckin' people." Leonardo spun on Russo. "We came here in the hopes of being *civil*. Of getting to the bottom of whatever the fuck is going on, and you pull this shit?"

Russo stepped closer. "You need to relax. I'll tell you right now, with absolute honesty, that if you come with me for a short tour, you'll be laughing about this on your flight home. We're not bad guys, but we're also not patsies. You're the fed, and you've got the big guns. Indulge us our primitive securities, and I promise you will *not* be disappointed."

With that, Russo turned back and departed in the direction from which he came. Leonardo watched him walk away for a moment before turning to his team. "Stay here, stay low, keep a fucking eye on that asshole," he said, pointing to Oliver. "If I don't come back, don't make any deals."

He turned and followed Russo.

****

97…

98…

99…

100…

Stark collapsed on his chest. Sweat soaked through his shirt and trickled in a steady stream off his brow, pooling on the cool, concrete floor beneath his beard.

"Where do you get this much energy?" Tulimak asked

wearily from the next cell over.

Stark ignored him and rolled over onto his back, curling his knees and beginning to do crunches.

1…

2…

3…

He had always been the athletic type. But his current calisthenics routine wasn't for keeping in shape. He needed to burn away the anxiety that plagued the dark corners of his mind. He needed to exhaust himself to the brink of passing out in the desperate hope that the bursts of useless adrenaline that accompanied his panicked thoughts of the Homestead would sting just a little less.

83…

84…

The door to the sheriff's office creaked open. Stark ignored it, continuing to pull his elbows up to his knees and focusing on the burning in his abdomen. The deputy on duty would doubtlessly leave whatever slop of a meal they brought for him in the opening between the bars.

89…

90…

"Stand up," an unfamiliar voice ordered.

He stopped and glanced over his shoulder through the bars. Two men flanked deputy Carr, who had a befuddled look on his face.

Or maybe that's just his face?

"Stand up!" one commanded. He was huge, pale, and ogreish, in contrast to his slight, dark-skinned partner, whose whole face squeezed forward into a long, upturned nose like a rodent.

Stark stood. Both men were clad in matching black polos two sizes too small that were tucked into cargo pants.

"Stand against the wall, hands above your head," the larger, bald one continued, typing a code into the wall-mounted controls. The box beeped and the door slid open.

Stark obeyed, but kept his eyes locked on the deputy. There was definitely confusion in his expression, even more than usual. But there was also something else…

Fear.

The rat-faced man's hand darted to his hip. There was a *pop* and he felt the two tiny prongs of the Tazer stab into his ribs. Before he could react, the blast of electricity, amplified by the coating of sweat, caused his body to seize violently. His mind fizzled like a broken TV and he dropped to the floor. In a second, his hands were wrenched behind his back and a thick bag was pulled over his head.

The routine felt too familiar.

****

"We call this building the Koutla," Russo said, opening the door to the log hall. "I guess you could say it's our community center."

"Why do you call it that?" Leonardo's anger at being toyed with was still there, but as he followed Russo through the compound, the man's patronizing tone had faded, and Leonardo was beginning to feel a bit more at ease.

"It's actually a funny story. We started off calling it the COC, military jargon, but that was a shitty name for a 'great hall' like this. One of our people suggested calling it the 'Koutla' after the Tswana word for 'meeting place.' Something he picked up after spending a lot of his youth doing mission trips to Africa — he was a really giving soul — so we all agreed to call it that."

"Am I going to meet this 'giving soul' today?" Leonardo

asked sarcastically. He had yet to see a single person outside of his two-man greeting party. His number one goal for the incursion had been, and remained, to create a dossier of the odd little community's inhabitants.

Russo stopped alongside the table that spanned the length of the hall and turned back to Leonardo. "You already have. His name was Donald Jameson."

A tingle shot up Leonardo's spine. It was the way Russo had said it. Cold, distant, non-accusatory, like the monotone voice of a court stenographer reading back the accusations of a wronged party. The complete lack of malice in his voice was disturbing.

Russo continued, his voice regaining its chipper tone. "This is where we meet, eat, celebrate, mourn. This is the central area of our community. Go ahead and have a look around. It's pretty open. Under the platform up front we have some food storage, and there's a tool shed around back, but other than that, what you see is what you get."

Despite his situation Leonardo couldn't help but be impressed with the adept construction of the long hall. Whoever these people really were — terrorists or just woodsy freaks — they had a knack for building. The inside of the hall itself was barren, and when Leonardo pulled open the hatch that revealed the storage space, he found nothing more than a row of canned goods. He paced along the table, examining the intricate carvings on the walls. The subject matter was eclectic to say the least: a handful of hulking beasts from every corner of the world stood in an assortment of poses, many locked in battle with everything from Vikings, to astronauts, to a very obvious knock-off of the children's character Gumby, only bearing a shield and brandishing what appeared to be an M60 machine gun.

"The winters are long here. We all have our projects to

keep us busy," Russo called from where he sat by the hearth after noting Leonardo's fascination with the bizarre engravings. "I read, Oliver drinks, Stark carves."

"What's the deal with the machete?"

Russo glanced up at the three-foot blade that hung above the hearth and grinned. "You wouldn't believe me if I told you."

"Try me."

Russo chuckled and stepped back from the brick threshold. "It's Stark's. He carried it in Afghanistan. Were you in the service?"

Leonardo shook his head.

"I'm surprised." Russo gave a disappointed shake of his head. "We were all infantry. It's a… strange culture. A bunch of violent teenagers thrown together from all over the country and sent to the worst hell holes on Earth… people pick up weird habits. In every Marine platoon, there ends up being at least one knife guy. Normally, he's a weirdo, sometimes he's just a hillbilly, but it goes without fail that one kid in the platoon always has at least one big stupid knife strapped to his flak. Now, fighting the Taliban, you'll never get close enough to poke 'em with one of those things, so the knife guy just dreams of the day he gets to let loose and use it. Stark was a knife guy.

"He was also a squad leader on his second pump. He knew his Area of Operations like the back of his hand. A few months in, he takes his guys on a routine security patrol through a relatively low-key village where they'd made some decent contacts and had a good rapport with the locals. His platoon commander, this real antsy little prick of a lieutenant who had no place in the Corps, decided to tag along. So, they were patrolling through these compounds and *boom,* an IED pops off in the middle of their column. Nobody's hurt, but this Lieutenant freaks out. He jumps behind a mud wall and starts panicking. In the field beyond the wall, there's a farmer and his young son tilling their land, and they stop and stare at the smoke. The LT, in his panicked state, pops his head over the wall, sees this man and his kid, and decides that they're the ones who triggered the IED. He opens fire on them.

"Stark runs over, see's what's going on, and forces the LT to stop, but the farmer is already on the ground. The next compound over has a group of people sticking their heads out of their mud hut trying to see what's going on. The LT freaks out again, steadies the end of his rifle against the mud wall in front of him, and takes aim at the far compound's entrance."

Leonardo listened to the story intently, but let his eyes wander around the great hall, letting every detail soak into his memory.

"Stark knows this particular compound; it belongs to a family that routinely fed him info on IED locations, information that likely saved his guys more than a few times," Russo went on. "So without a second thought, he pulls out this machete and brings it down on the LT's rifle, smashing the optic and flaying the shit out of the LT's arm.

"Shit like this is a huge deal, especially in the Corps. Shit like this gets you 30 in Leavenworth. In the end, the LT understood that if he tried to get Stark court marshaled, the platoon would bite him back. But that didn't stop him from doing everything in his power to ruin Stark's career."

"That's a good story, but I'm a little lost on the point. You're saying Stark's a good guy?" Leonardo asked.

"I would never say that." Russo chuckled. "He *did* put his freedom on the line to save those Afghans, and that would be noble for anyone. But that's not why he did it. He knew that if they killed those civilians, that would be the end of their relationship with that village, and that his chances of losing one of his men would go up exponentially. He came down on that LT without a second thought because he knew it could potentially save the lives of his brothers. I sincerely don't think he gave a fuck about the lives of those villagers. He definitely didn't give a fuck about a court martial. Understanding that moment is definitive in understanding the man; the only thing he gives a shit about is protecting the people he cares about, and if you threaten that, reason has a tendency to go to the wayside."

Leonardo felt like he was beginning to see what Russo was getting at.

"That's what happened in Harkstaff," Russo said. "Jameson was in Stark's squad during all of that. He was repaying that loyalty when your people cut him down. We know what's going on, with Masterson and the FBI. We know you're holding him on bullshit charges so Lockstone can steal this land. We *hope* that you, as *an individual,* are not a part of it, which is why we've allowed you to come today."

"Your sniper in the tower, that was Oliver?" Leonardo asked. "He was missing my people on purpose, wasn't he?"

Russo nodded. "Suppressive fire, keeping your heads down for us to get out of there. Trust me, nobody in this place wants to be responsible for the death of a federal agent."

The pieces began to click together in Leonardo's head. He leaned against the table and contemplated the new perspective, then pointed to a pair of clubs hung over a plaque reading "Trial by Combat"

"What's the story behind that?"

"Pretty self-explanatory, isn't it?" Russo said. "Just because we're out here to escape the bureaucracy doesn't mean we can't have justice."

"Yeah…" Leonardo muttered.

Justice.

"No time to dick around." Russo resumed his chipper "tour guide" voice. "On to the barn!"

****

17…

18…

19…

Water dribbled up his nose and filled his sinuses as he ran out of air to exhale. He tried desperately to suck more in through the soaked rag pressed over his face. Stark knew exactly what was happening. He was acutely aware of the inclined plywood board stabbing splinters into his bare back and tried to focus on the reality that he was not drowning.

22…

…

23…

He'd managed to maintain his grip on reality through the first three sessions of waterboarding, but this time he couldn't control the spasm of panic rising from deep inside. Suddenly he was back on that helicopter, spinning haphazardly through the ocean, the icy water surrounding him and ripping the breath from his lungs. He needed to unclasp the harness that squeezed him in a death grip against the horrifyingly solid metal bench, but his hands were trapped behind his back, locked tight by the metal handcuffs.

Then it was over.

Reality came rushing back as the rag was pulled away and he saw the gleaming bald head of his tormenter above him. A devilish grin spread across the man's ugly, pale features.

Stark sucked at the air, reveling in its life-giving purity. He would quit smoking. He would enjoy every last second of breathing he could. He would never take that glorious relief of filling his lungs with oxygen for granted again.

"Had enough yet, boy?" the shining dome drawled.

Stark closed his eyes and prepared himself. "You're a fuckin' pussy," he rasped out, and in an instant, the rag slapped back over his face and he was back in that horrifying, unforgiving ocean.

1...

2…

3…

****

Leonardo followed Russo through the barn and into the paddock, taking note of the different types of animals and their numbers. There was definitely a good number of people living here based on the amount of work it would take to maintain just the livestock.

They strolled through the bunker-like BAS and doubled back past the charred remains of a satellite dish and into the residence hall. Russo guided him to a quaint bedroom with a crib in the corner. The furnishings were humble: a book case, a desk, a single bed, and a nightstand. The walls were covered in a child's drawings. One stood out: a blue woman with a smiling face and the crudely written word "Stafiny" beneath it.

"Who's Stephanie?" Leonardo motioned to the drawing.

"Don't worry about her. Do you know who that is?" Russo asked from the doorway, pointing at the photo displayed on the nightstand. Leonardo immediately recognized Jameson holding a toddler.

He picked it up and stared at the two brightly smiling

faces for a moment before nodding.

"Why did you people build all this?"

Russo shrugged, then casually flicked a finger at Leonardo. "You remind me of my brother Nick."

"How so?" Leonardo asked.

"He was a man of the law. A real stickler for the rules. He was a few years older than me and fought in Fallujah. That was a big part of the reason I enlisted in the first place. He was always doing the right thing, by the book, impressing his superiors, moving up in the world. He got onto the Boston PD pretty easily and worked his way up. We didn't always have the best relationship, I kind of thought he was a dick when I was younger, but I loved him nonetheless."

There was a long pause as Russo visibly collected his thoughts. When he spoke again, his voice was hesitant. "He was my age when he killed himself. It was the day after a Christmas party. The whole family came together the night before to drink and have a good time. He seemed fine: his normal, reserved self. The next day, we all went out to breakfast. I had a surprise gift for my mother that I forgot back at the house, a little turtle broach I'd picked up the week before in Athens. I snuck off halfway through the meal to go back to my parents' house and grab it. That's when I found him.

"He did it in their kitchen. My dad had an old revolver that my grandfather brought back from World War Two. Nick put one of those ancient bullets through the back of his head and splattered his brains all over a painting my aunt had done of us as children. I…"

Russo's voice almost broke, but he took a deep breath and maintained his composure. Leonardo knew he was listening to a story that had likely never been told aloud.

"I called it in. I tried to get them to clean it before my

parents came home, but that's not how forensics scenes work. My mother saw it, we couldn't stop her. My father didn't even cry. But after that, something broke in him… I… I checked the gun myself. The bullets in it were originals from the 40s. The two rounds before the one he fired had imprints on their primers. Do you know what that means? It means he pulled that trigger three times before it went off. Twice he felt that hammer fall and nothing happened. Twice he was granted a new lease on life. But something was so fucked up inside of him that he just kept pulling.

"You asked me why I'm here, and I'll tell you right now that I can't explain it… But I felt something, living back there in the city, forcing myself to play the game day in, day out. Something that I'm afraid my brother felt. Something sick and twisted clawing at my insides. A pain I can't describe. A numb, throbbing void in my soul and I couldn't sit there and let it consume me like it did him."

Russo stood, arms crossed, staring at the floor. Any semblance of his showman-esque aura had evaporated.

"So, coming here, it made that pain go away," Leonardo stated.

"It helped," Russo said with a sad smile. "It still comes back. Something tells me it always will. But this place definitely helped." He looked up at Leonardo. "That's why I'm here. That's why most of us are here. The forest — it heals old wounds."

****

"Tell us about the compound," the rat-faced torturer's tone was entirely professional.

Good cop, Stark thought, though he wasn't really the good cop to the Ogre's bad cop, just a *less* bad cop.

"I'll tell you whatever you want, but first you tell me who you work for," Stark responded. This must have been the dozenth time he'd demanded the information.

They were in the makeshift interrogation room. The plywood board and a half-empty bucket of dirty water lay in the corner. Stark sat across the table from the Rat, while the Ogre paced the room behind him.

The Rat shook his pointed face in disappointment. "Do we have to go back to the board? You held out well for a while, honestly the longest I've ever seen. But don't pretend those last few sessions didn't get to you."

"NSA? DHS? I would say CIA but we're on American soil, not that that means anything…" Stark said and looked over his shoulder at the bald man.

"Don't look at him, look at me," the Rat snapped.

"I'll tell you what you want to know when you tell me who I'm talking to."

The Ogre slapped him upside the head and leaned in close. "We're your worst nightmare."

Stark forced a mocking laugh. "Seriously? Ok, Bruce Willis, have it your way. Break out the fuckin' board."

The Ogre looped a pale arm around Stark's throat and squeezed, cutting off his air flow but missing the arteries on the sides of his neck.

"How 'bout I squeeze a little harder and we see how long before you get brain damage?" the Ogre growled.

Stark noticed a winged symbol tattooed on the meaty forearm under his jaw, then looked at the man across the table and rolled his eyes.

"Enough," the Rat ordered. The arm released.

Stark cleared his burning throat. "What kind of a choke hold was that, Q-tip? And is that an Air Force tattoo? Who the fuck gets an Air Force tattoo?"

Stark could tell by the cautioning look from the Rat that the Ogre almost retaliated violently. He smiled and went on. "More importantly, who the fuck *hires* someone out of the Air Force as muscle? Jesus, you guys aren't even government, are you? Fucking amateur hour…"

This time the Rat didn't stop the Ogre. A bony fist slammed into the left side of Stark's head. He recovered quickly with a laugh that sent a splatter of blood onto the plastic table.

****

Leonardo and Russo walked shoulder-to-shoulder back across the clearing to the helicopter. The FBI team was sitting in the sun-soaked field while Oliver leaned against the helicopter's side, twirling the grenade's pin on his finger and whistling an indistinguishable tune.

"Everything alright, Leo?" Ferrara asked once he was within earshot.

"Yeah, everything's fine, Ferrara," Leonardo responded with a disarming look. "Load up, guys. We're done here… for now."

The team cautiously stood and patted the crumbled earth off their pants before filing back into the helicopter. Leonardo looked at Oliver, then at the grenade clasped in his hand. Something occurred to him that cast a shadow of doubt over his newfound understanding of the situation.

"I want to believe you, Russo," Leonardo said, "but the fact that you have illegal military ordinance up here makes me tempted to re-evaluate…"

Russo gave a mischievous smile and nodded to Oliver, who limped forward and held the explosive out toward Leonardo.

"Take it," Russo urged. "Trust me."

Leonardo carefully reached his hands out and cupped the heavy metal ball, making sure to keep the spoon held tightly against its coarse metal side. Once Oliver had fully released, he and Russo shared a hearty laugh. Confused and a bit alarmed, Leonardo stared at the device in his hands.

"Turn it over, dickhead," Oliver grumbled in a strange voice.

Leonardo reluctantly complied. There was a hole in the bottom of the metal sphere, exposing its hollow insides.

"It's decommissioned," Russo said. "It's a paperweight. You can get 'em at any Army Navy store. Trust me, Leonardo, the craziest thing you'll find here is a couple assault rifles. We're not terrorists, just Marines."

The helicopter engine hummed to life and its blades began their slow spin as Leonardo watched the two men walk away toward the Homestead. He couldn't help but let out a disbelieving chuckle as he stuffed the paperweight into his pocket and climbed back aboard the helicopter.

"What happened out there?" Ferrara yelled as they rose off the patch of dirt.

Leonardo shook his head. "We've been coming at this from the wrong angle."

Something tells me that the only terrorist out here is Masterson.

****

Stephanie crouched behind a boulder at the base of the Fist and watched the navy-blue helicopter glide away from the Homestead. As it faded into an obscure dot in the southern sky, she rose and looked back toward the ravine that currently sheltered the rest of the Homesteaders.

"Stay down!" Dave hissed next to her, but she brushed

him off.

"They're gone, Dave." She gave his shoulder a reassuring squeeze. He grunted but remained, almost comically trying to hide his massive frame behind a pine sapling. He was clearly not the type of man who was used to running or hiding, and their escape had turned him, as well as many of the others, into a rough tangle of frayed nerves.

Their flight from the Homestead the night before had been a chaotic mess. The need to remain clandestine required strict light discipline, and the faint glow of the half-moon barely made it through the canopy of the surrounding forest. Stephanie had no doubt that more than a few things had been lost in the darkness, and could only hope that they weren't leaving a breadcrumb trail for the FBI to eventually follow.

She left Dave in his precarious hiding spot and made her way into the rock walled ravine that marked the beginning of the hidden path across the mountain. Most of the Homesteaders were spread out on the mossy earth attempting to catch a nap before the sun sank low enough for them to continue their arduous march. Alwan and Maya hovered over Frank, who was strapped to a metal stretcher, still unconscious from Russo's strike.

"Are you sure?" Maya whispered to the doctor as Stephanie joined them.

"I'm afraid so. He won't make it through the night," Alwan stated regretfully, pulling his wire rimmed glasses from his face and massaging the swollen bags under his eyes. If the journey was hard on the rest of them, whose age averaged in the late twenties, then Stephanie could hardly imagine how exhausted the sixty-seven-year-old was.

"What are you saying?" Emma peeped up from just out of earshot of their whispers.

Alwan looked at Maya and flicked his head in Emma's

direction. "You're her best friend. Better you to tell her than me."

Emma was silent as Maya gave her the prognosis.

"Are you alright?" Stephanie asked Alwan, who had sat back against a boulder and stared off into the distance.

"Yeah..." he responded absentmindedly. "Babylon has finally come to find us."

She snorted, remembering their conversation in the garden, then sat next to him and pulled out the pack of Lucky Strikes she had grabbed from Stark's cabin. The doctor cast her a cockeyed glance and clicked his tongue disapprovingly as she lit one.

"Oh, fuck off," she said before coughing hard at the acrid smoke.

After a moment, he shifted uncomfortably and she realized her smoke was blowing straight into his face.

"Sorry," she said quickly. "I'll move."

"No, no, no." He stood slowly, motioning her to sit. "I need to prepare for tonight. Speak to Maya. She's having a hard time coping with all of this."

He left, and Maya returned and took his place. Stephanie looked at her best friend and knew exactly what Alwan had meant. Maya had never been any good at hiding her feelings, but now she sat stone-faced and silent, staring into the distance without the slightest hint of emotion.

"What is it?" Stephanie asked after a moment, drawing Maya from her trance.

"Nothing," Maya insisted, making a bad attempt at a smile.

"*Maya...*"

"I just," Maya began, then stopped. Her eyes began to well with tears. She was still doing her best to hold herself together. "I just have this feeling that I'm never going to see Andrew again."

"Don't be ridiculous." Stephanie wrapped a comforting arm around her. "I doubt there's anything in the world that can keep that man from getting back to you."

Maya nodded, but Stephanie knew her words gave little comfort.

"Listen," Stephanie said softly. "You'll be back together in a couple weeks, three at the most. All he's waiting on is for us to get to safety before the three of them make a break for it. Just focus on getting through the night and remember that the faster we move, the sooner you'll have him back."

With that, the dam broke and the waterworks began to flow. Maya spoke haltingly between teary gasps. "But their plan, it's so *stupid!* What makes them think they can outrun the FBI even if they set this whole valley on fire? What if the police are waiting for us on the other side of this mountain? What if the FBI comes tomorrow before we're even halfway there and he tries to be a goddamn hero? I'm scared he's going to be a *fucking martyr,* Stephanie!"

"Maya, that's insane. Give me one good reason he would stay for even a second longer than it takes us to get over this mountain."

"You wouldn't understand," Maya came back, regaining control of her speech and looking hard at Stephanie. "You're a runner, Steph, you always have been. This is what you do — you escape when things get to be too much. Andrew's not like that. He's taking this whole thing too far because they killed his friends. He's going to get himself killed. I *know* it."

Stephanie paused and pondered her best friend's statement.

Maya read the look on her face and rolled her teary eyes dramatically. "Stephanie, you *are*. That's why you can't understand; you ran away from Montana to Florida, you came *here* with us, you've run from every relationship and every major commitment the moment it got too serious. That's who you are and I love you for it, but you need to understand that what we're doing now isn't natural for Andrew like it is for you. He's never run from anything in his life."

While she couldn't argue the logic in Maya's words, Stephanie felt a deep sense of belligerence welling up inside of her.

"You're being stupid, Maya. I can understand just fine, and I promise you that Andrew isn't going to stay behind out of some sick desire to avenge Jameson or Stark. That's ridiculous… you *have* to see that."

Maya slumped against the boulder and stared at her feet. "His loyalty is just as much to those fucking Marines as it is to me. I've known it for a long time. I came here because of it and spent the last three years trying to cope with it. It hurts every day but, in the end, I've accepted it. If something happens and he has the opportunity to try and fix this, or get revenge, he's going to take it… And I'm going to be a widow."

Stephanie squeezed Maya closer and stroked her hair. As much as she hated to admit it, Maya was right. About everything. Stephanie was a lifelong runner in an endless sprint away from anything that scared her, and Russo was as loyal and steadfast a man as there ever was. Maya had successfully flanked herself with two people who were polar opposites, and now she was preparing to lose one of them.

But what about Stephanie? Was she really as flippant as everyone around her seemed to believe? She had run from Montana, there was no question there. The endless days of boredom that defined her youth had her searching for an escape as soon as she was old enough to grow tired of Barbie dolls and ponies. Florida had been a wonderful reprieve from all of that… but she had run from there too. What was she was running away from?

Maybe she wasn't running away. Maybe she was running *toward* something.

The thought seemed strange at first, but as she sat there and consoled her friend, it grew in her mind like a weed. The Homestead was the one place Stephanie had *truly* felt comfortable. It had been the puzzle piece that completed her, the thing she had always been desperately searching for. It was a family — a tribe with members pulled from every walk of life — that fought wildly against the forces of nature with the single goal of persevering and taking care of each other. Even in fleeting moments when she'd considered leaving, she'd immediately doubled back on the idea.

This was her home.

These people were her family.

And they were in danger.

"I'm going to prove you wrong," Stephanie whispered as the tips of the distant tree line emanated the warm orange glow of dusk.

"What?"

"I'm going back," Stephanie whispered, and stood. Maya clung to her hand and gave it a desperate pull.

"Stop, what the hell are you talking about?"

Stephanie looked down at her best friend. "I'm going back to the Homestead to make sure your husband doesn't do anything stupid. He won't risk it if I'm there."

"Absolutely not," Hunt barked out behind her. She hadn't heard him approach.

"Try and stop me."

"Stephanie, please, that's so stupid," Maya whispered. Stephanie squeezed her hand but didn't look back down at her.

No more running.

13

Same Day

The helicopter glided over Harkstaff and came to a gentle hover above the airstrip. Leonardo had used the return flight as an opportunity to digest what he had learned, as well as begin to plan out his next step.

"Who the hell is this?" Ferrara pointed out the window as the craft touched down.

His gaze followed her finger and he reiterated the question in his own mind. Half a dozen fat, black helicopters sat in a perfect line along the edge of the airfield. They had no insignia or identifying marks, but reminded Leonardo of the Army Blackhawks he'd seen in movies.

No, he realized as the dusk sun glinted off the nearest helicopter's perfectly shined flank, military choppers wouldn't be this pristine. Who in the hell would—

The sudden realization sent a shock of fury through his chest.

Masterson.

They landed, and Leonardo caught sight of the agent he'd left to guard Stark, Edd Tomlinson, trying to brace himself against the rotor wash. Leonardo ripped the door open and made a B-line for the young agent.

"What the hell is this?" Leonardo shouted above the rush of air, pointing at the airstrip's new additions.

"What?" Tomlinson yelled back as Leonardo approached, cupping his ear but quickly pulling his hand away as the roar of the helicopter overwhelmed him.

Leonardo reached Tomlinson, grabbing him by the shoulder and pulling him close so that he was yelling directly in his ear. "What is this?" He accentuated every syllable with a jab of his finger.

"I don't know!" Tomlinson replied hesitantly. "They won't say who they are! We got orders from Washington though; we're supposed to do whatever they say!"

At first, Leonardo thought he misheard, but with a quick scan of Tomlinson's face, he knew better.

"They've set up shop at the inn! That oil guy, Masterson, he had the Director on the phone, told me to have you report in when you got back!"

Of course.

"There's more," Tomlinson continued. The roar of the helicopter had died down to a dull throb as the blades wound to a halt. "They've got Stark. They're... doing shit to him... I don't know exactly what, but it's bad."

Leonardo pushed past him and climbed in one of their waiting SUVs. He threw it in drive and took off across the tarmac toward the small town, not bothering to wait for Tomlinson or the others.

Masterson was lounging on the couch inside the sheriff's station when Leonardo shouldered open the door. The old man began to stand to address the agent, but Leonardo put him down with a sinister look.

"Agent Leonardo, things have cha—"

"Who the fuck are they? Spooks? NSA?" Leonardo demanded, poking an accusatory finger into Masterson's chest. "What have you got your grimy fucking hands into, Masterson?"

Vehemence crossed Masterson's features and seeped into his voice. "Now listen here, boy, you stand down. You couldn't get the job done. Now someone's here who can."

Behind the door marked "evidence locker" came a muffled shout. Leonardo's eyes shot to it then back to Masterson's.

"Don't you dare…" Masterson began.

Leonardo ignored him, crossing the room and wrenching the handle. It stuck. Without a second thought, he reared back and kicked it. The wooden frame around the lock splintered and the door flew open, revealing Stark's half naked body draped over an inclined plywood board. A man held a rag over Stark's face while another doused it with a steady stream of water.

It took Leonardo a second to grasp what he was witnessing. He'd read the papers, he *knew* what it was. But it was so surreal in person that he froze in place and gawked at the scene.

The larger of the two men, an ugly, pale abomination, yanked the bucket back and glared at him while his partner looked up casually.

"Can we help you, agent?" the smaller man asked as if he was just watering daisies.

"Get that shit off him! Now!" Leonardo growled and stepped forward, but the mongoloid was surprisingly quick, dropping the bucket and cutting him off.

"Go talk to your boss," he said, motioning back through the door.

"Let him go," Leonardo said slowly. His hand drifted to

the pistol at his hip. Fuck the FBI and whoever this was —
there was no way he was going to watch these spooks torture
a man.

The massive creature saw the movement and tensed.

Behind the giant came the gentle voice of his companion.
"Henry, relax…" He stood and placed a hand on the larger
man's shoulder, pushing him toward the open door and
casting Leonardo a grimy smile. "Agent Leonardo, he's all
yours."

Leonardo slammed the door behind them before rushing
over to Stark, who was convulsing under the soaked rag. Stark
let out a sputtering cough as Leonardo pulled it away and
collapsed sideways off the plank. He hit the floor face first
and gasped for air. His back was smeared crimson, scattered
with dozens of splinters from thrashing against the rough
wooden plank.

"Jesus Christ…" Leonardo muttered, taking a knee in the
pool of pink water that covered the concrete floor. He began
to pat Stark's back in an effort to help get the water out, but
was immediately met with a wild-eyed glare.

"You cunt…" Stark coughed out.

"This has nothing to do with me," Leonardo insisted. "I
swear I had no knowledge of this shit. I would never—"

"Fuck off."

Leonardo helped Stark sit up. Stark pressed the swollen
bruises that coated the left side of his face against the
coolness of the concrete wall and wrestled with the handcuffs
behind him. Leonardo knew there was no chance the man
would trust him now, but he needed to try and fix this.

"I met Russo," Leonardo started. Stark stopped fidgeting
with the cuffs and looked at him. "I saw your Homestead. I
believe you now."

Am I really saying this?

"These assholes, they aren't FBI," Leonardo continued. "I don't know who they are but they're done now. Masterson's trying to go over my head as we speak, but I'd rather resign and spread the truth than let this shit go on. What did you tell them?"

Stark smirked. "I didn't tell them shit. I got the feeling they aren't here for info though."

"They didn't question you?"

"Nah, not really, too busy drowning my ass."

Leonardo shook his head.

"If they got in here past your boys, then they have clearance." Stark pulled his face away from the wall, leaving a bloody smear. "I'm guessing by their antics that they're contractors. Low-rent goons hired out by some dark corner of the government."

"Well they're done now," Leonardo reiterated. He stood and pulled Stark to his feet. "I'll get to the bottom of it. Don't worry."

Stark let out a hearty laugh. "You won't be able to do shit. They're here to replace you. You're gonna walk out that door and every motherfucker in your chain of command will be waiting on the phone to chew your ass out for interfering."

"We'll see."

Stark jerked his head toward his cuffed hands. "How about you be a pal and loosen these so I can feel my fingers again."

"We're not on that level yet, *pal*."

Stark smirked, and Leonardo crossed the room and yanked open the broken door. A dozen black-clad men stood in the main office before him, a handful of them bearing M4 assault rifles at the ready. He pulled the door shut behind him and faced the rodent-like interrogator who stood at their forefront.

"If you're finished in there, Agent Leonardo, we'd like to resume." His voice was nasally and sharp. He had an air of sleazy professionalism, and came off as more of a villainous henchman than a government employee.

How appropriate.

"You're done here," Leonardo stated.

The interrogator shook his head and sighed, then clicked his tongue disapprovingly. "I'm afraid not. Things have changed. We're taking over this… ordeal. You will continue your investigation, but under our direct supervision and command."

"Like hell…" Leonardo growled.

The interrogator extended his hand. In it was a satellite phone. "Take it."

Leonardo snatched up the phone. "Hello?"

"Special Agent John Leonardo?" The voice on the other end of the line was deep and raspy. The wheezing smoker's breaths gave away its owner.

"Yes sir. I—"

"Shut the fuck up and listen," the FBI Director cut him off. *"Did you just threaten these men with your sidearm? Did you not receive a direct order to get in contact with your superior as soon as you landed?"*

"Sir, they're torturing—"

"Shut the fuck up! Don't use that fucking word with me. Not now. Not ever. These men are here to deal with the high-level terrorist threat that you have yet to resolve. You will give them your full cooperation and assist them in whatever," he said the word with emphasis, *"they damn well need. Do you understand?"*

Leonardo glared at the sly grin displayed across the interrogator's face.

"Do you understand?"

"No. I don't."

"What the— Son, you do know who you're speaking to, correct?

Do I need to explain to you how stupid—*"* The Director let out an exasperated grunt. When he spoke again, his voice was even. *"Agent Leonardo. You've given the past fifteen years of your life to this organization and to this country. Right now, you need to think about that, because if you continue on this path of insubordination, all of that is going to disappear, understand? You don't want to flush any hopes at continuing your career in law enforcement, hell, any career, down the drain over some misguided sense of morality. There are things at play here that are way over your head. These people, they are very bad people; they're domestic terrorists and will be dealt with as such. We don't have the resources or the time to deal with this debacle before that whole area is snowed in. So, in the spirit of inter-agency cooperation, the CIA has supplied us with some of their best assets. You will do as they say and nothing more or less. Are we clear, Agent?"*

Leonardo's mind flicked over the choice before him. Fifteen years, fifteen *long* years as well as his entire future was at stake.

"I led an incursion into the area today," he began. "I have good reason to believe that we're being manipulated in order for—"

"Goddamnit!" the Director shouted through the tiny speaker. *"Put Chen on. Now."*

"Chen?"

"Yeah," Chen piped up. Leonardo hadn't noticed him sitting nonchalantly behind the sheriff's desk. Chen beckoned for the phone.

Leonardo tossed it to him.

"Chen speaking." His voice was muffled by his swollen jaw. "Yes sir… Yes sir… Absolutely, sir, you can count on me… Yes sir, I'll tell him… Thank you, sir. I won't let you down."

Chen tossed the phone back with a sly grin. Leonardo raised it back to his ear.

"Chen's in charge now. Any insubordination will be met with immediate termination." The Director paused. *"Son, I know you're a good agent and I understand you feel conflicted, but if you fuck this up, I will personally bury you."*

The phone clicked as the Director hung up.

The head contractor was still smiling at him. "So, may we proceed, agent?"

Leonardo stood fast, blocking the door.

Chen spoke up from his seat. "Yeah, go ahead, he's all yours. You'll be working directly with me from now on." His voice was festive. "Agent Leonardo, go prepare a debrief at the inn. I want the exact layout of the terrorist encampment and IDs for everyone you encountered. Also, let the team know there's a new boss."

When Leonardo still didn't budge, Chen clicked his tongue, imitating the interrogator. "Don't be an idiot, Leo. You seem a little too friendly with Stark. I don't want to get the impression that you're working with the bad guys now."

Leonardo fantasized yanking his pistol out and emptying it into the smug prick, then begrudgingly stepped aside. He watched the two interrogators reenter the room and for a brief second caught the look on Stark's face before they pushed the door shut behind them.

Stark was smiling, as if to say *I told you so.*

****

The trek back through the moonlit forest seemed to drag on forever. Every snapping twig and distant howl brought back the image of Jackson's mutilated corpse. Stephanie clutched the rifle Hunt had given her in a white-knuckled grip. She knew the basics of handling the AR-15; Stark had run her through the drills a handful of times over the years, teaching her proper handling and clearing procedures in case of a jam. But the cold plastic grip offered little comfort against the all-encompassing darkness of the wilderness.

It was nearly eleven by the time the ghostly glow of the Homestead's outdoor lighting melted through the trees. At first, she was surprised that the boys still had the complex lit up, but quickly remembered that was the whole point of their staying behind: to make the area look inhabited.

The unmistakable clack of a rifle being cocked made her jump.

"Drop it," a menacing voice snapped. She immediately recognized it as Irniq's.

"Jesus Christ, it's me." She sucked in a deep breath to calm her racing heart.

"Stephanie?"

"Yeah, who the hell did you think it was?"

Irniq emerged onto the ATV-worn path. Even in the dim moonlight she could see the confusion on his face. "I don't know, the FBI again? Where are the others? What went wrong?"

She held up a hand to silence him. "Where's Russo?"

Irniq fidgeted nervously. "He's in the Koutla with Oliver. Stephanie, why are you here?"

She stepped past him and continued walking. He surveyed the darkness for a moment then rushed after her.

"Stephanie, why did you—"

"To speak to Russo."

"Is it about Frank?"

"Frank's dead." The ice in her voice drew a regretful sigh from the teenager.

"Jesus, Stephanie, I didn't mean for—"

"Yeah, I get it, but he's dead and there are more important things to deal with now." She was caught off guard by her own callousness. Today was a day of surprising herself.

Irniq shut up and fell in step behind her. They emerged into the small cluster of buildings and crossed the courtyard to the Koutla. For the first time in the three years she'd spent nestled in the remote village she felt an overwhelming emptiness. All the feelings of warmth and comfort that had hallmarked her time there seemed like distant memories, giving way to an eerie, empty ambiance that made it difficult for her to recognize the structures around her.

She pulled open the door to the Koutla. Russo and Oliver hunched over a pile of papers at the head of the table. They didn't bother to look up.

"Irniq, you've got another three hours of watch, kid," Russo called out.

"I'm back," Stephanie said.

Russo and Oliver both jumped at the sound of the woman's voice and gave her a confounded look.

"Why did you turn back? Where the fuck is Hunt?" Russo asked, mirroring Irniq's initial reaction and marching toward her.

"It's just me," Stephanie reassured him. "The rest of the group is still on track."

"Why are you here?" Russo's voice shifted from concern to anger.

"I'm here to make sure you idiots don't pull anything stupid."

"Aw shi—"

"Not now, Oliver!" Russo yelled over his shoulder, then grabbed Stephanie by the arm. She flung him off.

"Why the fuck are you here, Stephanie? This is no place for you right now!"

"Fuck off, Andrew, I'll go wherever I please."

"Did Maya put you up to this?"

"No. But she knows as well as I do that the chances of you morons trying to fight goes from exponentially high to nil if I'm here to weigh you down. So that's exactly what I'm doing. Think of me as insurance that your wife will get to see you again."

Russo belted out a series of curses and began to furiously pace the hall.

"That goes for you too, Oliver," she yelled.

Oliver gave her a casual thumbs-up and turned his focus back to the papers in front of him.

"And you, for what it's worth," she said quietly to Irniq.

It took a few minutes for Russo to calm down. In the meantime, she crossed the room and examined the haphazard mess of plans strewn over the table. The crude, half-labeled drawings took only a moment to decipher.

"You're setting up a defense…" she muttered. Oliver nodded. "I take it the meeting with the FBI didn't go too well…"

"It went fine!" Russo ejaculated, finally abandoning his pacing and joining them. "It doesn't matter though, we have to prepare for the worst."

"Define *fine*," she said.

"Fine as in fine. As far as I can tell, the agent in charge is starting to put the pieces together. There's a decent chance that this whole thing might go away, but we can't count on that yet."

"You're saying that they're going to let you guys off the hook for trying to break Stark out?" She didn't allow the flutter of hope in her heart to seep into her voice.

"No. I don't know, but this whole 'terrorism' nonsense will probably go away. This Leonardo seems to have his head screwed on the right way."

"What're these?" She pointed to a series of scribbles that

looked like upside-down muffins.

"Pungee pits," Oliver told her proudly.

"Pungee pits?"

"Yeah, pungee pits," Russo explained. "Dig a hole, bury some spikes, pull a tarp over it with some loose dirt — pungee pits. Charlie used them in Vietnam. If we need to egress in a hurry, a few of these on the main trails might buy us some time."

"You realize how weak that sounds, right?" Stephanie asked, bewildered by the *Home Alone* tactics.

"Those were my idea, you dick," Oliver grunted. She cast an apologetic look and patted him on the head. Despite being entirely aware that he was a fully functioning adult, she always indulged the urge to treat him like a lost puppy.

"You need to go back," Russo said flatly.

"The only way I'm going back is with you all," Stephanie snapped. "Even if you convinced me it was the right thing to do, which you won't, the rest of the group is too far gone. I'd never catch up to them and I can't navigate that mountain on my own."

He mulled it over, then slapped the table in resignation. "You know what? It's a good thing you and Stark never got pregnant. That kid would've been the most hard-headed, belligerent, tenacious little asshole in the world."

"So basically, they'd be just like you." Stephanie smirked, then took on a more serious tone. "What did the FBI say about Stark?"

All three men stopped moving and glanced at each other. She got the distinct feeling that she wasn't going to like the answer.

"He's alive," Russo said haltingly. "But, Stephanie, you have to let him go."

"You said that you think they'll drop the charges..."

"I did, and there is that possibility, but we had to do something... a backup plan."

"What kind of a backup plan?" She didn't like his tone: it was too apologetic.

Russo stared at the floor. She turned to Oliver.

"Oliver, tell me what he's talking about."

Oliver shifted uncomfortably. His face was still swollen from his tumble out of the bell tower so when she grabbed his chin to turn it toward her he winced.

"Oliver..."

He pulled his head away. "Unless we get reason to believe that the FBI has gone full circle and are on our side, Hunt's going to make a call... a call that will bring hell down on Harkstaff." His voice was strangely regular, which sent a chill down Stephanie's spine.

"Who is he going to call?"

This time Russo spoke up. "A cartel. A group of Mexican drug lords that will go through hell or high water to get to Stark, even if they have to take out the whole team of feds to do it."

Stephanie was lost for words. The memory of Stark's puzzling interrogation of Franklin Summerset came to mind. She knew she'd heard the word.

Cartel.

14

The mild odor of bleach lingered in the dingy room of the Harkstaff Inn. Leonardo had been forced to relocate to a smaller room at Chen's orders so that they could make room for the two dozen contractors who now seemed to occupy every available nook and cranny of the tiny town. He sat at the head of his bed, leaning back against the scuffed headboard and staring at the boxy tube TV in front of him. Agents Tomlinson and Ferrara sat around the room with him, all three sipping a disgusting combination of Bacardi 151 and Coke.

They all needed a strong drink after the third day of Chen's over-the-top orders and incessant brown-nosing to Masterson and the contractors. With Tulimak still imprisoned and his store out of commission, the grocery burned to rubble, and the airstrip shut down to civilian resupplies, Leonardo had considered himself lucky when the inn keeper offered to sell him the bottle of overpowering liquor for ten times the retail price.

He brought the plastic solo cup to his lips and took a long sip of the concoction. As he muscled the burning liquor down, he couldn't help but take a sharp inhale through his nose.

Big mistake.

The pungent fumes curled up his nostrils and made him gag. He coughed a mouthful of the black liquid back into the cup, then pulled it away and cleared his throat repeatedly, unable to expel the enduring bite of the cocktail from his senses.

Ferrara and Tomlinson both pretended not to notice, but eyed their own drinks cautiously.

A run of the mill network crime show was on the TV: two women playing federal agents were arguing outside of a suspected kidnapper's house. The blonde one, who was clearly the rookie in the show's universe, told off her superior with a melodramatic flip of her hair and charged into the building, her gun drawn, shouting something along the lines of "screw your warrant: I'm here to save lives!"

Ferrara snickered. "If only it was that easy… What do you think would actually happen to her at the debrief?"

"She'd get the axe faster than I'd give her the D," Tomlinson grunted.

Ferrara snorted. "But seriously, how many times have you seen people get fried by the Bureau for pulling shit half that stupid?"

Leonardo knew what she was getting at though she was taking the long way there. Since Chen had taken over, the three of them had adopted the role of dissenters. There was a clear divide among the team: those who approved of Chen's aggressive strategies and those who didn't. Leonardo was surrounded by the latter.

This wasn't the time for that discussion though. If it came down to it, Leonardo didn't want Ferrara and Tomlinson, both much younger agents in age and career, jumping aboard his sinking ship of righteous indignation.

"You gotta have the willing suspension of disbelief to

enjoy shit like this." Leonardo forced down another sip of the diesel fuel tasting cocktail and shuddered. "Of course it's not realistic, every episode would be five minutes of pissing in cups on stakeouts, fifty minutes of paperwork, then five minutes of getting screamed at by their alcoholic, shit for brains boss."

The other two nodded. One of the agents on the TV was in a car chase with a tattoo-covered, bare-chested Hispanic man on a motorcycle. After a few seconds, the agent managed to shoot out the bike's rear tire, bringing him to a crashing halt against a wire fence. Amazingly he appeared unharmed as she slapped cuffs around his wrists.

"You know, my mom still believes I do shit like that for a living," Tomlinson said.

"Yeah, I bet you don't correct her on it either," Ferrara chimed in with a knowing glance in his direction.

"Eh, I let her think what she wants, but it's not like I tell her bullshit stories or anything."

"Are you going to tell her how you singlehandedly brought down a steeple with a nine, then chased a bunch of terrorists off into the woods?" Ferrara asked sarcastically.

"No. I don't know if I'll ever tell anyone about that," Tomlinson muttered.

"Why?" Leonardo had been trying to ignore the back and forth but Tomlinson's statement caught him off guard.

"Well, it just doesn't seem that exciting when you say it out loud. Like, don't think for a second I wasn't shitting my pants the whole time. That was singlehandedly the craziest thing I've ever seen, but when you compare it to *this,*" he pointed at the TV, "it just doesn't seem that... cool?"

"That's because we're all numb to real life," Leonardo said. "Trust me, kid, nothing you'll do in this job, or even in your life, will ever equate to the garbage you see on TV.

Everyone is so used to being spoon fed these overly-dramatic bullshit tropes that they lose touch with reality. Perfect example: how many people have you seen killed on TV?"

Tomlinson shrugged.

"Let's say a thousand, hell, even five hundred. Let's say you and every other American has seen five hundred people killed in these crazy primetime shows, and that's a humble estimate. Now, Tomlinson, how many people have you seen die in real life? Not just dead bodies, this job can make you numb to that on its own, but people actually dying in front of you?"

"One," Tomlinson said. Ferrara raised her eyebrow, prompting him to go on. "When I was a beat cop in LA, we pulled a guy over for speeding. At first, he pulled the race card, yelling about how we were profiling and shit, I mean the guy was Asian. I didn't even know that kind of profiling was a thing. Anyways, when we weren't having it he pulls out a gun. I wasn't paying attention but my partner caught it, put two rounds into the guy's ear point blank. It was a fucking mess…"

Leonardo let the story hang in the air for a moment before going on. "Ok, and what was that like?"

"What was it like?" Tomlinson asked, slightly indignant.

"Yeah, I mean, was it like they show on TV, like those five hundred people you've seen die so dramatically?"

"Fuck no."

"Exactly. It was fucked, I'm sure. But if you try to explain that to someone, *anyone* who hasn't seen what you've seen firsthand, they're going to pull from their experience to understand. It's empathy, human nature. The problem is that the experience they're pulling from is that clean, crisp, plot pushing death they saw so many times on TV, and they won't think twice to try and understand your experience as anything more than that. It's not just with killing, it's everything else too. For the majority of people today, the human experience has been whittled down to what they see and hear on their screens."

Tomlinson grunted.

Leonardo was afraid he'd lost him. "Do you get what I'm trying to say?"

"That I'll never be as cool as the people on TV?"

Leonardo sighed. "Yeah, you'll never be as cool as the people on TV. And more importantly, nobody aside from the people in this hotel will ever truly understand what we did that night. To expect them to see it for the terrifying shit show of an event that it was is a fool's errand."

Ferrara spoke up. "You've thought about this a lot."

"Yeah, I have…" Leonardo had begun to slide down against the headboard. When he pulled himself back up to correct his posture, he felt the slightest wave of a buzz coming on. "My old man was in 'Nam before I was born. Growing up I always harassed him about it. I wanted to know if it was like the movies and the crazy war stories from the other guys' dads. One day when I was ten, he was sober long enough to sit me down and tell me how all the other dads that told those stories were full of shit, and how that the only time I'd ever hear about what he did over there was after I'd killed a man myself. Hell of a thing to tell a ten-year-old."

There was an awkward pause, then Tomlinson spoke up. "Well, you should call him up and ask now." His voice was beginning to slur.

Ferrara hissed at him, and he gave her a confused look before realizing that it might be a soft spot for Leonardo.

"I'm sorry, Leo…" Tomlinson began but Leonardo gave him a disarming smile.

"It's fine, kid, and honestly I would, if he hadn't drank

himself to death before I graduated high school. The point is, I came to learn that the reason he was so reserved about that shit, even back then, was because I had no capacity to understand the things he would've told me. All those horrible and enlightening details would have rolled right over my head while I sat there and thought 'neat-o, blood and gore!'"

The room once again filled with silence. Leonardo shifted his attention back to the curvaceous agent on TV, now clad in a bikini and flirting with an absurdly muscular beach-goer.

"Is that why you've been so eager to stick up for these guys? Because they're vets and they remind you of your dad?" Ferrara asked, her face immediately turning red after she'd finished. "I'm sorry, Leo, that came out wrong…"

"No, it's fine," he responded. The alcohol was loosening their tongues. "Honestly, I've been asking myself that same question, trying to figure out if my judgment's been compromised. I won't lie, they do remind me of him in a way."

He took a big gulp of his drink, drained it, and stared at the bottom on the white plastic cup. "It's weird. Growing up I always thought he was trying to escape from me and my mom in the bottom of a bottle. I figured there was the whole shell shock thing from 'Nam, the Agent Orange and what not, but how could he be so fucked up when there were guys from Iwo Jima and Normandy who experienced the hell of World War Two and came out fine? I labelled him as a piece of shit for a long time. Then one day I heard a statistic, saying something about how the vast majority of guys in World War Two didn't take the shot when they had it, how they chose *not* to kill. Something clicked. My old man wasn't like that. He was a volunteer. He wasn't the guy who'd take his finger off the trigger. Hell, I always got the feeling that he *missed* pulling that trigger, but that he was ashamed of it.

"I think that's how it works nowadays. We train these young kids full of piss and vinegar to relish in killing the enemy, but then after the war's over and everything's settled, we tell them it's wrong — the killing and hate and violence. It was ok when they did it over there, but now it's wrong. That's where I see my old man when I look back: a fighting dog that's been put through the ring again and again, and then one day they just pulled him out and told him he could never fight again. That the thing he's been bred to do was wrong and evil. They stuck him in a nice, warm, loving home with no doors or windows to escape out of, and we suffocated him with hugs and love and soft toys. But he was still a fighting dog. He dreamed of getting back in that ring but had no means to get there... Maybe he would have ended up in a place like this..."

He straightened himself and the room around him spun. He was definitely drunk.

"If he just wanted to go back to war, why didn't he reenlist?" Tomlinson slurred out from where he now lay on the floor at the foot of the bed.

"The war was over. I don't think it was that easy. Hell, I don't even know if he wanted to go back to war, or if he even knew what he wanted. I think he just experienced something incredibly intense, that no one in his life back home could relate to or understand. I think maybe he felt like he *should* have been ashamed of what he'd done, but that he wasn't, and because he wasn't, he *still* felt ashamed nonetheless. I remember him telling me how those dads spitting off grandiose war stories were all admin guys who never saw combat. He was so vehement when he talked about them. It was like they were cheapening what he was going through, his own dilemma that even he couldn't understand."

Tomlinson let out a grunting snore from beyond the foot

of the bed, but Ferrara was leaning forward in her chair listening intently.

"I see that same lost… shit… in these guys," Leonardo mumbled. His mind was swimming.

Fucking 151.

"It's like they don't know what they're looking for, but they found some part of it here. They ran away to this wilderness and found the… will? Yeah, the *will* to keep going. Maybe it's the challenge of doing it, maybe it's the community, fuck, I don't know. I have no idea… All I know at this point is that they managed to escape society, and we're the assholes who've been sent to punish them for it…"

He hiccupped and felt the frozen pizza he'd had for dinner start to boil back up. Ferrara must have been in the same boat. She leapt from her seat and disappeared into the bathroom. He could hear her let out a belching burst of vomit.

Shit.

Leonardo found that just stringing together thoughts was becoming difficult.

We might be the bad guys.

****

"I'm getting tired of asking the same questions, Augustin," the Rat said, his voice never shifting from its monotonous, nasally whine.

"I told you a dozen times, only my mother gets to call me that," Stark responded. "Call me Stark."

He was seated once again in the interrogation room, his arms extended to his sides and cuffed to the plastic table's legs, exposing his aching ribs. The contractors had weighed down the table with cinderblocks on the corners to hold it steady. Underneath the table, Stark's feet were submerged in a five-gallon bucket of ice water. The Ogre behind him slammed a thick phonebook against his side, drawing a loud, stinging slap. Stark winced, and his elbow naturally recoiled to protect his exposed ribs, shifting the table toward him. As soon as the table scuffed against the floor, a jolting shock of electricity blasted through his legs. The Rat smiled, toying with the remote for the electric dog collar secured around Stark's ankle.

"What mother? You have no family on record. It's like the moment you came into all of that money everything about your past aside from your military file was expunged from all databases. How much did that clean start cost you? Millions? We found your little piggy bank in New York. I have to tell you, if I had nine figures lying around, I definitely wouldn't be in a place like this… So, why the clean start?"

Stark tried not to let the boiling hatred creep into his expression. He'd been able to maintain control over the past four days of intermittent torture and sleep deprivation, but now his grasp on reality was loosening. He felt himself slipping closer and closer to the chasm that he'd tumbled down long before in Mexico, into a deep pit of hate that he knew bottomed out to a state of terrifying chaos.

"How about her name? Your mother, what's her name?" the Rat asked from across the table.

When Stark still didn't respond, the Rat nodded for the Ogre to continue. The phonebook cracked loudly in his ears, but this time Stark managed not to flinch. The Rat waited a moment, surprised that the table hadn't shifted, then shocked Stark's soaked, numb feet anyways.

"Ok, fine. Have it your way." The Rat checked his watch. "I think it's time to change methods again. How about we get the board back out?"

"Henry," Stark said, addressing the man behind him.

The Ogre slapped him on the back of the head. "You don't get to say my name."

"Henry, are you married?" Stark asked. He'd noted the titanium band on the man's hand a day before.

The Ogre laughed in disbelief. "This fuckface doesn't stop, does he?"

"Henry, does your wife stay faithful when you leave?"

This brought another heavy blow from the phonebook, followed by the accompanying shock.

"It's just—" Stark began, but he was cut off as his head was thrown forward and bounced off the plastic table.

"Fuck! Alright, I'll make a deal," Stark said, staring with wide-eyed exasperation at the man across the table.

"We aren't really the deal making type, Augustin."

"Try it for once, trust me, it's better than just letting little… little… douche bald guy? I don't know, it's better than letting little Henry here wear himself out."

Another slap upside the head. The patronizing cuffing brought on more rage than the phonebook.

Maintain control.

"What deal do you want to make?"

"I'll tell you what you want to know, all of it: who's out there, the buildings' layout, their defenses, everything. And you can even keep this weak ass 'leave no marks' torture routine… But I want to take a guess at how much Air Force One's wife weighs."

The Rat snorted; it was the first time he'd lost his bearing. Stark heard a distinct click behind him, and a second later, as the Rat reached out in alarm, he knew it was the sound of a knife blade locking in place.

The pain was sharp. It seared through his temple and as it made its way to his jawline, he felt the heavy flow of warm liquid cascading down his cheek and shoulder. He gritted his teeth in order to keep from screaming as the Ogre tossed his dismembered ear on the table in front of him and pressed the knife against his throat.

"I'll leave all the marks I want, you little shit," his tormentor spouted out furiously. Stark caught the stink of his breath full in the face. "You're going to die here. I fucking promise you that."

"Henry!" the Rat roared, his voice surprisingly powerful.

Stark didn't smile. He didn't quip. He closed his eyes and accepted the pain, letting it flow into his heart where it coagulated and mutated into a boiling rage. Staring down into the chasm of hatred inside him, he let go, and toppled over the edge.

"Jesus Christ," the Rat muttered, pointing at the corner. "Back the fuck off!" He pulled out a satellite phone from his cargo pocket and dialed. A moment later, as Stark felt the warm pool of blood that was forming in his lap soak through his pants, the Rat spoke into the device. "Sir, Nazzir here. There's been a... complication.... Yes, sir, he's alive, a little worse for wear though... we're going in the morning after tomorrow, he hasn't given us much info but the FBI has a layout for us... I think that's the best option, sir... Yes, I'll make sure it happens... Yes, sir, no more mistakes."

He hung up, then looked angrily at his partner. "Get a notepad, now."

The Ogre complied, leaving the room with a spiteful grin toward Stark. But Stark barely noticed. He wasn't in the room anymore, not fully. That man was buried somewhere deep inside. The thing chained to the table was no longer Augustin Stark.

"Thing's just got really simple. You're going to write out a confession and sign it. If you comply, we'll toss you back in your cell and leave you to deal with the federal prison system." The Rat had regained his creepily calm voice.

He's lying.

They're going to kill you.

The Rat reached over and knocked the pink hunk of flesh off the table onto Stark's lap, where it landed with a wet splat. He used a rag to wipe the blood away, leaving nothing but a faint pink smear on the white plastic.

The Ogre returned and tossed the notepad down where the ear had been.

The Rat pulled apart a pen and slid its stem across the table. "Good luck turning that into a weapon," he said absentmindedly, then turned to his partner, who was preparing to uncuff Stark's right hand. "Henry, is this your first fucking day?"

The Ogre gave him a queer look before realizing his mistake. He pulled out his pistol and handed it to the Rat. They seemed to be taking every possible precaution to ensure Stark couldn't lash out.

The Ogre released Stark's right hand. Stark slowly reached in front of him and grasped the flimsy pen stem. It bowed in his grip.

"Write as I say," the Rat commanded, leaning back and thinking hard. "I, Augustin Stark, hereby profess my guilt to the crimes of terrorism, murder, racketeering…"

He paused as Stark scratched barely legible words into the notepad's soft yellow surface.

"Your handwriting is shit. We better be able to read that… racketeering, possession of illegal substances including drugs and weapons, as well as explosives…" the Rat paused again, giving the notepad a glance before motioning to the Ogre. "What the fuck is he writing?"

The Ogre leaned over Stark's shoulder, squinting at the chicken scratch. "I can't read that shit… 'All'… something…

'and no ploy'?"

The Rat grunted and snatched the notepad away. He held it up in front of him and moved his mouth as he deciphered the words.

The tempest that raged inside Stark was climaxing. He felt the quickly drying blood that covered his face crack apart as his features spread into an evil, uncontrollable grin.

"All work and no play makes Stark a mad boy?" the Rat read, his confusion emanating from his voice. "Who the fuck are you, Stephen Ki—"

Stark balled his fist around the flimsy ink shaft so the point protruded between his knuckles and slammed it into the Ogre's crotch, drawing a gasping scream. The man doubled over. With lightning speed, Stark grabbed the slippery bald head and brought it smashing full force into the corner of the nearest cinderblock.

The Rat flinched as a spurt of blood from his partner's scalp sprayed across his face. Stark kicked the bucket off of his feet and grabbed the concrete block. He flung it into the seated man's chest, sending him toppling back in his chair. Stark stood, his numb feet slipping on the wet floor, and grasped the table's edge. With a throaty growl, he flipped it forward. It landed on the Rat's chest, pinning him to the ground. Stark slid his remaining handcuff off of the overturned table leg, then dropped to his knees atop the pinned rodent. The Rat's obnoxiously calm demeanor was gone, lost in the ocean of terror that now swarmed in his eyes.

1…

2…

3…

4…

Stark's fist came down like an oil pumpjack. With every punch he could feel the Rat's skull flexing against the concrete floor.

6…

7…

The terror was gone from the Rat's face, replaced by a bulging, blank eyed stare at the wall.

9…

10…

The skull gave way with a raucous crunch.

13…

14...

"Nazzir?"

A voice from just beyond the door to the sheriff's main office snapped Stark back to the present. He kicked the upturned table out from under him and grabbed the Rat's pistol with swollen, brain spattered hands. There was a moment of silence, then footsteps echoed from just across the sealed door's threshold. There was a knock.

Stark fired five times, twice at chest level and three more times down the length of the thin wooden door. A satisfying thud met his ears as he scrambled to his feet and flung it open.

A dead contractor lay in front of him. The screen door slapped against the office's main entryway and he saw the lanky frame of Deputy Carr sprinting away toward the inn. He leveled the pistol.

No.

Stark stopped. He unclenched his vice-like jaw and let in a breath. He was already off the deep end. He knew that he needed to reel himself back in, to regain control. Through the red haze that was suffocating his thoughts, he recalled the Rat's phone call: *They're going in the morning after tomorrow.*

Across the room, the shortwave radio sat atop the sheriff's desk. He stumbled as his feet began to regain feeling. Each step sent jolting shots of pain up his calves. The radio was still on the Homestead's frequency.

He keyed the mic. "Homestead! Homestead! This is Stark!"

The radio was silent, but outside he could hear yelling coming from the direction of the inn.

"Answer the fucking radio!" he roared into the receiver.

"—*ly shit, Stark? What's happening?*" Irniq's panicked voice came through the speaker.

"They're coming. Morning after tomorrow. Get everyone out. It's not the FBI anymore, they have military contractors—"

The window next to him shattered and he was surrounded by the distinct snap of bullets.

He ducked down beneath the desk and continued hastily. "They're armed to the teeth, they won't take any prisoners."

Outside he heard a repeated call: *the antenna.*

The sound of the rounds snapping overhead turned into a cascade of heavy thumps above him as the contractors shifted their fire to the antenna on the roof.

"*Gen-pop is already out! Stark, are you—*" The transmission cut off.

"Irniq can you hear me?" Stark asked desperately, but there was no reply.

He threw the handset and bear-crawled back to the interrogation room. His hands and feet slipped on the thick trail of blood that still poured from where his ear had been. He could hear the gunfire getting closer as bullets chewed at the walls of the main office.

This was it. This was the end.

He clawed through the Rat's pockets to find the satellite phone, then pulled the nearly headless corpse in front of him like a barricade and aimed the pistol out the front door.

A shadow shot across the alleyway outside. He fired three

times into the darkness, then called out as loud as he could, "I have one of your men! Stay the fuck back!"

He flipped open the phone. It dripped with water from the overturned bucket.

It had to work.

His fingers dialed the number he'd memorized so many years before. The phone rang once and someone picked up, but the line remained silent.

"This is Augustin Stark. Listen very carefully, because this is the one chance you'll have to find me. I'm in Alaska, east of Fairbanks, near the border. A town called Harkstaff. You have until tomorrow to get here—"

The outside door lit up with a flash of gunfire, Stark blasted back, emptying a handful of rounds into the darkness. "Get here now and you can have it all, the money and me."

The line remained silent and Stark feared for a second that he had misdialed. Then a crackling, drawn out voice spoke.

"Mr. Stark. It's good to hear from you. By the sound of it, you have your hands quite full. We have already been alerted to your location. I believe you'll be seeing an old friend soon."

"Get here by tomorrow or I'll already be gone," Stark spat.

"Yes… we'll see."

The line went dead. Stark slammed it down on the wet floor. When it didn't break, he fired a round into it point blank. The small phone popped off the ground and skittered across the room.

Stark followed it with his eyes and saw the Ogre shifting in the corner, slowly waking. He pulled a hand up to the gushing wound on top of his head. Stark whistled. The Ogre looked up in confusion before Stark shot him in the face.

****

Oliver sat across the Koutla table from Stephanie, eyeing the half-empty bottle of eighteen-year-old Glenlivet between them.

"Your turn," she said. She'd just finished regaling him with the story of her father scaring away one of her high school boyfriends.

"I don't know, most of my best stories don't really appeal to girls," Oliver said with a sly grin.

In the corner Russo snored loudly atop one of the mattresses they'd dragged over from the residence hall. It was 2 AM, but Stephanie wasn't particularly tired and knew Oliver's anxiety over his wife and two-year-old son wouldn't allow him to sleep until he knew they were safe over the mountain.

"Tell me about when you first met Alasie."

Oliver looked down and smiled. "It's not that good of a story. Pretty mundane actually."

"Try me."

Oliver pulled the bottle of scotch in and took a sip. "When Stark hit me up I was laying brick outside of Philly. Civilian life wasn't really working out that well for me, and I honestly had no idea what all of this," he spun his finger in a little circle, "would turn out to be. But I liked the idea he had, so I came with him. You know the story. We did a few scouting trips out here trying to figure out exactly what we were getting into. About a week in, we ended up hiring this guide from Tallsway, the next town over from Harkstaff, to kind of teach us about the Alaskan bush."

"That was Irniq and Alasie's father, wasn't it?"

Oliver smiled and nodded. "Yeah, Sivoy. He was crazy, man. Contrary to popular belief, the Marine Corps doesn't make you anything close to a survival expert. If anything, it just teaches you to be at peace with being uncomfortable for long periods of time. We spent three weeks with this guy and he taught us a lot, I mean *a lot,* about everything from the local hunting game, what kind of wood to build with, and the best ways to keep from going crazy in the winters. We liked him so much that by the end of it, Stark tried to give him a cold million bucks."

Stephanie snorted. She, along with most of the Homesteaders outside the immediate group of founders, had no idea how much money Stark had. Only that it was a lot, and that he had no qualms about spending it.

"Sivoy told him to fuck off, and refused to take anything over his standard fee. So, we asked if there was anything we could do for him to repay the lessons he'd taught us. He told us to come stay with him at his home for a week and help him build a new dog house. Yeah, yeah, at first, I thought he meant like a little Snoopy shack too, but Sivoy had what was basically a small barn to house his mutts. There must have been at least thirty of them, and he trained them all as sled dogs. So, we show up at his place after two weeks in the forest, and the first thing I see when we pull up is this girl sitting on the porch with the *nicest* pair of tits I've ever—"

"Oh my god, shut the fuck up."

"Ok, ok," Oliver laughed. Stephanie realized that she had never really seen this side of him. "No, really, I saw her sitting on the porch and I couldn't look away. She was fucking beautiful. I mean, I don't really have to explain, you've *seen* her. I've never been much of a romantic, but I knew, right then and there, that—"

"Where's Russo?!" The door banged open and Irniq rushed in.

Oliver leapt to his feet, wincing as he put too much weight on his badly sprained knee. "What is it?"

"Stark just called, he said they're coming the morning after tomorrow!"

"What the hell…" Russo muttered groggily, sitting up on the mattress and rubbing his eyes.

Even before Irniq continued, Stephanie could tell by the look on the young Inuit's face that this visit from the FBI wasn't going to be as amiable as the last.

"He said it's not FBI, they have military contractors or something and they're coming for blood!"

Russo snapped awake. He jumped off the mattress and crossed the room to the table. "What exactly did he say?"

"He said the morning after tomorrow contractors are coming, armed to the teeth, and they aren't going to take any prisoners."

What the fuck happened?

"Jesus," Russo said under his breath. Stephanie saw the flood of fear in his face that had terrified Maya weeks before.

"How many pungee pits do we have so far?" Russo madly shuffled through the papers that were scattered across the table.

"Three finished on the eastern trails, another two half-dug to the south," Oliver responded. The rare vulnerability from a moment before had dissolved.

"Forget them. Fuck." Russo glanced at his watch. "We can only give ourselves twenty-two hours. We need to adjust our plan and adjust our defenses. Irniq, what did he say about the contractors? Did he give you numbers?"

"Nothing. He literally got off what I told you then the line went dead."

"Fuck," Russo paused and closed his eyes, focusing. "If they're military contractors we have to assume they're going to have a lot more firepower than we planned for. Probably more than one bird, too. Oliver, any ideas?"

"We need to shut down any landing zones. If they get

boots on the ground in the paddock or the garden, we're done."

"True. We still have to assume that they'll send in a ground element from the western clearings to cordon us to the west and south." Russo slapped the table as a lightbulb came on in his head. "How much steel cord do we have left over from the paddock fence?"

"A fuck ton," Oliver responded with a curious look.

"If we use a grinder to cut embrasures into the Connex box in the paddock—"

"Embrasures?" Stephanie asked. It was becoming increasingly difficult for her to keep up with these tactical plans. They were Marines. She was just a nurse from Montana.

"Arrow slits, thin ass windows to shoot out of that are hard as shit to shoot back at. If we can cut embrasures into the Connex box, then that will provide cover for someone to defend the paddock. Then we can string the steel cable in a net over the garden, like this." He grabbed a paper and scribbled a rough sketch of the garden, crisscrossed with a handful of lines that represented the steel cables. "We string them tight from the trees at a ten-foot height. No choppers are going to be able to land in that shit."

"What's going to stop them from rappelling in? And what if they have something that can penetrate the Connex box? That steel isn't exactly armor..." Oliver didn't sound particularly happy with the idea. Stephanie apparently wasn't alone in getting the hint that it would be him sitting in the thin metal container.

"You're right," Russo said, not slowing down. "But if we can electrify the cables—"

"No one here can do that. Dave was the electrician and he's long gone," Oliver came back.

"Fuck. Ok. Can you put together a pressure plate ignition system?"

Oliver nodded. "Yeah, for what though?"

"If we leave a gap big enough to where they *think* they can land, we can make a fire trap."

"Russo stop—"

"We mix the gasoline stores with Styrofoam. Fuck, we don't have any Styrofoam. If we can get an ignition system for when the helo lands, then we can find something around here that will explode—"

"Russo, stop!" Oliver yelled it this time.

Russo glanced up at him.

"You need to relax, dickhead." Oliver's gravelly voice made a reappearance, as it often did in times of great stress.

"There's no time to relax, bud," Russo said slowly, turning to the others. "We only have an hour to plan out a full defense against an unknown enemy, then another twenty-one to put it in place. If anyone has any bright ideas, now's the time to share."

"We can't keep them from roping out of the helicopters," Irniq said after a moment of silence. He was eerily calm, staring at the scattered plans before them. "And we can't leave right now, or even tomorrow. If they get the hint that we're not here anymore, then they'll have the Canadians combing the border searching for the rest of us. We need to stick to the plan. We need to wait until the last possible second, when they think they have us cornered, then burn it all and disappear in the smoke."

"Agreed," Oliver said.

"Yeah," Russo nodded then pointed to the drawing of the wire netted garden. "I honestly believe this'll make it awkward enough for them to get boots on the ground, especially with us taking pot shots at them."

Oliver nodded. "So, we string the wire tonight. We're going to need to get moving."

"You and I," Russo said pointing at Oliver. "We'll do that now. Even if they've got a satellite watching us, the darkness should cover our movement. Irniq, I need you to gather every piece of flammable material and arrange it on the western side of the river over by Stark's cabin. When the time gets close, we'll soak that shit in kerosene and gas. I get the feeling those pines are gonna go up no problem. Stephanie—"

She looked up from the papers in surprise. Though she was keenly aware of the events unfolding around her, she felt entirely detached from reality.

"I need you to make half a dozen dummies. Use blankets and shit from the residence hall to stuff clothes, then stage them in the stables."

"Why?" she asked, her voice weak.

"When we light this place, we're going to need diversions. We set the horses free and they'll scatter. If it looks like there are riders on their backs, it'll take those helos a while to realize it ain't us. Let's go." Russo waved at Oliver to follow him. Together they bolted through the door, Irniq in pursuit.

Suddenly Stephanie found herself alone in the giant hall. She looked down and realized that she was clenching the chair back in front of her in a white knuckled grip. She released it, and her hands began to shake. Reality set in, accompanied by a wave of nausea. She vomited hot bile and scotch onto the floor, then collapsed next to the putrid puddle and curled into a ball.

This was it. There were men coming to kill them. The boys were preparing to light a whole forest on fire. This was absurd. Hadn't it just been a backup plan? A "what if?" Now it was painfully real and absolutely terrifying. Why had she turned back? Why wasn't she safe and warm with the others with a mountain between her and all this mayhem? Why the fuck had she come here in the first place?

She cursed herself and squeezed her legs tighter against her heaving chest. All the bravado and confidence was gone from her mind, replaced by an overwhelming sensation of doom. She wished Stark was with her. He always had an answer. She knew he was full of shit half the time, but his confident words were the only thing she could imagine soothing the deep-rooted terror she felt ripping her mind apart.

Beyond the thick table leg in front of her, she saw the intricately carved mural of a lionskin-clad woman thrusting a spear into a rearing bear. Stark had etched it into the Koutla's wall the previous winter, insisting through the whole process that it was purely ornamental. But everyone had joked about the snarling woman's striking resemblance to Stephanie.

She remembered the night he finished it. He'd snuck to her room in the residence hall and carried her through the snow, half asleep and bundled in blankets, to the Koutla. He'd told her that it was his favorite of the dozens of carvings that spanned the hall, and that he only wished that he could have captured more of her raw power. She'd laughed at him and insisted that he'd completely misjudged her, but he'd refused to believe it. He'd said how she was far stronger than she knew. That despite her lack of inner confidence, she had the heart of a fighter.

At the time, Stephanie had brushed off the comment as a means for Stark to get laid. But now, looking at the ferocious woman standing against the massive, snarling bear, she took it to heart, and willed it to be true.

She rose. She walked out of the Koutla as calmly and steadily as her shaking legs would hold her. There were defenses to prepare.

****

Leonardo woke with a start. The banging on the door was incessant: he could hear one of his agent's voices yelling beyond it. He sat up too quickly and the room around him spun. Crimping his eyes shut and shaking away the instant nausea, he stood and unlocked the door. It shot open, nearly sending him toppling backwards. Agent Christoff's plump frame filled the entryway.

"Agent Leonardo," Christoff panted out, grabbing the wall and slumping over. "Gear up. They need you at the sheriff station. Something's happened."

Leonardo grabbed his pistol from the desk beside the still playing TV and kicked Tomlinson, who looked up with beet red eyes.

"What the hell is going on?" Leonardo asked. He could smell the alcohol on his own breath.

"Stark's taken hostages," Christoff wheezed. "He's demanding to speak with you."

No.

No! Not tonight…

Even with the rush of adrenaline that accompanied the news, Leonardo could still feel the rum fuzzing out the edges of his thoughts. Drinking had been a mistake, a moment of agitated self-medication which he seldom indulged. Now he was fucked.

He was still drunk.

"What the hell is going on…" Ferrara groaned from the corner, trying to stand but stumbling back and knocking a lamp off the nightstand.

"We fucked up." It was the best way Leonardo could articulate the storm of regret bubbling in his stomach.

He followed Christoff down the hallway and almost fell while trying to navigate the stairwell to the ground floor. By the time he emerged into the crisp night air of Harkstaff, he had come to the conclusion that he was too inebriated to operate in any sort of tactical situation, much less negotiate with the cryptex that was Augustin Stark.

Christoff led him across the street to the burned grocery store. Chen was crouched next to a burly contractor named Joe. The two men were arguing over protocol when Leonardo dropped to a knee beside them.

"What the fuck is going on?" he asked.

"Quiet," Chen hissed, attempting to continue his dialogue.

The contractor turned to Leonardo. "Stark escaped. He claims he has one of our men hostage in there... he's demanding to speak to you."

"There is no goddamn way I'm sending *him* in there." Chen's child-king demeanor as he snapped the order solidified Leonardo's decision before he even considered the alternatives.

"I'll do it."

"You're not even a trained negotiator." Chen gave a dismissive flip of his hand.

"I've been doing this for fifteen years. You know—" Leonardo hiccupped. "You know how many hostage negotiations I've handled?"

The real answer was none.

"You're under my command—" Chen began.

"And you're under his," Leonardo cut him off.

The contractor mulled it over in his mind.

"There is no way in hell–" Chen started, but the contractor held up a hand to silence him.

"Go. If you fuck this up, it's on you."

"No, it's on me!" Chen protested.

Leonardo ignored him, pulling out his pistol and his wallet and handing them off to Joe, who held up the wallet and gave him a cockeyed look.

"I don't know,,," Leonardo hiccupped again and stood.

He did his best to walk a straight line as he made his way along the burned storefront, across the alley, and to the sheriff station's entrance. As he came close, one of the contractors, crouched behind the same dumpster Leonardo had taken cover behind a week before, hissed at him to get back.

Leonardo held up a reassuring hand and called out. "Stark, its's Agent Leonardo. They said you wanted to speak to me."

Silence.

"Stark!"

"Enter." Stark's voice seemed different, guttural. Missing its usual ring of sarcastic arrogance.

Leonardo stepped into the entryway. The only light in the room came from the computer screen in the corner, but he could just barely make out Stark crouched behind a human shield just beyond the door to the interrogation room.

"Stop!" Stark commanded. Leonardo froze.

"I'm unarmed, I promise."

"Prove it, strip."

"Are you serious?"

"*Do it!*" The words rasped out between gritted teeth.

Leonardo pulled off the cheap button-down dress shirt, held his arms in the air, and spun in a slow circle. "Happy? Because I'm not losing the pants or the undershirt."

"Who are these pieces of shit?" Stark growled from the darkness behind the door, like a lion cornered in a cave.

"You were right, they're contractors. Private sector guys the CIA uses overseas. I doubt any of this is legitimately legal, but I doubt even more that anybody outside of this shit town

THE HOMESTEAD   225

is ever going to hear anything about it."

Stark was silent.

"What's your plan here?" Leonardo was doing his best to maintain his composure despite the rum bubbling its way back up his esophagus.

Silence.

"Why did you want me here?" Leonardo demanded.

He started forward, closing the fifteen-foot gap between him and Stark to ten.

"Stop!" The raw ferocity of Stark's voice compelled him to obey. "I won't tell you again."

Leonardo grabbed a spindly wooden chair beside him and leaned on it hard. As his eyes adjusted to the darkness, he looked closer at the man Stark had propped in front of him. It was the pale, monstrous interrogator. A thin line of dark liquid trickled from a hole under the contractor's right eye.

"He's dead. You don't have a hostage at all," Leonardo thought out loud as the realization dawned on him.

"I do now." Stark pulled his pistol away from the dead contractor's temple and leveled it with Leonardo.

Shit.

"You know they won't let you out of here alive, Stark. Hell, at this point they'd probably be just as happy to kill me as they will you."

"They'll have to."

"Oh, for fuck's sake!" Leonardo rolled his head back and groaned. "You're really going to give them this? You think this isn't exactly what they want?"

Stark pulled back the hammer of the Sig Sauer.

"Go ahead then, shoot me, you fucking animal." Leonardo gave a resigned sigh. "I thought you were smarter than this, but if in your mind this is coming off as some sort of heroic last stand, then go ahead. Shoot me and they'll come in here and shoot you and then they'll go up there and kill your friends, and nobody will be left to tell what really happened. Masterson will walk away from this with a nice new hunk of land and not a care in the world, and you'll just be another lifeless bag of meat who tried to martyr himself for no fucking reason. Pull the fucking trigger, you stupid little shit."

The room was silent, but Leonardo could hardly hear Stark's sharp breathing over the sound of his own racing heart. Maybe it was the liquor. Maybe the previous week's ordeal had changed something in him. He didn't know, and in that moment, he didn't care. Stark wasn't going to kill him. It would be stupid, irrational, moronic. If there was one thing Stark had exhibited in his dealing with Leonardo, it had been an incredible amount of self-control in the face of a threat.

"Pull the fucking trigger!"

Leonardo flung the wooden chair with all his strength through the door, immediately lunging in after it and throwing all his weight into a football tackle. He slammed hard into a mass of body, pinning it against the wall, entirely unsure whether it was Stark or the dead contractor. Reaching out blindly, Leonardo grasped a head full of matted, wet hair and pulled it toward him. He balled his other hand into a fist and brought it crashing down. The punch landed, then he felt his legs fly out from under him.

It was odd, amidst the rush of adrenaline amplified by the alcohol-fueled indifference to his own health, the sensation of falling affected him more than the mind shattering impact with the cold, wet concrete floor. In a second, Stark was atop him, pinning him to the ground and grinding the cold metal of the pistol barrel into his cheek bone.

The ambient light from the computer in the next room glinted off Stark's wild eyes. They were shark eyes: dead, empty, soulless orbs. Leonardo stared into them and came to the horrifying realization that he had drastically miscalculated. There was no control there. He was about to die.

"Stephanie!" he gargled out as Stark's hand crimped down on his throat. He didn't know why he said it. Somewhere in the panicked flurry of desperate pleas brought on in the face of certain death, the misspelled name scrawled beneath the child's drawing had manifesting itself and forced its way out of his constricted vocal cords.

Stark's eyes twitched. Leonardo wasn't sure if he was clinging to the last desperate hope of life or if he saw a hint of recognition pass through them. The barrel pulled back ever so slightly, and the grip on his throat loosened.

The explosion filled his ears. It drove down their thin canals and smashed against his eardrums with deafening power. Everything went white.

Part 3

15

The hokey dining room of the Harkstaff Inn had been transformed into a headquarters for the contractors. Leonardo sat in the last of five rows of folding chairs trying to listen over the incessant ringing in his ears as the contractor named Joe outlined the plan for the next morning's incursion into the Homestead.

Despite the relatively warm temperatures, the National Weather Service had issued a blizzard warning for the next afternoon. Joe kicked off the brief with an assurance that they had only the morning to conduct the raid and secure the Homestead for the FBI, then be wheels up and departed from Harkstaff by noon. The timeline may have seemed ridiculous, but the mission outline itself took the cake.

The eight-man FBI team would be split into two groups, each four-man team reinforced with contractors. Leonardo, along with Ferrara, Tomlinson, and Christoff, would make up the FBI component of the unit that would land in the clearing along the northern edge of the lake that separated the valley from the tundra. They were to push northeast and arrive at the river that skirted the Homestead by approximately 8 AM. There, they would set in a cordon to keep the Homesteaders from escaping south. A team of twelve contractors would land in the westernmost clearing, marked by Masterson's burned helicopter, and push eastbound directly into the Homestead. Two teams of contractors would fly in low over the treetops above the compound and provide covering fire, landing and dismounting a six-man team each if the opportunity arose. The latest satellite imagery provided by the military showed that the Homesteaders had established some sort of grid system over the garden area. Joe guessed it was a primitive attempt to keep them from landing. He ordered his men to be ready to rappel down if the occasion called for it.

Lastly, Joe called on Chen and the other three remaining members of the FBI team. They would accompany him and the rest of the contractors to a remote clearing on the opposite side of the mountain. They were to disembark that night.

"You can't make it over that mountain on foot in ten hours," Ferrara pointed out.

"Don't worry about that. You do your jobs and be in your assigned positions by zero eight hundred," Joe told her.

It didn't make sense to Leonardo. The contractors seemed to be under the impression that they could scale the mountain, make it down the other side, and meet the westernmost element in the middle, coming into the Homestead in a pincer move. Leonardo had been there; he had seen the terrain and was entirely sure such tactics were flawed from the ground up.

But he remained silent. A big part of him hoped the contractors would fuck up. He had no illusions as to their goal: to wipe the Homestead clean, leaving a pile of bodies to bury along with any evidence of their involvement.

When Ferrara spoke up again asking about rules of engagement, Joe motioned to his men with a chuckle. "Same as Libya," he told them. He turned to her, presenting a more serious face. "We're only to engage direct threats. However, with the overwhelming amount of evidence to support it, we've come to the conclusion that those residing in the terrorist compound are *all* likely to be direct threats."

"So, shoot first, ask questions later?" she retorted. Her snarky attitude made Leonardo proud.

"You don't have to worry about it," Joe assured her. "You'll be with the cordon team. Your only job here is to prevent anyone from crossing over that river and breaking away south. If you want to use a Tazer instead of a rifle, go ahead, but you *won't* let anyone through that cordon. The south is their only viable egress. Keep them from using it."

The brief finished and broke down into a question and answer session. The contractors seemed to be speaking their own language, debating methods of breaching and possible defenses. Leonardo felt slightly reassured that their largest weapon was a pair of door-mounted M60 machine guns for the helicopters that would provide overhead fire. He'd half expected their arsenal to include napalm.

As the debate moved on to which method of rappelling they would use, Leonardo couldn't help but zone out. The flash bang grenade that had saved his life the night before had nearly deafened him, and his head still pounded from the concussion.

But had it really saved his life?

He'd asked himself that question a dozen times. The image of Stark's face contorted in animalistic rage lingered in his thoughts. Those eyes. Those soulless, dead eyes. He instinctively brushed a hand against his cheekbone, which was still sore from where Stark jammed the .40-millimeter Sig Sauer's barrel. Leonardo had been so sure he was about to die. What had stopped Stark? Who was Stephanie? Who was she to him?

"Leonardo!" Chen hissed at him from the front row.

He glanced up. Chen motioned toward Joe with a look that screamed *pay attention.*

Leonardo had to stop himself from rolling his eyes in Chen's face. He knew the arrogant, power hungry junior agent would use any excuse to leave him behind on this mission.

****

Russo finished taping the last kerosene-filled Mason jar to the base of the residence hall's outer wall and nudged it with his foot to make sure it was secure. Aside from the ten jugs of gasoline that lay in intervals beside the wall of torn cloth, hay, and tinder along the western riverbank, they had rationed their flammable liquids evenly among the Homestead's buildings. Oliver had built a pressure switch under the singular 30x30-foot opening they'd left in the wire netting over the garden. It would initiate a makeshift ignition system that would ignite the gasoline-soaked tinder hidden beneath.

However the next morning panned out, one thing was inevitable: the Homestead wasn't going to be there come nightfall.

It was strange. Throughout the mad hustle to emplace the defenses Russo had found himself eerily at ease. As if the process itself had set him into some natural rhythm. The regular pangs of anxiety had all but subsided, muffled by the job at hand. As he crossed through the thin stretch of forest toward the garden, he wondered if this was, in fact, his natural state.

That was absurd though. He was just too busy to let the nerves in. There was too much at stake.

But what if that *was* it? What if the one thing that made

him most at ease was the idea that there was nothing beyond the next day? He had felt entirely at home holed up in the mud huts and Hesco barrier enclosed patrol bases in Afghanistan. As a matter of fact, he'd felt more at home there than he had anywhere in his whole life. What if the key to his happiness lay directly in the face of danger? What if, by some cruel divine irony, his only hope to escape the demons in his own head was the crushing weight of mortal jeopardy?

At that moment, his world existed entirely within the next twenty-four hours. There was nothing beyond it. There was no future to plan for, no past to reflect on, simply the here and now, and the imminent battle ahead. The thought was strangely comforting.

If that was the case, Russo mused, then he was fucked. If he had finally found the spiritual balance he'd been looking for all these years, then it was balanced on the bladed edge of life and death.

He emerged through the trees and carefully skirted the piece of hidden plywood, knowing that a single misstep would ignite the immediate area in a ball of flames. This wasn't the time to figure his issues out. It was the time to prepare. He grinned as he bent and pulled the concealing hay back, revealing a trail of wires that lead away from the pressure plate and back to an ATV battery hidden in the forest.

The plan was simple. Stupid, but simple. The garden was his to defend. Oliver had the paddock from inside the cover of the Connex box. Irniq would hide in Stark's cabin to the west, waiting until the last possible second to ignite one of the many glass jars full of kerosene that hung amongst the trees. Stephanie would stand by, waiting with the ATVs for the escape and be ready to triage.

Russo chuckled out loud.

What could go wrong?

****

"Chen!" Leonardo had tailed his former subordinate after the debrief concluded, following Chen up to his room where he had begun to don his gear.

"Not now, Leo. I have to be at the airstrip in twenty." Chen was especially irritable. Despite his best efforts to hide it, Leonardo could tell that the pressure was getting to him.

"We need to talk, please."

"What do you want?" Chen asked with exasperation, flipping the M4 carbine that the contractors had lent him in his hand and racking the bolt back several times. Leonardo doubted he'd ever used one before.

"This is insane. You know as well as I do that these sadistic bastards have orders to kill everyone up there. How can you go along with this?"

Chen turned to him furiously. "This is our *job*. I don't fucking care if you have a soft spot for these assholes. They're terrorists. Stark already killed *three men*, and he was about to kill you when these 'sadistic bastards' saved your life. I've been given my orders, the same as you, and I intend to follow them. Same. As. You."

"He wasn't going to kill me," Leonardo insisted. "Listen to me, man, this is fucked. Take me off the cordon and put me in the compound. I'm the only one who's been there."

Chen scoffed. "I have direct orders *not* to let you into that compound. You really pissed off some people with your over-the-top morality bullshit, Leo. You're sticking to the bench on this one."

"I'm the only one who knows the layout, goddammit!" Leonardo needed to convince Chen to let him go along, to put him in a position where he could prevent as many casualties as possible.

"No." Chen turned his attention back to the rifle in his hands.

"You're being a fucking idiot!" The dam of reason in Leonardo's head was giving way to a flood of anger. "How the hell do you think you'll be able to make it over that mountain in a night? They're playing you! You're going to be sitting on the wrong side of that mountain like a chump when they fly in and massacre those people. Terrorists or not, this *isn't right!* How are you going to explain when you show up a day late to a fucking bloodbath then get held responsible? Can't you see what's going on?"

"You always assume you know everything, huh, Leo? You really think we're going to climb that mountain?"

Leonardo paused. His thoughts scrambled over the past week's events as he tried to figure out what he'd missed. Chen seemed to revel in the confusion on his face.

After letting Leonardo stew for a moment, Chen spoke up. "We have intel from the Canadians. They picked up a woman on the other side of the border. She came to them, saying she'd escaped the Homestead and wanted to make a deal."

"What woman?"

"Some hot little piece of ass named Maya Russo. She said her and her hubby got roped into the whole thing by Stark, and offered us intel if we granted her and her husband immunity. You know what she gave up?"

The name hung heavy in Leonardo's mind.

Russo.

"How she got out," Leonardo muttered.

"Yeah. There's a pass that cuts through the mountain. She gave us a direct route to the Homestead from the east and the

Canadians are signing off on us using it. We're going to blindside them. Those terrorist fuckers won't know what hit them."

"Did your friends torture that information out of her?" Leonardo asked, disgusted.

Chen rolled his eyes. "Please, she's still in Canadian custody. These guys couldn't lay a finger on her if they wanted to."

"And you trust that she's jumped ship? That you aren't being played and that this isn't part of their plan?"

"Joe sent a team of five out last night. They've already scouted the area and we're in the clear. Apparently, she'd had enough with all the bullshit. No fury like a woman scorned, eh?" Chen's smile might have been revolting if it didn't betray how nervous he was about the whole situation.

"*Ephialtes…*" Leonardo muttered.

"What?"

"Nothing..." He tried desperately to come up with some argument, some way to convince Chen to see the light. "Chen, I've met this woman's husband. He was the one who showed me the Homestead. I can tell you with complete honesty that I do not believe he is the type of man that you think he is. Please tell me you plan on honoring that bargain. You *need* to keep these contractors from obliterating those people. If that happens, then you *know* this will spread, and *you'll* be the one who answers for it."

Chen pulled on a heavy flak jacket, another item lent to him by the contractors, and clipped the butt stock of the M4 to a carabiner on its front. He looked up at Leonardo and shook his head.

"You're bitching about stupid shit, Leo. The Director has already assured me that whatever the outcome, it will be dealt with accordingly. As long as I follow the contractors lead, we'll come out clean. Why are you having such a hard time following that?"

The antagonism in Chen's voice had waned. Leonardo suddenly realized the man's apprehension might not just be due to pre-mission jitters. He thought he saw some shred of mortality breaking through Chen's pompous exterior.

"You want to know where my head is at, Chen?" Leonardo asked, trying his best to appeal to the man's emotions. "We were sent here on a wild goose chase to help a corrupt man steal a piece of land. Things got shitty, people on both sides died. Now a bunch of bureaucrats who've never spilled a drop of blood in their lives are sending us to *slaughter* a group of people who haven't been convicted of anything. People who haven't even been given so much as an opportunity to explain themselves. They put you in charge when I resisted, and they're going to use you as a scapegoat when these trigger-happy assholes disappear into the wind. Ever heard of Waco? *That's* where my head's at right now."

Chen swallowed hard and for a second, Leonardo thought his words had broken through.

"I told you, I have personal assurances from the Director that whatever hap—"

"The Director is complicit in all of this! What the fuck is his *word* worth when he's about to let *this* happen?" Leonardo yelled.

"Apparently, it's worth an Assistant Director's position." Chen steeled his expression. "Move. I have a flight to catch."

****

Stephanie pushed the small brass .556 bullets into one of the dozen magazines spread on the table before her. Her fingertips were bright red and aching, but she'd finally reached the last one. Next to her, Oliver hummed as he gleefully distributed his own loadout: a hundred .50 caliber rounds for the hulking Barrett 82A1 that rested on the ground next to him.

She eyed the massive rifle. Never in the three years she'd spent in the Homestead had she seen it, and she had the sneaking suspicion that the boys had kept it hidden on purpose.

"We brought it up when we first started construction," Oliver said, noticing her staring.

"Why?"

"We figured it would be good to have around in case of bears. I mean, one shot from this baby, phew..." He pantomimed an explosion with his hands. "But in the end, we figured out that the best way to take a bear is with a good ole fashion hunting rifle. Doesn't destroy the meat."

"We've never eaten bear."

"*You've* never eaten bear."

"Neither have you."

"Shut up," Oliver grumbled, snatching the magazine out of her hands and looking down the twin rows of ammunition inside. "You should be loading the tracers every five rounds. Those ones, with the red tips. That way, if you see something we don't, you can point it out to us."

"Forgive me," she said sarcastically. "I'm new to this."

She'd been on a roll since the night before. After her brief episode of overwhelming panic, she'd made it a point to fake confidence for the sake of the others. In the past twenty-two hours, she'd made the dummies, helped build the flammable wall along the far side of the river, rigged the barn with enough gasoline to burn a whole town, thoroughly trashed everything inside of the BAS and, most importantly, she'd almost managed to convince herself that everything would be okay.

She took the magazine back from Oliver and finished loading it, then reached over and plucked one of his .50 caliber rounds off the table. Its cold metal casing filled her entire hand.

"Have you ever seen one of these hit someone?" she asked.

"Ohhh yeah…" Oliver gave a deviant chuckle.

She immediately decided to let that line of questioning end there.

The duo continued to prepare. Just as her stomach began to grumble, Russo's voice came over the radio clipped to the belt of her jeans.

"Guys, what's your favorite meat?"

They looked at each other, each knowing the other's response.

"Venison, duh," Stephanie said into the radio, drawing a grin from Oliver.

"My girl. When you're done in there, come out to the fire pit. Irniq's got the spit set up. I'm going to grab some meats from the cold storage in the BAS. Stephanie, you didn't destroy the cold storage yet, did you?"

"No," she responded. "I figured we'd have one last family dinner."

In reality, she'd totally forgotten the subterranean storage area dug into the BAS's basement. But she was glad she had.

Half an hour later, after she'd finished modifying her favorite winter jacket with a half dozen pockets to hold the freshly loaded magazines, Stephanie and Oliver emerged into the cool night air and crossed the empty compound to the fire pit. Irniq and Russo sat on chairs they had brought out of the residences, and Stephanie noticed they'd dragged Alwan's oversized recliner out for her.

She sat, sinking into the soft leather with relief. Aside from

Russo's short nap the night before, none of them had slept in what seemed like forever. The rich scent of the slowly spinning venison flank rolled over her, and she smiled at the others.

What a fucked up little dinner party.

"Like you said, Steph, our very own *Last Supper*." Russo chuckled.

"If only Stark was here to paint us," she mused.

She looked over and saw Oliver staring absentmindedly into the fire. The knowledge that the party carrying his son and wife still hadn't reported in was eating away at him.

"Remember when Oki was born?" Russo asked, clearly sensing the same thing.

"No shit I remember, dickhead." The garbled accent was back.

"What was it you said that made her slap you again?" Russo asked with a laugh. "The kid came out, and the first thing you said was 'aw shit' or 'babyshit' or something, right?"

"It was 'aw shit'," Stephanie interjected. "Alasie flipped out. Left a nice red handprint on your face if I remember right."

"She was mad that that was the first thing the little dickhead heard," Oliver said with a grin.

"Where did that even come from? Like the weird voice and all that?" Stephanie asked. She'd always wondered but no one seemed to know the answer.

"It's from an old internet series, the Tourettes Guy," Russo explained. "He was pretty much the first viral star, way back before all the social media bullshit. He'd talk like that and just say random shit and flip out for no reason. He was pretty much Oliver, but with more self-control."

"Shut up, dickhead."

"Ok," Stephanie said, mulling it over. "But why?"

"Now *that's* an enigma." Russo laughed. "We need a drink. I know we used most of the glass bottles for Molotovs, but there should still be a couple gallons of Oliver's piss-liquor holed up in the Koutla."

"It's toilet wine, you jerk." Oliver feigned indignation. "I know where it is. I'll grab it."

Oliver left and returned moments later with his questionably edible concoction. He passed a jug to each of them. Russo took a heavy swig, then coughed, spitting a mouthful into the fire, which ignited in a plume of flames.

"Jesus Christ! We should've rigged this in the garden!" Russo rasped out.

Oliver smiled and raised a pinky as he sipped daintily out of his own gallon jug.

"Do you think they made it through the mountain alright?" Irniq piped up from where he sat across the fire, sobering the group's attitude.

Russo cleared his throat several times. "They'll be fine. They've got Hunt to lead them. We knew there was a good chance they wouldn't be able to find a radio to call us on. This is one of those times where no news is good news."

"Except for Frank…" Irniq muttered.

"That's not your fault—" Stephanie said reactively, cutting herself off when Oliver glared at her.

"It *is* your fault, Irniq," Oliver said. "You're my brother-in-law and all, but I'm not going to coat it in daisies and kitten shits. What you did was about as fucked up as it gets."

Irniq slumped forward and stared at his feet.

"It happened. It's over. All that matters is tomorrow," Russo said, trying to shift the direction of the conversation.

"No. When we get out of here, *if* we get out of here, he's still my wife's brother. My son's uncle. I need to know, Irniq, was it worth it?" Oliver asked.

"Oliver! He's nineteen!" Stephanie ejaculated.

Oliver cut her off with a raised hand. "When we were his age we were fighting in a war. He's a fucking man. Irniq, do you love her? Is that what it is?"

Irniq shifted uncomfortably in his chair.

"This is your last chance to speak up, kid," Oliver said. "If you go under tomorrow, what you say now will define you."

Irniq spoke after a long pause. "I don't expect you to believe me, any of you. But yeah, yeah, I do love her. I swear I didn't mean for it to go down the way it did. You guys know I didn't really get much of an education growing up. I could hunt just about anything by the time I was ten, but I couldn't write a fucking letter to save my life. When I was fourteen they figured out I was dyslexic. That's when I dropped out. No bullshit public school is worth a two-and-a-half-hour commute when you can't even read your assignments.

"Emma... She was teaching me. She was a middle school teacher back in Massachusetts. It just kind of happened. I guess Frank wasn't really treating her right, and I got the feeling she didn't really want to be here. When it started... I don't know, man. I never meant to break the rules. I swear. I can't explain it looking back, but it felt right at the time..."

Irniq drifted off into silence, but when Stephanie glanced back at Oliver, she saw that his glare had softened.

"Things like this happen," she said tenderly. Irniq's situation was already delicate enough. There was no need to dwell on the past now. "Sometimes you can't help it. Frank died because he put his own anger in front of the group's safety. You didn't kill him." She paused and looked directly at Russo. "And neither did *you*. He killed himself when he swung that club. All we can do is try and remember him for who he was before all of that and focus on what's coming tomorrow."

What is *coming tomorrow?*

"I killed him," Russo stated flatly. "He chose his path and I put him in the dirt. It happens." He raised his jug. "To Frank Erikson: he was a decent man!"

Stephanie raised her own jug to the odd toast, then recoiled when the lukewarm moonshine rolled over her tongue.

Oliver raised his jug again after taking a heavy swig. "To Stark: for getting us back in the action!"

He and Russo laughed. They all drank.

"To the Homestead," Irniq bellowed from across the fire, raising his jug for a third time. "Our broken utopia!"

Stephanie could hardly breath after the third gulp, but she knew it was her turn. She raised the jug of nasty liquor before her and looked at each of the men. "To us. To our family over the mountain. And to tomorrow."

The men nodded approvingly and gulped Oliver's home-brewed moonshine.

That night, the four of them feasted on roasted venison flank, laughed heartily, and regaled each other with memories from a life they knew had come to an end. Afterwards, the men retired; Stephanie had volunteered to take the first shift of watch while they slept in the warmth of the Koutla.

She sat back in the plump leather recliner and gazed at the stars through the treetops above. As the fire died down, she pulled a thick wool blanket over herself. The winter came quickly in this part of the country, and despite the fact that the days were still moderately warm, she had little doubt that the first snow would come soon.

As she stared upwards at the glimmering dots in the sky, her mind wandered to Stark. He was alive after all. Wherever he was, he was alive, and maybe he was staring at that same night sky. The thought ignited a warmth in her belly that she hadn't felt in weeks.

There was still hope.

16

The Blackhawk helicopter was far less comfortable than the Bell 429 Leonardo had taken on his first incursion into the Homestead. The vibrating metal and canvas seats under him brought to mind the first time he had flown over the choppy lake that passed beneath them. Craning his neck to see out of the open side door, he wished he could recapture that sense of awe and splendor that had overtaken him only a week before. But it wasn't there. Instead, the approaching clearing seemed dark and foreboding in the early morning light.

The man standing between the two rows of seats, who told the FBI agents to simply refer to him as "Chief," held up two fingers.

Two minutes until they landed, then another two hours of trying to navigate the thick forest by GPS to set in the cordon. The secondary assault element, as Joe had so casually named it, had landed in the northwestern clearing hours before, and were currently halfway to the Homestead. Joe's own team, which included Chen, had called in moments before Leonardo's flight took off. They were nearly in position as well. As of yet, neither team had run into any trouble. Come eight o'clock, the two over-watch helicopters would assume their position, followed by the twin assault elements pinching down on the compound from either side.

The helicopter slowed as they approached the clearing, dropping down with a jolt onto the uneven terrain.

"Go! Go! Go! Get the fuck out! Go!" Chief screamed, pushing the agents forward as they scrambled to jump out of the mechanical beast.

Leonardo stumbled when he hit the ground; the rotor wash tossing him forward onto his face. By the time he pulled himself to his feet, the helicopter was already taking off, and within minutes it became a tiny speck in the southern sky.

"Let's go. We ain't got all day," a heavily tattooed contractor named Glen yelled out, waving for them to follow him to the tree line.

Leonardo knew that Glen wasn't his real name, just like "Joe" wasn't really "Joe." But it didn't matter. They all looked the same anyway: GI Joe figurines sporting sleeve tattoos and shirts five sizes too small to show off their roided out muscles to each other. They were doubtlessly veterans of the same wars that had shaped the men they now hunted.

The six contractors that reinforced Leonardo's own four-man team took off in a trot to follow their burly leader. Leonardo gave Ferrara a sidelong glance and shook his head before following them.

This is going to be bad.

****

Stephanie woke with a start to Oliver shouting over the radio. She was alone in the Koutla, curled up on a mattress next to the smoldering hearth. The radio next to her squawked incessantly as Oliver repeated the same call over and over again.

"Helos to the south! Helos to the south!"

She threw the wool blanket off and quickly donned her modified jacket, checking to make sure all of the magazines were secure before pulling the straps of her medical pack over her shoulders. Her mind raced over the situation at hand.

They were here. This was it.

She grabbed her AR-15 from the table and sprinted out of the Koutla, stopping immediately outside and scanning between the treetops.

Nothing.

Then she heard it: a faint chopping reverberated through the trees like a nightmarish war drum. The noise grew quickly until she made out two helicopters approaching low through the bristly pine tops.

Oh, Christ.

Oh, Jesus fucking Christ…

The façade she'd put up gave way and suddenly it was hard to breath. This was it. It was real. It was too real. They were coming to kill them.

She stumbled backwards, retreating into the Koutla without taking her eyes off the incoming helicopters. The warmth and security within the wooden walls did nothing to calm her. This was it.

She continued backwards, bumping against the table and leaning into it hard. The helicopters were loud now. She could hear their thumping rhythm pound the walls of the Koutla and encompass her. Her vision was suddenly blurry with tears. As she clenched her eyes shut, they cascaded down her cold cheeks.

From beside her came a soft voice.

"Yea, though I walk through the valley of the shadow of death, I will fear no evil."

She spun and stared at Russo. He knelt before the hearth,

his hand clasped around the golden crucifix that hung from his neck. He was praying. She'd never seen him pray.

"For thou art with me, thy rod and thy staff, they comfort me. Thou preparest a table before me in the presence of mine enemies. Give me the strength to protect these people. Please, give us the strength to do this…"

Stephanie watched, transfixed with terror as he rose and pulled the machete from its place above the mantle, looping the sheath through his belt. He drew the chipped, black blade and held it before him.

"I'm sorry I ever doubted you, brother," he whispered.

He slid the machete back into its sheath and picked up his AR-10. He turned to Stephanie and saw the horror in her face, then smiled sadly.

"Just stick to the plan, Steph. If it goes to shit, take an ATV and run. Don't look back."

With that, Russo disappeared through the door into the suddenly overwhelming brightness of the sunlit forest beyond.

******

"Five minutes," Russo muttered to himself as he jogged through the forest toward the garden.

The look on Stephanie's face had made him more nervous than anything else. He needed her to keep her shit together. The one thing that could undo all of this was the terror-stricken woman giving in to her panic.

He reached the wooded edge of the clearing and took his position, crouching behind a thick alder trunk and glancing at his watch.

4 minutes 27 seconds.

The timer ticked down slowly. Four and a half minutes

until they were atop their ATVs barreling away through the trees, leaving a fiery mess of chaos behind them.

If everything goes to plan.

The helicopters had done a lap above the Homestead and split up. One stuck above the paddock as the other swooped down low over the garden. Russo watched patiently as it came to a hover over the fire trap. The hanging wires had worked: the helicopter was forced to pick the one open landing zone.

Time stood still. Aside from the steady rhythm of the helicopter blades, the forest was completely silent. Russo raised the scope of his rifle up to his eye and watched the door along the side of the helicopter slide open. The men inside were outfitted in full battle rattle: black BDUs with ammo-laden flak jackets and rifles slung across their chests. Russo focused on the face of the nearest man as he leaned out of the helicopter and looked down. He was young, maybe Russo's age, with a long, scraggly beard and a shining bald head.

In another life, Russo could have been among them, a paid mercenary hired to get off on violence. Hell, at this point it didn't seem like the worst life path.

Russo watched through the crosshairs as the man stared at the ground thirty feet beneath him, then crouched back into the helicopter. A rush of adrenaline flowed through his veins. They were preparing to rappel.

Then the contractor emerged again, and Russo felt his heart plummet as the man tossed what appeared to be a cinderblock out the door toward the open earth below.

Without hesitation, Russo squeezed the trigger. The rifle bucked into his shoulder and the contractor collapsed backwards out of sight. In an instant, the earth beneath the helicopter erupted in a ball of fire as the cinderblock crashed down on the hidden plywood pressure plate. The curling flames launched skyward, licking the helicopter's bottom as it swung wildly to avoid them.

"Fuck."

The word was punctuated with the boom of Oliver's .50 caliber Barrett echoing from the paddock, immediately followed by a long burst of machine gun fire from above.

So it begins.

Russo followed the helicopter with his crosshairs as it rose above the garden. He squeezed the trigger of his rifle in a steady rhythm, focusing on controlling the adrenaline that coursed through him. The helicopter swung out in a short arc as his rounds clacked against its side, then disappeared behind the trees.

He grabbed his radio and spoke into it, trying to sound reassuring. "Irniq, you need to stay calm." Irniq had kept his head during the ordeal in Harkstaff. Now he could only hope the young man would match that as he hid in Stark's cabin. "You've got another two minutes before you light that shit. You copy?"

"Yeah," Irniq responded nervously. *"I got you man, I haven't see shi—"*

The radio cut out and keyed repeatedly. Oliver's screams broke through. *"The fucking Connex box ain't shit! They're cutting through this thing like paper!"*

Fuck.

Russo launched into action, sprinting away from the garden and toward the paddock where the repeated booms of Oliver's rifle were matched with the rattle of machine gun fire.

"Jesus fuckin' dicks! Jesus fuck, man!" Oliver's voice was desperate and shaky.

"Oliver!" Russo huffed out as he cut across the backside of the residence hall. "Oliver! Are you hit?"

"Motherfucker!" Oliver's roar warbled through the speaker as he unleashed a rapid series of .50 caliber rounds.

****

"Fuck this," Leonardo growled as he rose from his concealed position across the river from the small, outlying cabin. They'd held the cordon for nearly half an hour, but as the cacophony of gunfire kicked off across the rushing water he immediately lost his patience. "Ferrara, Tomlinson, Christoff, let's go!"

Glen the contractor grabbed his shoulder, but Leonardo tossed him off furiously. His agents leapt to their feet beside him and together they rushed forward toward the cabin. He *couldn't* just lay there and listen to this shit. Fuck the FBI. Fuck the Director. This was it. This was—

A distinct snap cut through the air and Ferrara screamed out in pain. She collapsed mid-stride and clutched her chest. Leonardo dove on top of her, bringing his shotgun to bear and searching the riverside ahead of him. From deep within the window of the cabin, he saw the flicker of a muzzle flash. Another snap. He heard the sound of shattering glass behind him and a wet substance splashed across his back. Another muzzle flash and a pocket of dirt exploded in his face.

In an instant, the air was filled with the sharp crackling of gunfire. Leonardo buried his face in the earth, doing his best to fully shield the squirming Ferrara beneath him. The stink of kerosene filled his nose and amid the deafening racket, he heard a heavy pop.

A brilliant light flashed above. Leonardo glanced skyward and watched a blinding orb dart over his head and into the forest from which they had emerged. Then there was the heat. Like the hot breath of a predator, it rushed over the nape of his neck as the trees behind him erupted in flame. He didn't stop to think how or what was happening. The only thing that rushed through his head was the innate understanding that they needed cover.

He scrambled through the dirt toward the river, blasting the semi-automatic shotgun from his hip, barely paying attention to where the 12-gauge buckshot landed. As he splashed into the knee-high swell, he caught the sizzling sound of flames being extinguished, and realized his back was on fire. He dove forward. The icy water sent a shock up his spine. Seconds later, he emerged on the opposite shoreline.

His soaked pants slapped heavily against his shins as he sprinted forward and dove head first into the cabin's open window, dropping the shotgun as he met the hard floor with a thud and wrestling his pistol from its holster.

The room was silent and still. Behind him, from the tree line, he heard the garbled screams of the contractors. A bright orange flare gun lay on the floor in front of him, still wafting a thin stream of smoke from its barrel. As his eyes adjusted to the darkness, he realized that the lump against the opposite wall was twitching. He stood and carefully approached it.

It was a young Inuit man. He couldn't have been more than twenty years old. His head flopped limply to the side and Leonardo saw one final, weak string of blood spray out from a gaping hole in his chest.

Behind Leonardo, the cabin door crashed open. He spun, pistol raised.

"Woah! Woah! Leo, it's us!" Tomlinson shouted, holding his hands up. Christoff shuffled in behind him with Ferrara draped across his shoulders.

"Put her on the table," Leonardo ordered, swiping a handful of rubbish off the cabin's one raised surface. "Where's she hit?"

"Ribs. Cut through her jacket like butter," Christoff grunted as he lowered her gently onto the table. "Her lung's collapsing — Holy fuck!" He spun and yanked out his sidearm, firing wildly into the already dead body.

"Stop!" Leonardo roared. "He's dead!"

Christoff stared at the corpse, perplexed. After a second, it twitched again and he swung the pistol back up.

Leonardo batted it down. "He's fucking dead, you imbecile!"

"Jesus Christ…" Christoff muttered in horror.

"I need plastic wrap and tape, *right now*," Tomlinson yelled. He was entirely focused on Ferrara. He'd pulled off her bullet-proof vest and ripped away her shirt. Blood pooled beneath her on the table and poured over its edge onto the floor.

She gasped in short, choppy breaths and clung to Leonardo's hand, staring up at him and desperately clawing at her chest. Outside the window beside him, the tree line raged bright orange.

****

Stephanie leaned back into the Koutla's table. She hadn't moved an inch since Russo had disappeared outside, but she'd heard it all. The radio at her side squawked furiously.

"Irniq!"

"Irniq!"

Russo was screaming. She could hear him firing in the paddock both through the speaker and through the open door.

"Stephanie!"

She knew he was calling her, but she couldn't move. Her hands were frozen, clenching the side of the table behind her.

"Stephanie! Goddammit, answer me!"

It's ok…

It's ok…

It's ok…

It's ok…

"Stephanie! We're fucking dying here! Get to the ATVs! Now!"

The ATVs…

The ATVs…

The forest…

The escape…

She had to move. She had to will herself to move.

"The forest is on fire! Oliver, I'm covering you, get to the barn!"

She slowly unclenched her hands and stood upright.

"Oliver!"

Get to the ATVs…

In the barn…

She walked forward, focusing her mind on the barn that lay only a dozen yards away.

"Oliver, goddammit, can you fucking hear me?"

The rifle…

She remembered the AR-15 on the table behind her. She turned and picked it up. It felt so heavy in her small hands.

"Stephanie," the voice through the radio was suddenly calm. *"Stephanie, please. We need you. Get to the barn and cover us. I need to go get Oliver. We need you."*

The gentleness of his voice cut through the fog of terror in her mind. She pulled the rifle to her chest and ran forward out the door. The barn was close. It only took her a few seconds to cross the courtyard and then she was back inside. The warm air and rich scent of manure filled her senses and, for a second, she was back home on her father's farm in Montana.

The horses bucked frantically in their stalls, their dummy

riders wobbling on their backs. She knew they must smell the same wood smoke drifting in from the west that she did.

On the other end of the barn, through the two wide open doors that lead outside, she saw the low flying helicopter skirting the opposite side of the paddock. It lit up as a side-mounted machine gun blasted holes in the Connex box at the clearing's center.

Russo was in the field.

He was running to the Connex box.

The machine gun cut off for a fraction of a second, then suddenly the dirt around the sprinting figure exploded in a flurry of gunfire.

****

Russo poured every ounce of his strength into each bounding stride. He'd never been much of a sprinter. In high school he ran cross country, and in the Marines he was accustomed to regular PT. Even in Afghanistan, in the midst of firefights he'd always considered himself to be a slow sprinter.

But not now.

His legs blurred underneath him as rounds snapped by. One glanced across his back, drawing a stabbing pain. Another slammed into his arm, tearing a hole through his bicep. It didn't matter. He was almost there.

He reached the Connex box and heaved the door open. A burst of machine gun fire clacked against the heavy door. Oliver lay on the sleek metal floor illuminated by a hundred slivers of light cutting through the bullet holes that riddled the double-layered steel box's side. He was curled in a ball clutching one of his legs and his stomach simultaneously. He looked up at Russo, his face a mask of confusion.

"I thought you said this shit was bulletproof, you fucking asshole!"

"Oh, Jesus… I thought it was," Russo muttered, more to himself than to his friend. Another burst of bullets ripped through the container's side, sending him sprawling in the growing puddle of Oliver's blood.

The dirt bike that had been Oliver's planned escape leaned against the far wall but the stench of gasoline immediately gave away the fact that its tank had been ruptured by the onslaught of bullets. Another barrage of fire cut a dozen more illuminated holes in the sidewall.

They were pinned down. There was no way Russo would be able to carry Oliver out of there and avoid the machine gun. Stephanie and Irniq weren't responding. This storage container would be their coffin.

He looked up at Oliver, who gave him a pathetic smile.

"I guess this is it, huh, dickhead?" Oliver croaked out in his gravelly voice, wincing as he spoke.

Russo couldn't help but grin in disbelief. The man was a legend. It was too bad nobody would live to tell about his last brave face.

"Run!"

At first, Russo thought he'd hallucinated it. He grabbed the radio from his belt and held it close to his ear as another barrage tore through the steel. A jagged piece of shrapnel drove into his arm.

"*Run! Now!*"

It was Stephanie, and it was real. Without hesitation, he leapt to his feet and pulled Oliver over his shoulder into a fireman carry. He heard the pop of her AR-15 belching rounds at the low hanging helicopter.

****

She could feel the spring in the rifle's stock recoiling and almost believed she could hear it constricting and stretching out under her cheek in slow motion. The deafening noise of its discharge, which had always been so abrasive when Stark taught her to shoot, seemed nonexistent as the distinct scent of burning grease and gun powder flooded her palate.

Her panic had evaporated when she had watched the rounds cut the earth around Russo, replaced by an incredible, protective tranquility.

Hammered pairs, she thought, taking aim at the helicopter's cabin and squeezing the trigger in consecutive, twin bursts. The machine gun mounted on its side momentarily stopped firing; she knew its gunner was searching for her.

The butt stock clapping back into her shoulder was calming. She watched as one of her tracer rounds arced over the field and bounced off the craft's windshield. The machine gun began again, and behind her the penned goats screamed as bullets snapped by.

Hammered pairs...

Russo had emerged from the Connex box, Oliver draped over his shoulder. He ran toward her.

Hammered pairs...

The rifle clicked in her hands. She needed to reload. She took a knee and grabbed one of the magazines from her jacket. She pressed the button on the rifle's side and watched the empty one slide out and clatter to the floor. As she calmly replaced it, the machine gun ceased, and the noise from the helicopter suddenly changed. She pressed the bolt release on the rifle's side, just as she had been taught. The bolt slid into place with a clack. She brought the rifle back up and took aim.

Just as she realigned the iron sights with the helicopter, it crashed sidelong into the opposing tree line with a resounding crunch. She lowered the rifle, watching in awe as the blades snapped off and flew away into the air while the fuselage tumbled haphazardly to the earth. In an instant, the paddock was silent.

Russo stumbled up to her, Oliver's blood cascading over his shoulders and down his shirt. He gave her a bewildered look, then stared back at the mangled heap of smoking metal.

"You beautiful woman. You beautiful fuckin' woman..." Russo rambled, unable to believe his eyes.

She wasn't quite sure what had happened. Something inside of her had snapped while watching Russo on the verge of death, almost cut down a dozen times on his mad dash to save Oliver. Something had changed inside of her. She found not only the will, but the need to fight back.

Nobody hurt her family.

As the strange new confidence washed over her, a bullet snapped by.

"Come on!" Russo grabbed a flare gun from one of the stalls and fired it into the waiting bale of hay.

Who was shooting? The helicopters were gone...

Another round snapped by and glanced the side of her pack, sending her spinning to the ground. She snatched her rifle back up and ran after Russo, slapping open the locks to the animal stalls as she passed.

The hay ignited quickly. The room was already filling with smoke as they made it to the end of the barn and released the panicking horses. Russo laid Oliver across the back of his ATV, which sat ready just inside the barn's side door.

"Load up, we're fucking out," he yelled to Stephanie. She leapt aboard her own, slamming the ignition and feeling the large steel beast between her legs roar to life.

"What about Irniq?" she called out above the din.

"He knows the fallback plan! If anyone can survive out

here, it's him!" Russo yelled back, and gunned the ATV out the door.

Their plan had been simple: to take one of three eastern hunting paths directly to the mountain pass where they would ditch the ATVs and disappear into the ravine. Aside from Irniq's disappearance, things seemed to be going as planned. But as Stephanie emerged from the barn, she saw something that made her heart stand still.

The entrance to the paths, *all* the paths, were lined with dark figures.

****

Stark huddled against the cold concrete of the cell wall. His heart pounded in his ears. His hands shook almost as violently as his jaw. A warm tingle clawed its way from his arms up to his scalp. The impotent rage that coursed through his veins was amplified by his inability to affect any change on the situation that was doubtlessly unfolding a hundred miles away.

Any capacity for joy had left him, and he was sure it could never return. His body seemed to be a vessel filled solely with hate. His regularly clear stream of consciousness ran thick with the mud of anxiety and his thoughts were few and hard to grasp for long enough to formulate an even somewhat comforting thought.

This was hell.

There was nowhere to go, nothing to do as the people he loved faced the odds of an excruciating death. His chest was strung so tight he thought he might snap. What would happen? What could happen? Would he die?

He wished.

Anything was better than this.

Fuck, *anything* was better than this.

As a man who believed he'd forsaken the ability to love, he suddenly recognized that he had miscalculated his own hard exterior. He loved. He loved deeply and thoroughly. He loved the family he'd created, his friends, his people. He loved every aspect of them. He loved them with every bit of himself. He realized in that horrible moment of agony that those people he had devoted every fiber of his soul to were on the brink of death, and not only was he incapable of saving them, but it was his fault.

And he hated himself for it.

He resigned himself to the hate. He let it corrupt every cell, every atom, every neuron. He let it become his food, his water, his religion, his soul. He accepted it fully, just like he had accepted it three years before.

He sat alone in the cold, dry cell and stared helplessly at his violently shaking hands.

The world didn't exist anymore. Nothing was real except the pain. He vomited, coughing up a thin stream of yellow bile. His stomach clenched. Clouds of confused anger suffocated his brain.

He didn't notice the muffled gunshots. He didn't notice Deputy Carr's agonizing scream cut short with a heavy thud. He didn't even notice the door to the sheriff's office swing open, or the three Hispanic men enter the hallway outside his cell.

A familiar voice brought him back from his tortured daze.

"Jesus, bro, long time no see."

He looked up slowly. His heartbeat pounded in his head, making the visage of the tall, square-jawed man before him throb along with it.

"You look like shit," the man said. He was well-built, sporting a plain black jacket and a pair of nondescript jeans.

In his hands he held a short, black assault rifle, its suppressor still pouring a thin line of smoke.

"You're too late…" Stark muttered, swallowing hard and shaking his head.

"Too late for what?" the man asked with a grin.

"Never mind…"

"So that's it? I come all the way up here to see my old boot camp buddy and you just brush me off? *Tsk tsk.*" The man wagged his finger, then took up a faux hurt look. "Don't tell me you've forgotten about me, devil dog?"

Stark hadn't forgotten the man. He'd haunted Stark's nightmares for the past three years. Every night Stark killed this man. Every night he bathed in this man's blood in the moonlight of his dreams.

"Juan, you got fat," Stark growled at him.

Juan laughed, looking at the stone-faced men that flanked him with a smile.

"You always did know the best way to get to people, huh?"

"Who the hell are you?" Tulimak spoke up from the next cell over.

Juan shook his head and pointed one of his men down the hall. A second later, the muffled thud of a suppressed rifle sounded. Stark winced as Tulimak let out a yelp. Another thud, then silence.

"I do hate interruptions." Juan leaned back against the opposite wall. "Now, what in the ever-living hell happened that made you call *us*? You had to have known that it wouldn't end well, right?"

"I have a deal for you." Stark met Juan's eyes for the first time. They were bright blue in stark contrast to his deep brown skin. Stark couldn't help but remember back to when he'd first met the man as rack mates in boot camp nearly a decade before.

"Oh, a deal? What kind of deal?" Juan asked. "You know, we heard you made off like a bandit with that little bitch's inheritance. Is that your bargaining chip?"

Stark felt nothing at the comment. He was already too full of hate. "Yeah. Just over a hundred million. It's yours, and so am I. All you have to do is kill a man."

"And just who am I supposed to kill?"

"An old fucker named Masterson. He's three buildings down across the street in the inn. Kill him, bring me his head, and I'll have the money transferred. Then you can kill me too."

Juan considered the proposal for a moment. "Why?"

Stark didn't answer.

"Why?" Juan's voice was hardening. Stark knew the chipper demeanor was a façade. Juan held just as much hate toward him as he had for Juan.

"For a hundred million you don't need to know why."

"Fuck your money." Juan spat on the ground. "Augustin Stark, killer of women and children. The scourge of the Habila Cartel... What the fuck have you gotten yourself into up in this shithole state? If killing this motherfucker is worth that much money to you, then letting him live is worth twice as much to me. Hell, I want to shake his fucking hand."

Stark's whole body tensed. They'd gotten here too late. It was all for nothing if Masterson didn't die too.

Juan leaned forward off the wall and grasped one of the thick steel bars. "You know," he whispered, "I don't blame you for killing my father. I don't even blame you for killing my brother. Retribution is part of the game. It's something men like me have to accept, doing the things I do.

"But I do blame you for murdering my mother. For murdering my sisters. For murdering my woman. I took something away from you, something small, some insignificant whore, and you burned my *fucking life*. Getting up here was a pain in the ass, trust me, but I enjoyed the flights and layovers, the long ass ride down the shit roads from Fairbanks, because I spent every second fantasizing about how I was going to slowly strip the skin from your bones, cut off your nasty little white pecker and make you choke on it. I had plans, man, big plans…"

He stopped, and looked directly into Stark's eyes.

"But I'm not going to do any of that. I mean, *look at you.* You're fucking miserable. Seeing you now, I know that there's nothing more I can do to you that wouldn't be some sort of relief. You *wish* I'd kill you." Juan gave a thin smile. "And that's why I won't."

"What are your bosses going to say when they find out you skipped out on a nine-figure payday?" Stark spat back.

Juan laughed. "When I tell them about the state you're in, they'll fucking applaud me. This is worth way more than money, even to them. Do you not remember what you did to them? *To their families?* Motherfucker, you are the most wanted man in the world as far as they're concerned. Don Marco lost his fucking mind after he came home and saw what you did to his wife. The man literally thinks you're *El Diablo* for Christ's sake! …No, you'll stay right here, or wherever they send you next. And we'll be watching, waiting, and enjoying as you *rot* from the inside out."

Stark rose and threw himself at the bars. Juan darted back deftly, holding his hand out to halt his accomplices, who had raised their rifles.

"It won't be fun, *hombre.* A long time ago we were brothers, then I fucked you over. You came back and destroyed everything I cared about, but you spared me, knowing full well that you left me an empty shell of a man… Now I have the *pleasure* of returning the favor."

Juan smiled wide and turned to leave.

"*Sackless bastard!*" Stark roared, stretching through the bars in a desperate attempt to grab him.

But he was gone just as immediately as he had appeared. From the open door to the sheriff's office, Stark could see the growing pool of blood around Carr's lifeless corpse.

He fell to his knees, grabbing the bars in front of him and smashing his head against them. Each mind-numbing strike brought a jolt of pain through his forehead and soon his face streamed with blood. Finally, he collapsed backwards, his mind racing clumsily through the storm of rage. He tried to cling to the throbbing pain of his head — it was so much better than the pain in his mind. Then a single thought cut through the fog. Something Irniq had said over the radio… *Gen-pop is out…*

They got out.

Stephanie got out.

Stephanie was safe.

Amid the teeming forces of overwhelming emotions, he decided right there, in that moment, that he was desperately, completely in love with her.

At least she's safe.

****

She knew they were trapped.

Russo had seen the men blocking their path as well, and in a split-second decision they had bailed from their escape plan and made for the residence hall. Together they carried Oliver inside the building's main room. No sooner had they entered than a deep voice projected from beyond the windows to the east.

"Stop! We know you're in there. Come out with your

hands above your heads if you want to live!"

They set Oliver down on the hardwood floor and she looked at Russo. His face was expressionless as he surveyed Oliver's wounds.

"What do we do?" she asked.

He gave her a stony glare. "They're gonna kill us, Steph. I'll hold them off for as long as I can while you patch him up. When he's ready to move, we light this bitch and go straight through them."

It was a bad plan, but she didn't have anything better.

"Yeah," she muttered, then tore away Oliver's clothes to see where he'd been hit.

"You have until the count of three!" the voice outside continued. "One!"

"Stephanie," Russo said, grabbing her arm. She looked back up at him. "He'd be proud of you. *I'm* proud of you."

"Two!"

The words burned like fuel inside her.

"Three!"

Russo squeezed her arm, then spun and raised his rifle, firing out the window. In a second, the room was full of noise and broken glass. Russo darted back and forth along its length, popping up to return fire at the oncoming horde.

Oliver's stomach bore a gaping wound and his left leg was nearly severed from a direct hit to the femur. She pulled off her medical pack and dumped it on the floor in front of her, madly sifting through its scattered contents in search of a tourniquet. She found one, a small nylon and Velcro ring with a plastic shaft attached. She slipped it up over Oliver's spasming thigh and wrenched it tight as close to his hip as possible.

He was muttering something. At first, she couldn't make out the words, but as she spun the small plastic rod to tighten the tourniquet, she realized she'd heard him sing it many times before.

"Show me the way to go home... I'm tired and I want to go to bed..."

She shifted her attention to the cavernous wound on his stomach, grabbing a bottle of water from the pack's side and dumping it on the quivering flesh to wash away the blood.

"I had a little drink about an hour ago, and it went straight to my head... Bum, bum, bum."

His abdominal wall had been ruptured. This was an exit wound — she could tell by the way his organs had exploded outwards.

"Wherever I may roam, on land or sea or foam..."

She grabbed a piece of gauze from the scattered instruments in front of her and pressed down on the bleeding mass. Oliver winced, but kept singing even as his voice grew weaker.

"You'll always hear me singing this song, yeah, show me the way to go home..."

Russo was reloading. The gunfire from outside stopped but the threat of countless rifles focused on the windows, waiting patiently for a shot, loomed over them. Stephanie got the distinct feeling that the dark figures outside knew they had the three of them cornered, and didn't want to bother wasting any more ammo.

"Stephanie," Oliver rasped weakly. She looked up from his wounds and saw that his face was smeared with tears. She'd never seem him cry. Hell, she'd never seen him do anything emotional. He was Oliver, the man who laughed in the face of danger and acted like a clown.

But not now. Streams of crystal clear teardrops cut through the blood and grit that coated his cheeks. His face clenched in desperate confusion, and he grabbed at her hands weakly.

"I don't want to die, Stephanie…" His voice was frail and cracking.

No.

He threw his head back against the floor and let out a gasping whimper, croaking out his son's name and shaking violently as sobs racked his body.

NO!

She stood. He was not dying here. Not this way, covered in his own innards and wailing. He was going to live, *goddammit*. She wouldn't let some faceless bastards take something so twisted and brilliant and beautiful from the world.

****

Russo heard Oliver's wail behind him. Stephanie had him, though. Russo needed to keep the wolves at bay. They had stopped returning fire moments before. He knew they probably had a secondary element circling the back of the residence hall in order to storm them. He needed to move fast. Popping up into the window, he fired a quick burst into one of the copses of trees he'd seen a man duck behind. They needed to make a break for it. One of the kerosene jars was just below the window. If he could break it somehow, and use the flare gun at his hip, then maybe they could escape behind the flames.

There was a snap as a bullet passed by, then behind him, something thumped to the ground.

He ignored it.

It could be anything.

Please, it could be anything.

Please, God, let it be something else…

"No!" Oliver's rasping cry confirmed Russo's fears. He turned slowly and saw her. She was laying on her back. Her golden-brown hair spread like a halo around her face, a dark pool of blood slowly seeping through it. One arm was splayed out to the side, while the other lay limp across her chest. A single crimson bullet hole marred her beautiful face.

The room was silent, and from somewhere outside Russo heard a triumphant voice shout, "I got one!"

Oliver gasped in pain as he tried to pull himself up, dragging his body toward Stephanie. Russo dropped to his knees and saw a hunk of pink flesh flop out of Oliver's torn shirt. It was his intestine.

Oliver pulled himself on top of Stephanie, resting his head on her chest and gasping in short, rapidly weaker breaths. Russo watched in stunned silence as his friend's breathing stopped.

Russo was alone.

****

They'd managed to stabilize Ferrara. Leonardo had ordered Tomlinson and Christoff to get her to the paddock area to be evacuated while he skirted the compounds to find Chen. He passed the flaming barn and emerged to the east behind a row of contractors. One spun and leveled a rifle at him.

"FBI, you cocksucker!" Leonardo shouted.

The contractor shook his head disapprovingly and barked for him to get down. Leonardo ignored him, scanning the dozen men crouched behind the cover of the trees. He spotted Chen, balled in the fetal position behind a mound of dirt.

He crossed between the trees, ignoring the constant

barking orders of the contractors to *get down* and *take cover*. There was no one shooting at them — the residence hall they faced was silent.

Chen was shaking uncontrollably when Leonardo grabbed him and flipped him over onto his back. The large man cowered beneath him.

"What the fuck is going on here?" Leonardo demanded.

Chen stared at him blankly. He was in shock.

"He's got sand in his pussy," Joe laughed from nearby. Leonardo looked at the man; he was grinning. This was just another day for him.

"We've got at least three pinned down inside. My guys think they tagged one of them. Now, for Christ's sake, get the fuck down before you get popped."

"What's your plan?" Leonardo asked evenly, remaining in place.

Joe sighed. "Moron... We lost contact with the western element—"

"They're dead."

"What!"

Leonardo pointed to the ocean of smoke flowing skyward beyond the roof of the residence hall. "Everything west of that river is burning. The men you left with me are dead, and the others are either falling back or dead too."

"Goddammit," Joe muttered, as if it was a simple inconvenience. "It doesn't matter right now. We have a team circling around to punch into the other side of the building and take 'em out."

"Call them off," Leonardo ordered.

Joe scoffed.

"Do it *now*. I don't give a fuck who you are or who you have behind you. I'm a federal agent, and I know your face. Either you call them off or I'll make it my life's mission to make sure that everyone in the fucking world knows what you did here today."

Joe laughed at him. "You don't know shit, you fed fuck. This forest is about to burn like a tinder box and we need to get this over with and exfil. Don't you understand that, you stupid bitch?"

Leonardo had heard enough. He turned and stepped out into the open area that bordered the residence hall. Behind him a handful of voices shouted for him to get back, but he ignored them.

"Russo!" he yelled out, praying that the man wouldn't pop up from beyond the window and cut him down. "It's Agent Leonardo! They're coming to kill you! Have your people surrender now and I *swear* I won't let them!"

The area was silent aside from the distant crackling of flames.

"Russo, please!" Leonardo called out.

The nearside door to the residence hall swung open. Russo stumbled out. He was drenched in deep red blood. His left hand hung limp at his side, but in the right, he clenched the machete that Leonardo recognized from the Koutla.

"Andrew…" Leonardo started softly, but he stopped.

The look on the man's face wasn't wild, it wasn't defeated, it wasn't even angry. It was dead. There was nothing: no hate or rage or trauma. He limped forward toward Leonardo, holding the machete at his side.

"Andrew, stop…" Leonardo continued softy, his hand drifting to the pistol on his hip. "Your wife, Andrew, think of Maya…"

The name did nothing to cut through the apathy displayed on the man's features.

"We have her, she turned herself in for your immunity. Please, think of her, think of the others. Just stop…"

Russo continued forward, slowly crossing the thirty-foot gap between them. Leonardo drew his pistol and leveled it.

"Russo, please. I don't want to do this. Please stop." Leonardo's voice cracked.

Russo closed in, and Leonardo saw a tear streak down his face.

Jesus.

It wasn't apathy.

He's already dead.

"I'm sorry…" Leonardo whispered, and the pistol bucked in his hand.

Russo fell.

17

Same Day

Leonardo flew back to Harkstaff on the last helicopter to leave the paddock. By the time he'd climbed aboard the bullet-riddled metal craft, the fire from the barn had spread, encompassing the Koutla and the residence halls. They had left the bodies where they lay to be incinerated by the cleansing flames.

As the craft rose above the forest, Leonardo looked down on the infernal blaze. The trees west of the river were fully engulfed in a raging forest fire. Tiny flecks of white floated down around them. At first Leonardo assumed it was ash, but as they left the area, he realized that the snow had started. It felt eerily appropriate as they sped away through the thick smoke that wafted over the treetops. Hell was freezing over.

Leonardo tried not to focus on the events that had just transpired, instead shifting his mind to the matter at hand; they'd only accounted for six of the Homesteaders including Stark and Maya Russo. Somewhere across the Canadian border, a whole mess of people had escaped. The contractors knew it, his team knew it, and the brain trust in Washington doubtlessly knew it too.

Then there was Stark. Leonardo held no illusions that the man would survive the night. As far as the masked forces pulling the strings were concerned, Stark had no doubt become a loose end. Leonardo had seen too much death that day, and as the helicopter touched down back on Harkstaff's airstrip, he knew that there was no way he could let them take Stark out.

Tomlinson was once again waiting for him on the tarmac when he climbed out of the helicopter.

"How is she?" Leonardo asked as they climbed into the waiting SUV.

"She'd still stable. The contractors stopped here to refuel and then flew her and the other wounded to Fairbanks. They think she's gonna make it."

Leonardo nodded his head gratefully.

"Something happened while we were gone, Leo."

"Stark?"

"He's alive... But the sheriffs, all of them, they're dead."

"What?"

"Tulimak too. Someone took out everyone in the station except Stark, then disappeared."

"How the fuck—"

"They left a note." Tomlinson pulled a crumpled wad of paper out of his pocket and handed it to Leonardo.

To our dear friends, whoever you are. Blame Mr. Stark for these corpses. Needless to say, they are just a few more names to add to the impressive list of death and destruction he has left behind him in his short 28 years. Please treat him nicely. Or don't. Either way, we'll be watching.

The note ended with a crudely draw smiley face winking at them.

"Do we have any idea who did this?" Leonardo asked in disbelief as they pulled up next to the inn.

Tomlinson shook his head. "All we know is that the innkeeper says he saw four 'darkies' leaving the station at around 10 AM.

Leonardo looked at the sheriff's station down the road. He could see the rest of his team, besides Chen, combing through it, searching for any clues as to who had added this new aspect of bloody chaos to the day.

"*This* motherfucker…" Tomlinson muttered.

Masterson walked out of the inn. His ghoulish subordinate, Franklin Summerset, followed him dragging an oversized suitcase. Masterson avoided meeting Leonardo's eyes as he walked toward a parked truck.

"Masterson." Leonardo climbed out of the SUV. The man ignored him.

Leonardo felt everything well up inside of him at once. He stormed over and slammed his fist against the truck's door as Masterson tried to open it.

"Where the fuck do you think you're going?" Leonardo demanded.

Masterson stared up at him in feigned shock. "I'm leaving, Agent. Is there a problem?"

"Yeah, there's a goddamn problem!" Leonardo came back, then realized that he had no legal ability to keep the old piece of shit from fleeing.

"And it is…?" Masterson asked slowly.

Leonardo paused, his brain scrambling. He glanced over the hood of the truck at the sheriff's station.

"Do you know what happened in there?"

"I heard," Masterson replied dryly.

"This whole town is compromised to hell. We can't keep Stark here any longer — the body count is already ridiculous. Death follows that man like a dog. I need you to take him to Fairbanks with you."

Masterson scoffed.

"*Think about it.* This place is about to turn into a blizzard, and God only knows how long it will take me and my team to deal with this mess. He *can't* be here. I know you have space on your helicopter. I'll provide an escort and—"

"Absolutely not." Masterson shook his head. "This is ridiculous. What the hell makes you think I'd let that animal onto my helicopter?"

Leonardo leaned in. "Because you and I both know this whole ordeal needs a fall guy. It's too big now for it to be just brushed under the rug. This hellhole will be teaming with reporters the second they get wind of this shit, and if you think for a second they won't latch onto the overly involved oil magnate as a bad guy, you're high as a fucking kite. *You* need Stark to live. *You* need him to be breathing so he can take the blame. If he gets on a helicopter with those contractors, especially after his people just slaughtered a dozen of theirs, he won't make it to Fairbanks."

Masterson mulled it over as he stared at the sheriff's station.

"Fifteen minutes," Leonardo insisted. "I'll give you Chen, he's no good to us here anyways. We'll chain Stark like an animal and Chen will be there the whole time. You know this has to happen."

Masterson gave a resigned sigh and nodded. "Have him to the airstrip in ten minutes. Any longer and I won't wait. I'm not getting stuck here by a blizzard."

Leonardo knocked twice on the truck's hood. "Good. Good. Ten minutes."

Masterson climbed into the oversized truck and drove away toward the airstrip.

"We're really sending Stark back with those assholes?" Tomlinson asked.

"Yeah, we don't have much of a choice," Leonardo replied. "Get him ready for transport. I'll meet you by the station in five minutes. I need to get these clothes off — they're soaked and it's freezing."

Two minutes later, Leonardo pulled on a thick blue cotton sweatshirt with the FBI insignia emblazoned on the chest. He looked down at it with disgust. In his fifteen years with the Bureau, amid all the bullshit he'd seen, he'd never come to hate the organization as he did now. As he pulled a pair of sneakers from his suitcase, his eyes wandered to the cardboard box on the desk. The words *Stark Evidence* were written in Ferrara's elegant handwriting across its front. He walked over and pulled off its lid. The contents were sparse, just the clothes and a few items Stark had been carrying on him when he was arrested.

Leonardo thought back to his first impression of Stark: a pompous, insane millionaire terrorist with a shit attitude. He played out their conversation in his head. The last words echoed through his mind.

Stark had called it.

Leonardo was the bad guy.

****

The black FBI SUV pulled up next to Masterson's helicopter. Stark sat in the back seat next to Leonardo. Leonardo had not spoken a word since Stark was dragged out of his cell in chains and tossed into the seat next to him. But the man's silence betrayed his regret.

Chen was waiting by the helicopter's door when the other agents pulled Stark out of the vehicle. Leonardo exited the

SUV and gave Stark one final pat down before nodding to the tall Asian man.

"Get in," Chen said. His voice was weak, almost as if the perpetual chip on his shoulder was gone.

Stark climbed into the luxurious aircraft and settled into the heavily cushioned seat across from Masterson. They sat facing each other as Chen climbed aboard and took his place beside Stark.

Over Masterson's shoulder, Stark watched the pilot flick a series of switches and the helicopter hummed to life. As the blades began gaining momentum, Franklin Summerset let out an uncomfortable grunt next to Masterson.

He would be scared of flying.

"You know," Masterson said solemnly, staring at Stark's face. "I told you I'd win. This could have all been avoided had you taken my offer in the first place."

Stark was silent, focusing on Masterson's beady eyes.

"It's going to be hard for you to accept, but this is all your fault. Those people that died, *all of them,* that's on you," Masterson went on as the helicopter rose. The confidence in his voice showed that he truly believed the statement.

Chen leaned forward and spoke politely. "Sir, I have to ask that you not speak with the prisoner."

Masterson laughed. "Oh, calm down, Chen. You've got a promotion coming your way!"

Chen sat back in his seat uncomfortably.

"Ok, ok, my friend. I'll do as you ask. But first there's something I need to find out, something I've been dying to know since this whole ordeal started. Permit me one question?"

Chen nodded.

"Fantastic." Masterson turned back to Stark, giving the scabbed wound where his ear had been a disgusted look. "I see they did work on you, boy. I want to know, though, how was it that you came into Anders Muller's land and fortune? You see, I knew the man. He was a self-righteous prick, almost as much so as you. One of his companies did some work for me decades ago. That's how I came to find out about this pretty little piece of land up here. Did you know he inherited this straight down from his great-great-grandfather? That family owned it since long before this land was even part of the United States. It was their little fallback, their inaccessible hunk of wilderness that their family clung to for generations. He told me off a dozen times when I tried to buy it from him, and when I found out he'd passed... Well, let's call it what it was, when he *killed himself,* I knew it was time that land was mine.

"Of course, this whole mess will take a couple years to blow over, but soon enough I'll have my prize. Through some friends in the law enforcement and intelligence communities I've learned that you had it in with his daughter before she disappeared. Tell me, did you kill her?"

Stark shook his head and smiled.

"Oh, come on now, boy, you're already off the deep end. Just tell me the truth: how did you steal that inheritance?"

"It's a long story," Stark began. His voice was raspy as he tried to organize the narrative in his head.

"We've got, what, two hours? Go ahead, don't be shy." Masterson flashed a patronizing grin.

"Alright. I'll tell you, but I don't think you'll like where it ends." Stark returned the smile. "I was a deviant growing up, and the Corps didn't help. But in college, I met Paige. That girl turned my life around. Since the first day we hooked up, we were inseparable: two broken, fucked up kids who only had each other. I was in a bad place back then and so was she. One night she OD'd on coke. Her dad said he was going to disown her if she didn't get her shit together. So, we decided to take a year off, travel the world, and get our heads on straight."

Stark leaned back on his cuffed hands, noting the surprise on Masterson's face that he'd opened up so easily. "We did Europe in a few months, had an incredible time, fell even deeper in love... That girl was the one good thing in a world of shit... But we wanted something more, not the cobblestone streets of London or the flooded alleys of Venice. That wasn't the *world,* those were just *places.* We needed something more visceral, an escape from modern life. So, we flew down to Argentina in the middle of the summer and worked our way from village to village, backpacking through the jungles and just living.

"By the time we hit Mexico, she'd gotten a little worried about safety. Neither one of us wanted to go back home yet — we weren't ready. But Mexico is a hairy place for a rich little white girl. I told her it'd be fine. I had a friend from the Marine Corps who'd returned home to Mexico after popping on a drug test in the School of Infantry. He was a good guy, honorable, loyal as a dog. His name was Juan Rodriguez. He was the one who killed those sheriffs."

Masterson's face darkened and Chen suddenly perked up, mouthing the name to remember it.

"So, we stayed with Juan and his family. Wonderful people. His father owned a used car lot just south of the border where he and his brother worked. They made enough money so that his mother could focus on raising his two teenage sisters the right way. But Juan wasn't content there.

"You see, Juan had joined the Marine Corps in the hopes of earning his citizenship and escaping the boring, day to day life that his family offered him. When he'd popped on that piss test, it crushed him. He insisted it was second hand high from being around pot smokers, but who the fuck really knows, right? Anyways, Juan wanted something more from life than he was getting, so when I showed up at his door with my beautiful wife-to-be — yes, we were engaged at that point — it only took him a minute to realize that she had come from money.

"We stayed with the Rodriguez family for three days. On the third night, while Juan and I went to the store to grab some more *cervesas*, Paige was kidnapped from their home by a group of armed men. I found out later that they had thrown her in the trunk of their car and taken her to a nearby vacant lot. It was in that lot that they raped her, cut off her fingers, and then shot her in the head before burning her body in an oil drum. Apparently, they didn't realize *how* rich her family was, because if they had, then they might have kept her alive while they contacted her father and demanded a ransom, rather than just sending the fingers as proof of life.

"When we got back from the store, I found out she'd been taken and I went straight to police. They were nearly as corrupt as you. They held me for three days, beat me, tried to get me to confess to being complicit in her kidnapping. Anders used his contacts to get me released, and told me that there was a ransom demand. He wanted me to be there when it went down, to bring his baby girl home to him. I went back to Juan's house and found his family. His father pulled me aside into the dining room and told me that Juan had disappeared. He told me that he believed his son had something to do with Paige's kidnapping. Then he told me about the burned woman's corpse that had been found in the nearby lot. He was trying to do the right thing. He was a good man."

Stark spoke casually, ignoring the searing pain at the base of his wrist.

"I hacked his head off with a dull steak knife, and when Juan's brother came in to see what the screaming was, I killed him too. I caught his mother and sisters cowering in the kitchen, and by the time Juan returned that night, they were everywhere."

Masterson's face showed the same confused fear that it had after Stark had destroyed his helicopter weeks before.

"I kept him alive, but I cut off his balls after he revealed the names of the men he'd told about her. I didn't spare him because he complied, or even out of pity. I spared him because I wanted him to see the image of his mutilated family every time he closed his eyes."

Stark smirked at the disgust on Franklin's face.

"Juan had given her up in the hope of being employed by the cartel that ran the area. I guess he thought it was a good sacrifice: one dead white girl for endless career opportunities. It took me a week to find the first man who'd taken her. He didn't cry. His family did, but he didn't. He told me how he raped her before they pulled the trigger, and how she was screaming out my name to come save her... The noise his bones made as I broke them... This sickening *pop*... The type of noise a man can never forget..."

The others failed to notice the very noise he was describing over the hum of the helicopter and their intent focus on his face. Franklin covered his ears. Masterson and Chen both stared at him in morbid fascination.

"Over the next three weeks, I killed twenty-three people. It got to a point where the Cartel had a multi-million-dollar bounty on my head. I didn't sleep. I didn't eat. I didn't do anything but stalk them and tear them and their loved ones to shreds. It was a Tuesday when they finally got me. A freak occurrence. They'd managed to get photos of me and distribute it among the locals and police. A gas station attendant shot me five times while I was filling up a car I'd stolen. I barely managed to make it across the border to an old friend who took care of me. His name is Hunt, Tim Hunt. Actually, I believe he escaped over the border just before you attacked my people."

Chen repeated the name, then raised an eyebrow. "Why are you telling us this?"

Stark broke his gaze away from Masterson's eyes for the first time since he'd sat down, looking out the window at the pearly blue lake beneath them. He felt the thick pool of fresh blood soaking into the back of his shirt. "Do you remember the story I told you the first time we met, Masterson?"

"Wha…" Masterson was lost for words. He looked at Chen, and Stark could sense his panic from across the cabin.

"About what happens when a helicopter hits the water? About the horror?"

Stark raised his arms in front of him. The intact handcuffs dangled from his right wrist.

Chen and Franklin recoiled in their seats as Stark's dismembered thumb tumbled to the cabin floor. Masterson stared in shocked disbelief at the bright red gushing wound where it had come from. In his right hand, Stark clenched the knife he had used to cut off his own thumb. The inscription on the blade glinted beneath its crimson coating:

FRS, with love

Chen flinched hard as Stark swung his arm back and buried the blade into his chest. Stark ripped the blade out, smiling at Masterson and standing. Franklin cried out, but Stark barely noticed.

The terror.

The sheer terror in Masterson's face washed over Stark's soul like a cleansing fire.

The pilot let out a gargling howl as Stark lunged forward over Masterson's shoulder and stabbed the blade repeatedly into his throat. The helicopter spun out of control, throwing the four passengers haphazardly around the cabin.

Stark latched onto Masterson's throat with a vice like grip, pulling him close as the helicopter careened downward toward the lake below.

"Nobody wins, *boy.*"

A Note from the Author to Veterans

I felt compelled to add this note at the end of this novel in the hopes that it might reach a veteran struggling to keep it together after rejoining the civilian world.

I served in 1st Battalion 9th Marines from 2008 to 2012. During that time, I was incredibly lucky to be part of an irreplaceable family of young men. We went to hell and back with nothing but each other. We fought together, ate together, shit together, we did everything together, and despite our petty differences, there was absolutely nothing in the world that could have torn us apart… at least until our EAS dates came along.

Four men whom I considered closer than brothers have taken their lives since then. Four wonderful, strong, iron-hearted men with everything to live for took that last step over the ledge and made that irreversible decision.

I can't tell you why they did it. Maybe a part of me knows. I'm sure many veterans reading this understand it on some level even if you can't find the words to express it. All I know is that the world is a much darker place for us without them.

I offer this humble plea hoping that should any of you reading this ever find yourself staring down into that dark abyss, you simply remember and consider it. I beg you to think of us. Your brothers. The men who stood beside you through any and everything. I beg that you consider us before you take that final step. Whatever you suffer from, whether the world around you has become muted and soulless, or terrifyingly sharp and painful, I want you to know that you are not alone. To do that irrevocable thing is to steal all that is good in you away from the people that love you. And there is still good in you. I promise. There is also still good in the world. It can be a sonofabitch to find, I know, but it exists. You owe it to *us* to keep on pushing, searching, clawing your way forward until you can't push any further, and then keep going.

And if you find yourself helpless, alone, or entirely destroyed, I *demand* that you reach out to us. Asking for help is never a sign of weakness. Contact those grimy bastards that you stood beside in formation and huddled together with for warmth in a foxhole. Let them know something is wrong, take a drive to see them, get yourself in touch with them in some way beyond a casual text or Facebook message, because they feel it too, and to lose you would break their hearts.

We need each other. We really do. To take yourself away from us is unforgivable.

Please remember this.

About the Author

Doug Hoover was raised in a small Maine town. On his eighteenth birthday, he enlisted in the United States Marine Corps infantry. Over the next four years, he served in 1st Battalion 9th Marines in a variety of locations including Africa, Jordan, and Helmand Province, Afghanistan. After receiving an honorable discharge in 2012, he attended the University of Massachusetts in Boston where he recently earned a bachelor's degree in Communications with a minor in Anthropology. He currently resides on Cape Cod with his beautiful girlfriend and their two pit bulls, Bug and Skootcha Nunchuck Monsterface.

Made in the USA
Middletown, DE
29 June 2021